# WITCH FIRE

*Also by Laura Powell*

Burn Mark

# WITCH FIRE

## LAURA POWELL

**BLOOMSBURY**

NEW YORK   LONDON   NEW DELHI   SYDNEY

First published in Great Britain in April 2013 by Bloomsbury Publishing Plc
Published in the United States of America in June 2013
by Bloomsbury Children's Books
www.bloomsbury.com

For information about permission to reproduce selections from this book, write to
Permissions, Bloomsbury Children's Books, 1385 Broadway, New York, New York 10018
Bloomsbury books may be purchased for business or promotional use.
For information on bulk purchases please contact Macmillan Corporate
and Premium Sales Department at specialmarkets@macmillan.com

Library of Congress Cataloging-in-Publication Data
Powell, Laura.
Witch fire / by Laura Powell. — 1st U.S. ed.
       p.     cm.
ISBN 978-1-61963-006-2 (hardcover) • ISBN 978-1-61963-044-4 (e-book)
   1. Witches—Juvenile fiction. 2. Missing persons—Juvenile fiction.
3. Friendship—Juvenile fiction. 4. London (England)—Juvenile fiction.
[1. Witches—Fiction. 2. Missing persons—Fiction. 3. Friendship—Fiction.
   4. London (England)—Fiction. 5. England—Fiction.] I. Title.
PZ7.P87757Wit 2013        823.92—dc23        2012038630

Typeset by Hewer Text UK Ltd., Edinburgh
Printed and bound in the U.S.A. by Thomson-Shore Inc., Dexter, Michigan
2 4 6 8 10 9 7 5 3 1

*For my Dutch family, Wim and Kikki Van Dam*

# PART 1

# CHAPTER 1

The two runners on the roof were barely visible in the dawn light. The sky was low and grey, except for a blush of primrose at the horizon. If anyone had been out on the street, the figures above would have been little more than shadows, moving quickly but unevenly as they skirted obstacles and ascended and descended slopes.

The city was never entirely quiet. But early on a Sunday morning, the throb and grind of it was a distant hum. Up on the rooftops, the running boy and girl were conscious only of their own gasps, the thump of their feet on slate, brick and stone.

It had been an even race, but now the boy was drawing ahead. The top of the building ended in a parapet wall and there was a gap of at least two metres between it and the slope of the neighbouring roof. The boy came to a halt a few steps back from the parapet. While he hesitated, his companion gained on him. 'Catch me if you can,' she called out gleefully as she hurtled past, barely slowing as she reached the wall and the dizzying drop beyond. She threw out her right arm and a small brown pebble flew through the air and fell with a clatter on to the pitched roof on the other side.

The girl flew after it. It was an elongated half-leap, half-glide, and slower in motion than an ordinary jump. But no ordinary jump would have covered the distance. The girl landed with a smack, tilting forward, her right palm slapping hard against the sloping tiles, her feet lodged against the stone gutter. It took a second or so to get her balance, then she scrambled up and over the peak and into the roof valley beyond. A few moments later the boy joined her.

'I won,' she said, breathless and triumphant. 'I knew it.'

'I was being polite. Ladies first.'

'You're so full of crap.' She laughed. ''Sides, I ain't no lady.'

Lucas and Glory were in training. They had the ability to sky-leap because they were witchkind, and permission to do so because it was part of a government-approved exercise. Both wore the blue uniform with the W on the back that WICA – the office of Witchkind Intelligence and Covert Affairs – wore when committing witchwork in public.

All witches were required to be registered, although legal witchwork had been decriminalised in Britain in 1753. Those who chose to be non-practising were bridled in iron cuffs that blocked their power. Those who continued to practise sought employment in the public sector. Witches of all kinds were monitored by the Inquisition. The Inquisition still burned witches convicted of the most serious crimes, and continued to hunt down those who operated outside the law.

Their race over, Glory and Lucas leaned against a chimney stack, gathering their breath. Their jackets had hoods to shield their faces from view. Glory pushed hers back, and shook out her white-blonde hair, which had got entangled in the hoops of her earrings. Lucas kept his own hood pulled low. His black hair stuck damply to his forehead. His face, naturally pale, was flushed. They had run hard.

London sprawled around them, smudged and sullen in the thin light. Glory fixed her eyes on the horizon.

'I could do this for ever,' she murmured. 'On and on, higher 'n higher . . . There's times I don't want to ever come down.'

Today was the first time they had sky-leaped unsupervised. It was not, however, the first time Glory had outdone Lucas in the exercise.

Witchkind's unnatural abilities, their Seventh Sense, or fae, as it was usually known, varied in strength. Lucas and Glory's fae was of the highest level: Type E, as registered in the Inquisition's files. Only about one person in a thousand turned witchkind, and most of these were in their twenties when it happened. Lucas and Glory were still only fifteen.

Glory saw the fae as her birthright. Her grandmother, Cora Starling, had been one half of the infamous Starling Twins, the beautiful blonde witch-sisters whose outfit, the Wednesday Coven, had dominated the East End during the sixties and seventies. In the criminal underworld, the twins were remembered as celebrities and heroines. Respectable society regarded them as dangerous felons.

Lucas's family were as respectable as it got. He came from a long line of witch-hunters and his father, Ashton Stearne, had been Chief Prosecutor at the Inquisition. The fae wasn't only rare; it was usually hereditary. For Lucas to be a witch should have been impossible. He had joined WICA in a daze of desperation, because he didn't know what else he could do.

It was while Lucas was on an undercover assignment in the coven world that he had met Glory, and the two of them had exposed a plot by corrupt inquisitors to frame Jack Rawdon, WICA's director, for witch-terrorism. Nearly three months on from the debacle, the Inquisition was struggling to deal with the fallout.

Only a handful of family members and state officials knew that Lucas and Glory were witchkind. In the intelligence world, they were valuable assets, as most people would assume they were too young to be witches. Yet their status at WICA was uncertain. Nobody seemed quite sure what to do with them. Most of their schedule was filled with ordinary lessons and with practising witchwork they already knew how to do. Occasionally they'd attend seminars on subjects such as Applied Behavioural Science, and Fae Theory and Witchcrime. But they had spent just one afternoon on firearms training, and over two weeks on Data Analysis. It was starting to look as if they'd be spending the next few years stuck behind a desk.

The night before their first sky-leaping session, Lucas had the old childish nightmare of flying, in which he spiralled helplessly away from the earth and everyone he knew.

Lucas had only seen sky-leapers in action once, when he was still at school, still living his old life, still sure of his destiny as a thirteenth-generation inquisitor, detecting and punishing witchcrime. Sky-leaping wasn't just rare; it was risky. In the old days of persecution, a witch would only use it as a means of escape as a last resort. Even Glory, brought up in a coven, hadn't tried it. The chance of exposure was too great. And when he asked her what was involved, all she'd say was 'It sorta works like magnets.' Lucas suspected she didn't actually know.

WICA's HQ was a warehouse in the London dock-lands. The sky-leaping induction, however, took place in an airfield in Surrey that had been converted into a training facility. Their instructor, Agent Austin, a small and rather stout woman who looked wholly unsuited to springing through space, began proceedings in the control tower's office.

'Now,' she said briskly, 'sky-leaping aside, what do you think is the most impressive act of witchwork?'

'Um . . . raising a wind?' Lucas offered.

'Crafting a poppet,' said Glory.

Agent Austin nodded. 'Good answers. Most people would agree that brewing up a storm, or using a doll to control another living being, are extraordinary feats. By comparison, simply moving a small object by force of fae doesn't seem so impressive. However, it's something very few witches can do.'

She placed a penny and a pebble on the desk in front of them, and smiled at Lucas. 'Try to move the coin with your fae.' She tapped the metal. 'Don't worry; you can touch it first.'

The Seventh Sense was a mental power, but it was channelled through people or objects. Bodily substances were key. Witchwork was often literally a matter of blood, sweat and tears.

So Lucas spat on his palm before picking up the coin. He used his right hand to roll it around his left in a smooth clockwise motion; creating a rhythm, forming a bond. As his mind focused on the task, he could feel the Devil's Kiss, the small inky blot that was the mark of a witch, begin to warm on his shoulder blade. His pulse quickened, and a second throb – the dark, hot pulse of fae – echoed in his head. The Seventh Sense was reaching out, uncoiling itself from the deepest, most secret part of him.

He placed the coin in the centre of the table. Brow furrowed with concentration, he put out his right hand, and beckoned to it. *Come*, he said in his mind.

Nothing happened.

He frowned harder, gathered up his fae and directed it with a glare towards the penny. *Come*, he commanded, still silently. *Now.*

The coin didn't so much as twitch. Maybe he wasn't going to be able to do this kind of witchwork after all. Maybe he couldn't sky-leap. Maybe he wasn't as powerful as everyone thought he was –

But Agent Austin was unfazed by his failure. 'Try it with the pebble.'

Lucas got ready to repeat the process. He wasn't optimistic, but right from the start the little stone began to clumsily roll towards him. All of a sudden it flew into his palm and stuck fast. His body tingled with the rush of fae: like adrenalin, but wilder.

Job done, he tried to pull the stone off, tugging at it

with his left hand. Glory smothered a laugh. It was as if the stone had been glued there.

He turned to Agent Austin. 'I don't get it. Why didn't this happen with the coin?'

'Because the penny was man-made. This kind of witch-work only works on small amounts of organic materials. So you could do it to a shell or twig or a bit of bone. But a pebble works best for our purposes. What you've created there is a lodestone.'

'What does that mean?'

'Something what holds the fae,' said Glory promptly, 'but ain't used for witchwork.'

Their instructor nodded. 'As you know, an object used to commit witchwork is an amulet, if it's been made from scratch, or a talisman, if it's something that's been adapted. But both these kinds of things are tools; a lodestone is simply a receptacle. To summon that pebble, you have "loaded" it with your Seventh Sense.'

Lucas was more interested in the fact the pebble was still wedged against his palm. 'How do I get it off?'

'Reverse the witchwork,' Agent Austin replied.

He thought for a moment, then spat on the back of his left hand. He rubbed it in an anticlockwise motion around the pebble which, sure enough, dropped free.

'Simple, right?' said Austin. 'But it's still a very powerful bond you created there. By putting your fae into that stone, and summoning it with your Seventh Sense, it became a part of you: your body and soul and fae.'

'So how does this work for sky-leaping?' Glory asked impatiently.

'Summon the pebble again,' Agent Austin said to Lucas, 'and I'll show you.'

He did as he was told, and he and Glory followed the instructor out of the office and into the hangar. The space where planes had once been stored was now a kind of oversized adventure playground, filled with ramps, blocks, walls and runways, all of differing materials and heights. Like all WICA facilities, it was monitored by CCTV and wired for sound. The eyes and ears of the Inquisition were never far away.

'Throw the lodestone over there.' Agent Austin pointed to one of the few flat spaces.

'I can't. Not without reversing the witchwork.' The pebble was once more stuck to Lucas's palm as if it had grown there.

'That's because you're only using your physical strength. Do it with the fae. Push the stone out of you; expel it.'

Lucas closed his eyes. He gathered his Seventh Sense, feeling it seethe inside his head, spark through his blood and his bone. His fingers gripped the stone and he raised his arm. Go, he said silently in his head. Out. As he swung his arm up and over, the fae rushed outwards and pushed, rather than threw, the pebble away. It shot forwards with unnatural force.

Lucas let himself relax. But the moment he did so, he was yanked forward too, inexorably pulled towards where the pebble had fallen. It was not a dignified motion. He stumbled and jerked, right arm out-thrust, and before he quite knew what had happened, was kneeling on the concrete floor, palm pressed on the lode-stone. Glory sniggered.

'OK, here's how it works,' Agent Austin said. 'You loaded the stone with fae to summon it, and it stuck fast because the lesser amount of fae in the pebble was attracted to the greater fae in you. The balance of fae was then reversed when you used it to throw the stone away. And so you were immediately drawn to the lodestone with the same force as it was originally drawn to you.'

'Cool,' said Glory.

Lucas said nothing. He was feeling a little wobbly.

Agent Austin took another pebble out of her pocket, and summoned it to her. Striding forward, she lobbed the lodestone to the top of one of the free-standing brick walls, about two metres high. A few seconds later, she had sprung up after it. The movement was exaggerated yet graceful, a near-vertical jump. In the blink of an eye, she was crouched on the top of the wall, the pebble fastened to her hand.

'Can I have a go?' Glory asked eagerly.

'That's what we're here for.' The lodestone clattered to the ground, and Agent Austin swooped down behind it. 'Let's take it slowly, though. You can start off on that low ramp over there.'

They spent the rest of the day practising. As Lucas had discovered, the force of fae that drew them to the lodestones wasn't of much value on flat ground. Its real advantage was in scaling heights and crossing space. Though a sky-leaper could only go as far and high as he or she could throw their lodestone, the force and direction of that throw could be enhanced by visualisation, using the mind's eye to guide the stone to a suitable landing spot. Once there, it would stay fixed to whatever surface it had fallen on, until the thrower reconnected with it.

There was a lot to coordinate. Lucas particularly struggled with the transition from gravity-restricted running, climbing and throwing to the outlandish jumps and swoops impelled by the lodestone. His stomach lurched unpleasantly the moment he felt the fae's pull, even though the surge of weightlessness was over almost as soon as it had begun. As a result, while Glory flung herself into space with reckless ease, Lucas's leaps were always more cautious, his landings more clumsy.

Yet as Lucas watched the sun rise over London, he understood Glory's reluctance to return to gravity. Up here, it was possible to imagine a world free of surveillance. Up here, there was always an escape route.

'Come on,' he said brusquely, because he knew this was an illusion. 'It's time we got back. There's a fire escape over there we can use.' He began to unzip the blue jacket, and got ready to become an ordinary citizen again.

Glory was still gazing at the horizon. The drab dawn was giving way to a beautiful summer's morning. 'There ain't nothing I want to go back to. Just a whole lot of procedures and protocols and nag, nag, nag.'

'I find it frustrating too –'

'It ain't the same for you,' Glory cut in impatiently. 'That gang at WICA don't like me, nor trust me neither. I'm just some stupid coven tart to them.'

Lucas didn't know what to say to this. WICA's officers

were trained to stay in the background. They moved smoothly through the hushed corridors; their witchwork was quiet and precise, and devoid of flourish. Whereas Glory was all swagger and brashness, with her big sulky mouth and flashing dark eyes, her clashing gold hoops and impractical heels . . . A gangster's moll, he'd heard one of the senior agents say to a colleague.

He touched the thin grey streak in his hair that witchwork had put in and nothing would take out. It was something he only did when he was ill at ease, or distracted. 'They're not used to working with people like us,' he said. 'I mean, we're a lot younger, for a start. And we weren't recruited through the conventional route.'

'We ain't got nothing to prove. If it weren't for us, Jack Rawdon would be toasted to cinders in the Burning Court, and there wouldn't even *be* no WICA. So I'm telling you now, I ain't going to sit back and take their crap for nothing.'

'How do you mean?'

'I mean I'm only sticking with this caper 'cause it's my best chance of tracking down my mum. I can't trust the covens with it. And WICA have the resources. If I stick with them, maybe I can even do things legit.'

Glory's mother Edie had disappeared when Glory was three. It was suspected she'd been murdered by her cousin, Charlie Morgan. He and his brothers had transformed the Wednesday Coven into the biggest and most brutal of Britain's criminal organisations. Because Edie was a powerful rival and witch, Glory believed Charlie had felt sufficiently threatened by her to have her killed.

But then Lucas had broken into the Inquisition's secret

files, and read that Edie Starling had been seen alive five years go. What's more, she had been on the Inquisition's payroll. Until she'd been reported as 'missing in action', she had been working on something called Operation Swan. One of the officers in charge of her case was Ashton Stearne, Lucas's father.

Lucas had told Glory that her mother might still be alive, and that she was on the National Witchkind Database. But that was all he had told her. He had not revealed Ashton's involvement, telling himself that he needed to get the facts straight and was waiting for the right time to ask his father. Yet today wasn't the first time she had raised the issue, and she was nothing if not determined.

With a sigh, Glory looked down at the pebble in her hand, and then over the cluttered roofs. 'She's out there, somewhere,' she said softly. 'Waiting for me to find her. If I run fast enough, leap high enough . . .' She turned to Lucas. 'You'll help me, won't you?'

# CHAPTER 2

After parting from Glory, Lucas went for a walk as fast-paced as it was aimless. He had nowhere he wanted to go. Once, his free time had been filled with activity clubs and house parties, sports matches and socials. As his life had become more complicated, it had also become emptier.

It wasn't only Lucas's life that had been turned upside down. His father had resigned from the Office of the Inquisitorial Court on the grounds that he was taking the fall for the collapse of a high-profile witch-trial. The real reason was that anyone with a witch-relative was barred from working in the Inquisition. In the normal course of things, the resignation of the Chief Prosecutor would have been big news. But in the wake of the witch-terrorism conspiracy, the newspapers had other headlines to splash.

Lucas knew his father did not blame him for the end of his inquisitorial career, but he still felt responsible. It was one of the reasons he was glad when WICA's schedule kept him away from home.

In addition to the guard at the gate, and other standard security measures, all the outside doors of the Stearne residence had iron bells encased over the threshold. They were wired to a central alarm system, ready to give warning if a witch hexing a bane approached. Witches were allergic to iron, and the iron in the bells was able to pick up on the fae used in harmful witchwork.

Although Lucas knew, rationally, he wasn't going to set off any alarms, he wasn't able to forget he was living in a house designed to withstand witches. Even the family portraits – all those witch-hunting heroes, pillars of society, defenders of the realm – were a reminder of how his place in the world had changed.

He found his stepsister Philomena in the kitchen, painting her nails. She wrinkled her nose at him.

'Ew. You need a shower. What on earth have you been doing?'

'I'd tell you,' he said, getting a carton of juice from the fridge and glugging it down, 'but then I'd have to kill you.'

'Ha bloody ha.' She tossed her hair. Philomena worked hard at many things (getting invited to the right parties, being seen with the right people, wearing the right clothes), but a really excellent head-toss was her greatest skill. With that one gesture, she could express flirtation, amusement, boredom or contempt. This was definitely contempt. 'I bet all you're doing at Spook Central is making coffee and filing, anyway.'

The truth was, Philomena felt hard done by. For all her artful head-tossing, her determination and charm, the whole getting-invited-to-the-right-parties-by-the-right-people business had always been easier for Lucas. The scandal of his fae was meant to redress the balance. Yet somehow her insufferable younger stepbrother had turned what should have been the ultimate disgrace to his own advantage. He didn't go to school. He didn't have a curfew. He got to be deliberately mysterious about everything he did. This was only more proof, thought Philomena Carrington, that life was monstrously unfair.

'The party last night was un-be-lievable, by the way,' she announced. 'Such a shame you couldn't be there.'

Lucas concentrated on buttering a mound of toast.

'Bea Allen asked after you. Quite a lot of people did. They're all dying to know what's going on. Nobody believes in this mysterious virus you're supposed to have had. Some people think it's a nervous breakdown. Others reckon it's drugs.'

'I'm guessing you did nothing to put them straight.'

She looked virtuous. 'I said that you're working through some personal issues, and it wouldn't be kind of me to say anything more.'

Lucas had been a witch for about four months. His initial absence from school had been explained away by a serious illness. He was supposed to still be recuperating, but Philomena had a point. It was time for a more sustainable cover story. Since his membership of WICA was secret, there was, in theory, no reason he couldn't resume his former friendships and occupations at some point. Yet he had no real desire to try. Too much had changed.

'The funny thing is,' Philomena continued, 'people would be less shocked if you turned into a druggie or nutjob than if you came out as a hag.'

Hag was a dirty word for witches. Lucas reached for

another piece of toast. 'Don't be vulgar, Philly, dear,' he said, using his stepmother's voice.

Another head-toss. 'Well, I'm sure I can come up with some amusing alternatives. Maybe I should start a rumour that you've had a lobotomy. Or a sex-change. I'll say you've asked us to start calling you Lucy.'

'Try that, and I'll hex you.'

'You wouldn't dare.'

'Wouldn't I? There's a bane to give a person breath like rotting meat. It's irreversible too. A lifetime of putrid breath: think about it.'

Philomena's reaction was extreme. 'No . . . please . . . don't hurt me . . .' She shrank away from him fearfully. Too late, Lucas realised they had an audience. His father was standing in the doorway behind him.

'My study,' Ashton said. 'Now.' As soon as his back was turned, Philomena smirked in triumph.

'She knew I was joking,' Lucas protested, once his father and he were alone. The study too was fae-proofed. The iron shutters over the windows and the iron panel on the door were in place to block witches trying to look in with a scrying bowl.

'It's no laughing matter.' Ashton Stearne's steely blue stare, legendary in court, was now turned on his son. 'Threatening people with witchwork is a criminal offence, and one the Inquisition takes very seriously. What if Philomena makes an official complaint?'

'But she's – we're – *family*.'

'The history of witch-trials is full of family denouncements.' His father sighed, then softened. 'Not that Philly would ever do such a thing. I have impressed upon her how important, and sensitive, your position is. And I know that she can be a little ... provoking ... at times. But please, Lucas. You're a professional now. A government agent. It's not only in your working life that you have to act older than your age.'

'Right. Sorry.'

'Anyway, that's not really what I got you in here to talk about. Take a seat, won't you – don't look so worried! I only want to hear how you're getting on. I know, of course, that WICA are pleased with you.'

'How do you know that?' Lucas was surprised. His father had been very reluctant to give his consent for Lucas to join the agency, and they rarely talked about his witch-work activities.

'Your witch warden makes regular reports.'

Lucas frowned. He hadn't realised Officer Branning was reporting his activities to his father as well as the Inquisition.

'I was glad to hear that you're keeping up with your academic studies too,' Ashton continued. 'So you're clearly settling well into your new life. However ... I did wonder ... We've never talked – not in detail, that is – about what happened with Gideon and that man Striker.'

Gideon Hale was a young inquisitor, and Striker a renegade witch-hunter, who had been involved in the witch-terrorism conspiracy. After Lucas fell into their hands, he had been subject to some of the Inquisition's more brutal techniques. He had got quite good at not think-ing about his time in the basement cell.

'There's not much to say. I had a lucky escape, all things considered.'

'So has Gideon. His lawyer did well to get him that plea bargain.'

'Yes. I heard.'

'And how do you feel about it?'

'Pissed off. But I'll get over it.'

'Hm. You've been rather quiet lately. And you look tired.'

'I've been . . . out for a run. Maybe I overdid it.'

'Are you sleeping properly?'

'Fine, thanks.'

Generally, this was true. He'd had the occasional flying dream, but no nightmares about his interrogation. The flashbacks came in the daytime, when he was least expecting them. He would be doing something ordinary, thinking entirely ordinary thoughts, and suddenly be caught by a drenching breathlessness, like a cold fist squeezing his lungs. And before he could blink the image away, there was Gideon, smiling. A hand on a lever. The leather straps. The iron and ice.

But these moments were over almost as soon as they'd begun. They were manageable.

'Anyway,' Lucas said, 'lots of people get ducked, all the time.'

Ashton Stearne would have ducked witches, or at least witnessed it. All inquisitors did at some point in their career. Perhaps he had taken photographs, or made notes, as the captive was strapped into the ducking-chair, and plunged backwards into the iron tank of cold water, again and again and again. It was the only way to drag the fae-stain out of a suspect witch.

'There was nothing conventional, let alone justified, about what those thugs did to you.' Was he imagining it, or did his father's voice have a defensive note? 'Using a bridle too – those contraptions have been outlawed since the last century. You were in danger of losing your life. There's no shame in admitting that's a difficult thing to deal with.'

'I'm not ashamed. Of anything.'

Their eyes met. Ashton cleared his throat. 'You know, Lucas, after your mother died, I worked very hard to keep my emotions at bay. I wasn't ready to admit I was angry, as well as grieving.'

Lucas's mother, Camilla Stearne, had been assassinated during the Endor witch-terrorist campaign in the late 1990s. Ashton had often talked to Lucas about his mother's life, but never about her death. The sudden introduction of the subject was disconcerting.

'In the end,' Ashton continued, 'I decided to take some time out and get help, professional help, to work through my feelings. Now, I'm not saying that you need –'

'Good,' Lucas interrupted. 'Because there's nothing wrong with me. My work at WICA's proof of that. Like you said, I'm doing well. I'm feeling well too. Everything's fine.'

'All right,' his father said. He rubbed his forehead, and tried to smile. 'All right, it's your call. As long as you can restrain yourself from turning your stepsister into a toad, then I suppose there's nothing to worry about.'

'Fair enough. And actually . . . since we're here . . .

there's something I've been meaning to ask you. It's to do with Glory.'

'Ah. Yes. A rather remarkable girl, by all accounts.'

'Has Jonah been reporting on her too?'

Ashton didn't answer directly. 'Talented though she is, Glory hasn't had your advantages: a stable home, a good education, moral guidance. Then there's her coven background. It's only to be expected her presence at WICA has ruffled a few feathers.'

'Gideon Hale had a good education and moral upbringing and the rest of it,' Lucas retorted. He paused. 'And Glory isn't just connected to the covens. Her mother worked for the Inquisition, didn't she?'

His father became very still, his voice very quiet. 'What do you know about that?'

So Lucas told him about using witchwork to hack into the classified section of the National Witchkind Database.

'I was trying to find out about Angeline Starling, you see. Then I saw that her file was linked to Edie's. There wasn't much information; only that she was recruited by the Witchcrime Directorate for something called Operation Swan. And that you were one of the inquisitors who supervised her case.'

Ashton did not say anything for a long while. His face was closed-off, concentrating. 'How much have you told Glory?'

'Not all of it. That is, she knows her mother could still be alive. And I told her that Edie'd been registered as a witch. But she's determined to find out more. I want to know more too.'

Lucas spoke more defiantly then he meant to, but his father didn't seem to notice. He started to speak, then lapsed into silence again. This hesitance was uncharacteristic, yet had been part of their interactions ever since the arrival of Lucas's fae.

'The other inquisitors involved in her case are retired, or else dead,' Ashton said at last, as if to himself. 'I will need authorisation. Your timing is unfortunate. But perhaps . . . inevitable. I'd better make some calls.'

And then he said something that sent a chill through Lucas's heart.

'I had my misgivings from the first. These things can't stay buried for ever.'

# CHAPTER 3

Glory did not return home with any more enthusiasm than Lucas had. After leaving the coven, the government had provided her and her father Patrick with a small council flat. Glory knew it was impossible for them to continue living at Cooper Street. But Grange House still felt like foreign territory.

Cooper Street was on the edge of the notorious Rockwood Estate, a concrete jungle of festering maisonettes and needle-strewn alleys, overshadowed by a lone tower block. The Grange was also located in the East End borough of Hallam, but at the opposite end. It was quiet and well-tended, respectable. Yet Glory was homesick for the old neighbourhood. Witchkind had always flourished on the margins of society, and Glory had walked tall through Rockwood's dark corners and grimy courts. She had been sure of herself then: a Starling Girl and coven witch, ready to claim her birthright.

As she put her key in the door to 24b she heard voices in the kitchen. Her dad had company. Someone from Cooper Street perhaps? Her stomach tightened. She missed them, in spite of herself: the quarrelsome, jostling boys, the hard-bitten men, and the fierce old lady who'd brought her up.

But their visitor was one of their new neighbours; a woman who lived on the floor below. She and Patrick were sitting at the kitchen table with mugs of tea. And a plate of the posh biscuits.

'Hello, love,' said her dad. 'You remember Peggy, don't you?'

Glory squinted at the woman suspiciously. Small, freckly and plain-faced, but cheerful with it. The busybody type, no doubt. 'Uh-huh.'

'What a nice colour you've got,' Peggy said brightly. 'Been out for a run?'

'Sorta.'

'I'm trying to get your dad involved in the Residents' Association,' Peggy explained. 'He used to be an account- ant, I hear. We could do with someone who's good with numbers.'

'Or at cooking the books,' Glory muttered, rummaging in a cupboard for tea. It was how Patrick had paid his way, back in the coven. 'Good luck with that,' she said in her normal voice.

Patrick had never got over his wife's disappearance. When Glory was small, he had been a kind and steady pres- ence, but as she grew older he had retreated further into his own world. He seemed content to stay in the background, as easy to tune out as the flashes and bleeps from his endless computer games. Glory, meanwhile, had been taken under the wing of her great-aunt. Before coming to the Grange, she and her father had gone for days at a time without exchanging more than a few words.

Glory looked at her dad's thinning hair and faded features with a familiar mix of exasperation and love. Maybe a project of some kind would be good for him. But she was reluctant to encourage this Peggy person – nosy neighbours meant trouble. It wasn't just their coven past the two of them had to conceal. Her work at WICA was even more of a secret. Patrick was one of the most private people she knew. Still, could he be trusted not to let something slip?

She announced she was going for a shower, hoping their visitor would take the hint and leave. She had homework to finish, after all.

The biggest shock on joining WICA was the news that she was expected to keep up her formal education. Yet Lucas took their study scheme in his stride, apparently effortlessly, and anything he could do, then so could she. For although Glory was as powerful a witch as Lucas, and every bit as smart and strong, she was beginning to realise that getting the same respect as him wasn't just about her fae. It was about sticking to the rules and ticking off checklists. It was also, apparently, about Spelling, Punctuation and Grammar.

But only five minutes after returning from the bathroom to her study files, her mobile beeped. It was a text from her Cousin Troy. 'Coffee?'

Glory smiled guiltily. She shouldn't be communicating with Troy, let alone meeting with him. If WICA found out, she'd be in real trouble.

Troy was not a witch, but an economics student. He

had no criminal record. He had helped Glory and Lucas to bring down Silas Paterson, the corrupt inquisitor who'd led the witch-terrorist conspiracy. But Troy was the grandson of Lily Starling, son of Charlie Morgan, and heir to the Wednesday Coven. That made him an enemy of the state.

Although the Inquisition led the fight against organised witchcrime, it had support from the police and other security services. WICA knew about Glory's background when they recruited her, but she had made it clear from the start that she wouldn't turn snitch. Even so, when Glory left the coven, she had not expected Troy to forgive the betrayal.

Yet, not for the first time, she had underestimated him. Somehow, they reached a compromise. Troy trusted she wouldn't use her knowledge of coven business and the Morgan family against them; Glory trusted he would keep the secret of her new life. In fact, he even helped maintain it – by spreading a rumour he was bankrolling her and Patrick after they'd been thrown out of Cooper Street.

She and Troy didn't meet very often. He was even busier than she was. Only twenty-one, he'd had to take a break from his postgraduate degree to oversee the running of the business while his father Charlie recovered from an attempt on his life. Although neither of them explicitly discussed their work, both understood what the other had given up as well as gained in assuming their new roles. Perhaps this was why they'd made the effort to stay friends.

Before going to meet Troy, Glory slipped an elusion

amulet into her shoe. It was crafted from a printout of a street map, on which she'd drawn a crazy maze in ink and spit, then bound it up in a tangle of thread. She always kept one ready-made and taped to the underside of the communal stairs, because it was the to and fro of passing feet that sealed the witchwork. If anyone tried to follow her, they would find themselves disorientated, then lost.

Would it be enough? An elusion only lasted for the duration of a single journey; WICA probably had all sorts of methods for monitoring her. Glory decided she didn't care. She had the right to see whoever she pleased.

Troy was busy typing on his laptop when Glory joined him in a café off Talbot Road. He looked, as ever, like a successful young executive in his expensive but sombre suit, briefcase by his side. All the Morgan males had reddish hair, but Troy's colouring was the darkest. He was auburn and angular, with narrow green eyes. Right now, they were frowning in concentration.

'With you in a moment, cuz,' he said. 'Go ahead and order.'

Excellent. Glory might prize her independence, but she had no problem with getting other people to pay her way. She scanned the menu for the most expensive pastry she could find. Troy could afford it. Hell, he could afford to buy the whole shop, if he was minded to.

He raised an eyebrow as she wolfed down the first of a trio of chocolate eclairs. 'I gather table manners don't feature on your new curriculum.'

'I'm a growing girl. Gotta keep my strength up,' she said

through a mouthful of cream. 'Come to that, green tea don't exactly scream macho.'

'You'd prefer me to swig bourbon in between polishing my knuckledusters, I suppose.' Troy took a sip from his cup. 'You need to move with the times, Glory. Even Dad insists on organic muesli these days.'

'How is the old sod?'

'Grouchy. He's going to be bed-bound for a good while, yet he's still trying to hold meetings and take calls. Mum's run ragged, even with the nurses we've brought in. She hasn't been able to get any proper work done for weeks.' Absently, Troy helped himself to a wodge of eclair. 'Oh, and get this – Candice broke out of her fancy rehab centre last week and has run off with some loser she met there. Nobody's told Dad, of course. It'll send him over the edge.'

Charlie's wife Kezia was head-witch of the Wednesday Coven, and so responsible for the management of all witch-work activities. Her eldest daughter Candice was a witch too, and in the normal course of things would be her apprentice. But Candice's only career aspiration was to be a professional party-girl.

'Do you know where Candy is now?'

'San Jerico, would you believe! She's refusing to come home.'

San Jerico was the capital of Cordoba, otherwise known as the Costa-del-Witchcrime. It also happened to be the party centre of South America.

Glory pulled a sympathetic face. 'Are the uncles any help?'

'Uncle Frank's been supportive. Vince . . . well. I'm not sure how happy he is taking direction from me.'

This wasn't surprising. Frank looked after the coven's financial affairs, while Vince was the enforcer. Of the three Morgan brothers, he was the most volatile. 'You don't think he'd make a bid for power, do you?' she asked.

Troy looked at her warily. Coven politics was dangerous ground, especially when family was involved. 'He wouldn't have the support – too much of a loose cannon. But I still need him onside. He's leading the investigation into Dad's car-bomb.'

'It were Paterson, I thought. Trying to start a coven blood feud by fixing it on the Wednesday's rivals.'

'Paterson was behind it, yeah. But he didn't get his hands dirty. We think he hired a couple of Russian freelancers – Vince has been talking to a contact of his in the Volkov Coven. So when it comes to payback, it'll be Vince who leads the charge.'

Glory grimaced. The Wednesday Coven had come a long way from its origins, when the Starling Twins had London enthralled by their outrageous heists, daring scams and razzle-dazzle charm.

'This isn't just about avenging Dad,' Troy told her. 'If I don't ensure the guilty parties are punished, I'll be seen not just as soft, but irresponsible. Governments do the same; they're just sneakier about it.'

She knew he was right. Witches made good assassins. Who knew what WICA might ask her to do one day, for Queen and Country?

'Anyway, enough about me,' Troy said. 'How's it going

with the witch-spooks? You must be disarming nuclear warheads on a regular basis by now.'

'Huh. I should be so lucky. All I'm doing at the moment is learning lists. Boring facts about boring countries and the boring people in charge of them. As bad as school, it is. Can't even go for a piss without asking permission.'

'And how's the Stearne boy?'

This, and 'the witch-pricker's kid', was how Troy usually referred to Lucas. His tone was amused as well as patronising.

'He's . . . OK, I guess. We've got different schedules most of the time – I reckon management think I'm a bad influence on him.'

Troy smiled. 'Oh, I do hope so.'

Sometimes Glory felt that she and Troy understood each other in a way that she and Lucas never could. Troy wasn't a witch, but they shared family and history, and an enemy too, for Glory's hostility to the Inquisition hadn't changed. She'd cooperate with them if and when the occasion demanded, but she'd never trust them. Not as long as they continued to pierce witches with needles, half drown them in tanks and burn them alive. Yet even after what had happened to Lucas, his faith in the institution held firm. It was one of the many incomprehensible things about him.

The fae was a mysterious and elemental force, and Glory had felt it spark between her and Lucas the first time they'd met. They had been through a great deal together in a very short space of time. As a result, they had a shared loyalty as well as rivalry, and a mutual, unadmitted need. Yet somehow their work together at WICA hadn't brought them closer. Aware that somebody was always listening and watching, a new formality had grown between them.

Troy heard her sigh. 'Never mind, princess. If you get fed up, there's always a place for you at the firm. You know that.'

Ever since Glory had discovered that the Morgans planned for her to marry Troy, consolidating the family alliance and enlisting her fae, talk of this kind made her uncomfortable. Now she was blushing, and Troy's green eyes had an amused glint. He always enjoyed making her squirm.

So she poked her tongue out at him. 'Or maybe I should sign you up to WICA. With all this admin experience you're getting, I reckon you'd make me a fine PA.'

Glory returned to the flat in a much better mood than when she'd left it, but the evil hour couldn't be put off for ever. She sat down at the kitchen table and got out her books. When her dad came in through the door, it looked as if she'd been studying for hours.

'You are good, Glory,' Patrick said admiringly. 'I must say, I didn't know you had it in you.'

'You and me both. Been stretching your legs?'

'Ah . . . ahem. Thought I'd, er, have a wander down to the old neighbourhood. See how they all were.'

'Cooper Street! Dad. You know we're supposed to be staying away.'

She'd heard from Troy that her former coven was going downhill. The boss was a drunk, his son a waster, and the elderly head-witch, Glory's Great-aunt Angeline, was increasingly frail.

Patrick sat down opposite her. 'Auntie Angel's still covering for us. All she's said to the others is that the two of you had a bust-up and she threw you out. There's been no mention of that business with Lucas Stearne, or your involvement with WICA.'

Angeline was the elder sister of the Starling Twins, and had raised Glory in their image. Yet Angeline had betrayed her sister Cora to the Inquisition, and lied about her niece Edie's disappearance. Glory knew her great-aunt wasn't protecting her out of loyalty; if Angeline grassed on Glory, then her own dealings with the Inquisition would be exposed.

Patrick didn't know this. It was one of the many things Glory protected him from. He still didn't know the full details of how and why Lucas had come to Cooper Street, and she had never told him her belief that Charlie Morgan had murdered her mother. When she realised this was one of Angeline's lies, her decision seemed justified. Patrick thought his wife was lost to them for ever. Now Glory wasn't so sure. But either way, it would be unbearably cruel to raise his hopes.

'Earl said that Angeline's got herself a new apprentice,' he told her. 'A witch from up north. Kelly-Anne, she's called. Twenty-something ex-hairdresser.'

So some other girl was being invited into the pink-striped sitting room, to drink cups of over-sweet tea and practise witchwork under the Starling Girls' shrine . . .

Patrick gave his daughter's hand a consoling pat. 'Word is, she's not up to much. But the old lady needs a project. You know how it is.'

'Yeah. Good luck to her.' The memory of their final confrontation still made her guts clench. Glory turned back to her essay, *The Changing Face of Witch-Terror: Endor and Extremism.* In spite of herself, the words blurred on the page.

# CHAPTER 4

Across London, Lucas was staring at the same essay title. He supposed the distraction was a good thing. The more time he spent on work, the less time he had to fixate on his father's cryptic remarks.

Endor, the subject of his essay, was not a dry academic problem. The organisation took its name from a witch in the Bible, whom King Saul consulted in his hour of need. It was founded in the seventies, in America's Deep South, and, like the covens, its original purpose was to protect witches from persecution. Later, its ideology became radicalised: its members believed witches to be a separate and superior race, and were intent on making them dominant. Endor's activities in the West peaked with a bloody terrorist campaign in the 1990s, but a concerted effort by the United Council of Inquisitors had managed to break up the network. It was now reduced to a variety of disconnected regional movements, mostly active in the developing world. However, the UK couldn't be complacent. Endor, the bogeyman of Lucas's childhood, still lurked in the shadows.

Over the next few days, Lucas finished his essay, but heard nothing more from his father on the subject of Edie Starling. On Wednesday, however, there was some good news: Ashton informed the family that he had been offered the post of Chief Witchkind Advisor to the government. He would be the consultant on witchkind-related policies to the Prime Minister and the Cabinet.

Apparently, Lucas's condition wasn't going to be a problem. The PM told Ashton he welcomed his first-hand experience of the issues facing the UK's witch population. Ashton still supported the Inquisition's ban on people with witch-relatives from joining the service. 'It's a necessary safeguard,' he said to his son. 'But the easing of some anti-witch restrictions is a sign of the times. We live in a more tolerant, less paranoid age. Your generation of witchkind has much to be thankful for.'

Lucas thought of the white-tiled Burning Court, of the interrogation suites beneath the Inquisition's lawns and courtyards. But he nodded all the same.

The following afternoon, a witch-consultant from one of London's general hospitals came to WICA to give Lucas and Glory a fae-healing session. They were practising staunching wounds and cooling fever through the laying-on of hands. It was difficult, messy work, for which neither showed much aptitude. Fae-healing was one of the few aspects of witchwork that didn't depend on a witch's overall power.

It didn't help that they were being supervised by their witch wardens, Officers Jonah Branning and Carmel Wilks. A warden's job was something between a social worker, a parole officer and a security guard. Lucas got on well with his, but it was a different story between Glory and Carmel.

Big, awkward Jonah, whose mild expression belied his intelligence, was watching their activities from a corner. Carmel, however, hovered by Glory's side, beady eyes narrowed in suspicion. 'Gather yourself, Gloriana,' she said as Glory, scowling and perspiring, struggled to stop the blood flowing from a self-inflicted cut to her arm. 'You know that when you lose your temper, you lose focus.'

'Maybe we should try cutting chunks outta *you* then,' Glory snapped. 'See how you like it.'

Carmel pursed her lips, and made a note in her little book. As soon as the session ended, Glory charged out of the room, trailing bloody bandages in her wake.

Lucas and Jonah exchanged looks. Once they were alone, Jonah said, 'By the way, the Director wants a word with you. He's in the Dee Room.'

'Sounds ominous.'

'I'm sure it's fine.' Jonah pulled on his coat. 'But your dad's there too.'

The two men were sitting at the table in silence. The contrast between them was striking: Ashton was tall, pale and aristocratic, whereas Jack Rawdon was burly and rugged, with a mop of grizzled hair.

In spite of his rough and ready appearance, Rawdon was a savvy political operator. He was one of the UK's most high-profile witches, due in part to his work against Endor when he was a young WICA agent, but also because of his outspoken media appearances. Over the last few weeks, he had seized the opportunity offered by the Paterson conspiracy to campaign for many of the restrictions on his agency to be lifted.

Even so, most of the WICA offices were monitored by CCTV, the phone lines were wiretapped and inquisitorial guards patrolled the building. WICA agents weren't even allowed to run their own operations. Instead, they were assigned to assist their colleagues in MI5 and MI6 on a case by case basis.

As it happened, the Dee Room was one of the few areas where the live feed going to the Inquisition surveillance team could be switched off. Lucas saw from the red light blinking on the communications panel that this had already been done.

'Have a seat,' Ashton said. He gave Lucas a small smile of encouragement, but only when Rawdon wasn't looking. Lucas understood. This meeting couldn't be a family affair.

Rawdon was the more senior figure. But as a former High Inquisitor, Ashton Stearne would always outrank even the most top-level witch. He was the one to sit at the head of the table. He was the one to say 'come in' to the next knock at the door.

A middle-aged woman entered the room. She was small and upright, wearing a sprightly red suit with a lacquered helmet of greying blonde hair. Her bright lipstick made her mouth look lacquered too. Lucas sat up a little straighter. This was Dorcas Hughes, the new Commander-in-Chief of the Inquisition's Witchcrime Directorate.

'So this is your son,' she said, as she joined Ashton at the head of the table. She examined Lucas with professional curiosity. 'Chip off the old block, by the looks of it. And yet he's a witch. Extraordinary.' She put her head on one side, as if to regard the specimen from a fresh angle, and pursed her shiny lips. 'Do you know why you're here, young man?'

'Because . . . because I've been asking about Edie Starling.'

'And we're here to give you some answers,' Rawdon said. 'However, there are conditions attached. What we're about to discuss is highly confidential. As one of my agents, I need to know I can depend on your silence when I ask for it.'

'The Inquisition deals severely with unauthorised disclosures.' Commander Hughes's tone was brisk rather than threatening. 'You will certainly be bridled and returned to civilian life. You might even be at risk of prosecution.'

His father leaned towards him. 'Lucas understands, don't you?'

Of course Lucas had no choice but to agree.

'All right,' said the Commander. 'Let's get on with it. Ashton, I think you should take it from here. After all, you're the only one of us to have been personally involved in the case.'

Ashton knitted his brows. 'In a minor capacity, it must be said. However, I'll begin with Cora Starling who, as we all know, founded the Wednesday Coven with her twin Lily. I don't need to tell anyone here that they were a pair of ruthless crooks who used celebrity and personal charm to, quite literally, get away with murder.

'Cora was the more reckless of the sisters. She had many affairs, several with prominent establishment figures, and there were rumours of alcohol and drug dependency. At any rate, in 1979 she quarrelled violently with Lily and disappeared, taking her daughter Edie with her. At that time, Edie was eight, her father unknown. Nobody heard from them for five years.'

Lucas nodded, trying to hide his impatience. He knew this already.

'By all accounts, they spent the next few years living a vagabond existence across Europe, using Cora's underworld contacts to evade the authorities. However, in 1983 Cora travelled to the United States, where she joined a New Age commune in Texas known as the Sisterhood of Divine Light. It was here she was recruited to Endor. She and her daughter spent three months in an Endor cell that was operating in Atlanta before Cora decided to return home. She may have been sent on a mission by Endor; she may have got bored, and left the organisation on a whim. She was, as I said, notoriously unreliable.

'Cora was immediately apprehended by the Inquisition on her return to England. Unfortunately, the officers in charge of her interrogation were overzealous in their efforts. She drowned in the course of a witch-ducking, before any significant information could be learned.'

Lucas had always been irritated by Glory's starry-eyed view of the Starling myth. Now, in spite of himself, he felt a sadness for the girl Glory's grandmother had once been. Cora the bad, Cora the beautiful. The half-crazy witch-girl who went dancing in stolen diamonds, and rinsed her hair in champagne to make it shine . . .

His father talked on, as placidly as if he was reading the

weather forecast. 'After Cora's death, Edie was adopted by Lily Starling and brought up inside the Wednesday Coven. It was Lily's intention to make Edie her heir, since none of her own children had the fae. But after Lily died, her three sons – led by Charlie Morgan and his wife Kezia – threw Edie out. She found refuge with her Aunt Angeline at the Cooper Street Coven. Though Angeline had hopes of using her niece's witchwork to restore the coven's fortunes, it appears Edie wanted to live an ordinary domestic life. She married and had a child: Gloriana.

'Edie was, of course, a person of interest to the Inquisition pretty much from the moment of her birth. But it was the time she spent as a child with Endor that made her such a potentially valuable asset. Accordingly, the Inquisition chose to keep her under surveillance rather than bringing her in for testing and registration. The strategy paid off. Sixteen years after she and her mother left Endor, Edie Starling was approached by one of their agents in London, and invited to join their cause. Initially, she refused.'

Lucas held his breath. So they were coming to the point at last.

'By then, the UK had endured three years of Endor terror: witch-hexed assassinations, sabotage, epidemics and banes. In Edie Starling, the Inquisition saw a unique opportunity to infiltrate the organisation. Her history and connections made her a natural convert to Endor's cause. And so "Operation Swan" was born.'

'You're saying Edie agreed to leave home and go undercover among a bunch of terrorists?' Lucas frowned. 'Just like that?'

Ashton didn't lower his eyes or alter his voice. Yet this time there was something effortful about his calm. 'Edie was . . . persuaded . . . it was in her family's best interest. The Inquisition had proof of her contact with a terrorist operative and this, in addition to her coven ties, would have been enough to put her away for a good number of years. Her associates at Cooper Street would also be vulnerable. By agreeing to work as a double agent, she was ensuring their continued safety, as well as that of the country at large.'

'I get it. She was blackmailed.' Lucas meant to sound impassive too, but the bitterness rose in his throat. 'And what was your role in this, Dad?'

'The Chief Prosecutor tasked me with preparing the legal case against Edie. I did not find out that it had been used to pressure her until later. When I did, I voiced my objections. Edie was an intelligent and capable young woman. But her background was murky, to say the least, and her character wayward. Whatever the ethics, it was a risky gamble.'

'It was for Edie, yeah.' His face was hot.

'Lucas.' His father's eyes looked tired, almost grey. 'I regret I did not object more strongly, and that events turned out as they did. But we were at war. It was a desperate, dangerous time. We all make our decisions without the power of hindsight.'

In those days, Ashton had been an ambitious young inquisitorial lawyer. He was also a widower. Two years prior to Edie Starling being brought into the Witchcrime Directorate, his wife's mind had been invaded by an Endor witch, and her body bound to a poppet crafted with fae.

Camilla Stearne had been forced to drive her own car off the road, to smash it into a twist of metal and flame. Lucas thought, as his father meant him to, of all the other families whose lives were left in ruins by Endor's campaign.

He swallowed. 'It was your war too,' he said to Jack Rawdon. 'When did you find out about this?'

Rawdon gave a small, apologetic shrug. 'Only after Glory applied to WICA. During Operation Swan, I was part of an anti-Endor task force that involved all branches of the security services, but communication was not always as . . . open . . . as it could have been. Especially where WICA was involved.'

He glanced quickly at Ashton and Commander Hughes. 'I suspect the fact that Edie was not a professional agent, and had no establishment or institutional ties, made her, in the Inquisition's eyes, easier to manage.'

*You mean easier to isolate and manipulate*, thought Lucas. Almost as if he had read his mind, Rawdon said, 'But you should know, Lucas, that in spite of the element of coercion involved, Edie showed a natural aptitude for undercover work. I've seen her files. In her contact with her handler she seemed, if anything, to relish the challenge.'

'A challenge that probably got her killed.' Edie had left a note to her abandoned family: *I love you, but it's better if I go. Forgive me.* Lucas remembered Glory's face when she told him, and his heart lurched.

'Well. That's the question,' said the Commander. She had spent most of the conversation tilting back on her chair, idly tap-tapping a pen against her teeth. Now she snapped upright. 'Operation Swan was initially a short-term assignment. Edie was asked to gather intelligence on a top-level Endor leader who was trying to enter the country. After this was achieved, she told her handler that she'd heard whispers relating to a potential attack on British interests overseas, and requested permission to follow the lead. She volunteered, in fact. It was only then that she left home.

'For three months, Edie Starling worked undercover in mainland Europe, from where she supplied the Inquisition with information that was used to prevent several attacks on British businesses and residences. Then she disappeared. It was feared she'd either been discovered and killed by Endor, or turned by them. But Endor was already moving its attention away from the UK. The immediate crisis had passed. One AWOL witch-agent didn't seem worth the trouble.

'However, five years ago, a source reported a sighting of Edie in southern Spain. It might not be the same woman, of course. But if there's a possibility she is still alive, there's a possibility she's now working for Endor. That makes her a potential threat – especially if she ever decides to contact her daughter.'

Lucas felt a new unease. 'It's been twelve years since she left. If she'd wanted to get in touch, wouldn't she have done so before?'

'Ah,' said the Commander, 'but Gloriana's almost grown-up now, and a powerful witch in her own right. If Edie discovers this, she might try to take advantage.'

'Seems to me she was the one who got taken advantage of. Bullied and blackmailed, then tossed aside – "not worth the trouble" of finding.' With effort, Lucas moderated his tone. 'That's how Glory would see it, anyway.'

The Commander smiled grimly. 'And that's why she

can't be told. Not yet. She's immature and wilful, with much to learn and even more to prove.'

'In the meantime,' said Rawdon, 'now that Glory is here and part of our team, we're in a good position to keep an eye on her. If Edie is alive, and *if* she decides to contact her daughter, then we'll know about it.'

'So Glory's being used as bait.'

And who were 'we', anyhow, Lucas wondered. WICA? The Inquisition? Did that mean him too?

Rawdon put up his hands reassuringly. 'Glory was recruited to this division for the same reasons you were. She's an outstandingly gifted witch who has already displayed great courage and resourcefulness in her work against the Paterson conspiracy.

'Yes, she has a few rough edges. She needs guidance and support. But I believe in her. What's more, I need her. Soon, I'll be calling on the two of you to put your talents to work outside the confines of this agency.'

Jack Rawdon gave the warm, frank smile that had made him the poster-boy for Socially Acceptable Witchkind. Lucas felt a spark of excitement in spite of himself. Did his boss have a mission for them at last?

'Of course, Glory needs to be told the truth one day,' Rawdon continued. 'But the likelihood of her mother being alive remains small, and the chance of her trying to get in contact is even smaller. I think we can afford to give Glory some more time to adjust to her new life. For now, the knowledge would be too heavy a burden.'

'You yourself have no right to that knowledge,' said Commander Hughes. 'Only the responsibility to safeguard it.'

'It's for Glory's own good,' said his father.

Once more, all three of them were leaning towards him, eyes fixed on his, expressions stern yet encouraging. Once more, he had little option but to agree.

In the aftermath of the meeting, Lucas tried to get a handle on Edie Starling and the kind of woman she'd been, but the various accounts he'd heard were too elusive and contradictory. He groped for indisputable facts, for clear judgements, and found none. Perhaps his father was right. It had been a war, and different rules applied.

Glory wouldn't see it like that, though. If she found out the story of Operation Swan, she'd leave at once and never look back. She would be lost . . . for ever.

He wasn't sure he believed that Edie had really volunteered to work as a double agent abroad. He wondered too if Rawdon and Hughes knew more about her whereabouts and activities than they were letting on. If so, was Glory in danger of being used in the same way as her mother had been? Either way, Lucas knew he was now part of the cover-up, however little choice he'd had in the matter.

But these concerns were already fading in the light of a new, more pressing question.

What kind of task did Jack Rawdon have in store for them?

# CHAPTER 5

Glory was dreaming of the Burning Court.

Its white-tiled walls sloped up to the mouth of the huge chimney that formed its ceiling. An audience of inquisitors waited behind a viewing pane.

She herself was waiting at the balefire's stake. Bundles of wood were stacked around her legs; an electric fuse led from under them to the observation room.

Glory stood in stillness and silence. She had no choice. She'd been given a drug to immobilise her body and numb the pain. While her heart hammered fit to burst, her reflection in the glass was perfectly serene.

She knew what was about to happen. She'd had the dream so many times that her subconscious mind could anticipate each step. That didn't mean she could stop it, though. That didn't mean she could escape the moment when her reflection changed, so that she was staring at another woman, a wide-eyed blonde, in the mirrored glass. Her mother.

And that moment was followed by the instant of true horror: when she realised the drug didn't work, that her nerves and senses hadn't been numbed, and she was about to burn alive . . .

As always, Glory tried to fight, to thrash, to scream. As always, she couldn't move. Not so much as a twitch of an eyelid, as the first spark leaped from the wood, and the fire swept upwards with a spit and cackle.

Through the rising smoke, she could see the audience in the observation room. This was the part of the dream that changed: the faces of the people who watched her burn. Tonight it was Lucas, standing next to Troy. Auntie Angel, arm in arm with Peggy.

As always, she tried to beg them to help. As always, they watched, patient, smiling, unconcerned, as the flames twisted towards her. At any moment, the fire was going to lick at her feet and writhe upwards through her flesh, flaying her to the bone.

Her tongue was frozen. So was the breath in her lungs. All the same, a scream, swollen, unstoppable, was bursting through her body –

Glory woke up. Her hair was damp with sweat, and she was breathing as hard as if she'd run a race. When she turned on the light, she nearly cried out for real. In the course of the nightmare, she must have been clawing at her arms, for the cuts and scratches left by yesterday's fae-healing session had opened again, and speckled the sheets with blood.

Cursing, she clambered out of bed. Wasn't she ever going to grow out of this thing? She was a legally registered witch. The Inquisition wasn't going to come for her in the night; boots on the stairs, fists on the door. Yet the old nightmare showed no signs of fading.

She glanced at the photograph of her mother she kept beside the bed. They didn't look much alike. Edie was a natural blonde, with small, delicate features, and a guarded smile. *The kind that always leaves, never looks back*, that's how Auntie Angel had described her. The only time her mother was truly vivid for Glory was in her dreams.

As Glory was leaving for work – late, as usual – she passed Peggy on the stairs. Patrick had attended his first Residents' Association meeting on Sunday evening, and had spent the following morning at a local computer club, teaching the oldies how to use the internet. Now he and Peggy were going to meet the construction crew who were refurbishing the children's play area. Maybe this was why he'd been so cheerful at breakfast. The fact her dad was up at all was a novelty. In Cooper Street, he had rarely surfaced before twelve. Glory noticed that Peggy was wearing a new lipstick, and frowned.

Normally, she quite enjoyed her docklands commute. This morning, the Thames glittered in the sun, and the sleek ranks of apartment blocks and offices glittered too. But Glory walked head down, too preoccupied to notice.

WICA was not a part of the shiny new developments. It was located in a Victorian warehouse on the edge of a run-down industrial estate. Unlike the other security service HQs, its location was kept anonymous. The sign over the main entrance was for *Avalon Atlantic Plc: International Shipping*. Since Glory and Lucas were too young to be plausibly employed by a shipping company, they entered the building through the so-called 'back door', an underground passageway that was accessed via a computer repair shop around the corner. This was as fake as the reception for Avalon Atlantic, and was also staffed by a WICA guard.

Glory sketched a greeting to the guard and made her way to the back of the shop, where there were stairs down to the subway. Lucas arrived just as she was typing in the access code. He didn't look as if he'd slept any better than she had. There were shadows under his eyes, and when he saw her, he seemed to hang back a little. But Glory made a point of waiting for him. As they walked along the narrow concrete passageway, she found herself confiding to him about Peggy.

'She's nice enough,' she said. 'It's just that she's a bit nosy for my liking. Bossy too, I bet. Those do-gooder types always are.'

'I thought you wanted your dad to meet new people. To get out more.'

'Yeah, but I reckon old Peg's after more than tea and sympathy. And Dad's so clueless he'll be the last to catch on.'

'Would it be so bad if Patrick met someone?' Lucas said cautiously. 'I mean, I wasn't too thrilled when Dad first got together with Marisa. But after I got used to the idea, I realised that it was probably a good thing.'

'I ain't stupid. Or selfish neither,' Glory retorted. ' 'Course I don't want Dad to be lonely – 'specially as I'm not going to stick around home for ever. But now I know my mum might be alive, that makes stuff complicated, don't it? Dad's still *married*, remember.'

Lucas was silent for a while. 'The thing is . . . even if

your mum . . . Well, if she wanted to get in touch, wouldn't she have done so by now?'

This was something Glory often wondered about, but didn't like to acknowledge. Her face tightened. 'That's the point: I don't *know*. I don't know *nothing*. If she were just another unhappy housewife who ran off then OK, fair enough. Maybe it'd be time to cut our losses. But there's more to it than that. I'm *sure* of it. Else she wouldn't be in them Inquisition files.'

Lucas looked uncomfortable. 'Anything's possible,' he said. 'But spend too much time wondering "what if?", and life has a way of moving on without you. Maybe your father's tired of putting his on hold.'

Glory knew that what Lucas said was perfectly reasonable, but she still resented him for it. It was probably just as well they were going their separate ways for the first lesson of the day. They each had to learn two modern languages and in this, as in so many things, Lucas's schooling put him ahead.

But Glory and her Spanish tutor had only just settled down to the latest vocab list when Jack Rawdon's PA knocked on the door. Glory was requested to attend a meeting in the Dee Room.

Uh-oh. Had they found out about her coffee with Troy? Or maybe this was about her strop with the fae-healer . . . She set off to the meeting with her best Rockwood Estate strut: head high, hips swinging, don't-mess-with-me scowl.

To her surprise, Lucas was there too. Maybe she wasn't in trouble after all. Jack Rawdon was leaning casually against the table, his shirt sleeves rolled up, unkempt hair falling over his eyes. There was another man sitting next to him. He was stringy and balding, in an ill-fitting suit. On the conferencing screen on the wall there was a woman in the scarlet and grey ceremonial uniform of a High Inquisitor.

'Glory,' Rawdon said. 'Good to see you. Let me introduce you to Commander Dorcas Hughes of the Witchcrime Directorate.'

Glory and the woman said stiff hellos.

'. . . and Guy Carmichael,' Rawdon continued, 'a colleague from Six.'

Glory went to shake the MI6 officer's hand. It was surprisingly firm for such a limp-looking man. As she sat down, Rawdon indicated the red light on the communications panel. 'This is a closed meeting. Your wardens will be appraised of what follows, but on a strictly need-to-know basis.'

Glory's stomach began to flutter pleasantly. She and Lucas exchanged looks, trying not to appear too obviously excited as Rawdon tossed them a couple of shiny brochures.

'*Welcome to Wildings Academy,*' Lucas read aloud. '*Distinction, Discretion, Diligence.*'

'It's a school,' said Glory, in the way other people might say 'it's a dead cat.'

'A very special, very *private* school,' said the man from Six.

Glory opened the first page. She was looking at a photograph of a narrow valley, shadowed by mountains and furred by trees. A cluster of grey towers and turrets rose up from the forest. It was a castle out of a fae-tale.

'*Wildings Academy,*' the introduction read, '*provides struc-ture and security for young people whose needs are not met by conventional education systems, and a refuge where troubled teen-agers can find shelter from the pressures of modern life.*'

'So it's a sin bin,' she said.

Rawdon looked amused. 'In a manner of speaking. But though you wouldn't know it from the brochure, its intake is exclusively witchkind.'

'Sounds like the place my stepmother wanted to send me to,' said Lucas.

Glory flicked through the pages. Wildings was appar-ently located in eastern Switzerland, somewhere near the Italian border, but there was no address or map, just a contact email. There wasn't any sign of the students either, in the glossy pictures of classrooms, science labs and sports facilities. The only people to feature in the brochure were a group of uniformed guards. 'Does the Inquisition run it, then?' she asked.

'It doesn't have jurisdiction,' Commander Hughes said from the screen. Her voice was acid. 'Switzerland does not legally recognise witches under the age of eighteen. Its own witchkind community is tiny: less than 0.05 per cent of the populace.'

'A loophole that Wildings Academy has been able to exploit,' Guy Carmichael put in. 'Wealthy families can purchase a special study visa from the Swiss government to send their offspring to the school, as long as they do so before the child's fae is officially detected and registered in their home country. Wildings' students are high-status – the sort who'd cause professional as well as personal difficulties for their parents if their condition was known. The academy operates a *Don't Ask, Don't Tell* policy, which is why it can get away with it.'

Glory snorted. 'I bet that kind of loophole don't come cheap.'

'Very true,' said Rawdon. 'Wildings is as expensive as it is secret and the intake is no more than ten students at any one time. You need powerful connections to even know about it.'

'So far,' said Commander Hughes, 'the Swiss government has resisted external pressure to shut the place down. Discipline there is tight: any student caught discussing witchwork, let alone practising it, is instantly expelled. They work hard to maintain good relations with their neighbours – in fact, the local village of Blumenwald gets regular "grants", i.e. bribes, from the academy. In the fifteen years it's been operating, there have been no security breaches. Or rather, none that we know about.

'However, our team at Intelligence Command has picked up chatter that the place has become of interest to Endor. There's a concern the academy could have been infiltrated, either among the students or staff. Since any collection of adolescent witches is a breeding ground for trouble, the more we can find out about what goes on there, the better.'

'So you're going to enrol us?' Lucas asked Rawdon.

But it was Guy Carmichael who answered. 'It would be a straightforward search-and-report –'

'Observation only,' Commander Hughes said over him. 'You will leave any follow-up action to us.'

Rawdon smiled wryly. 'Indeed. The operation is going to be led by the Witchcrime Directorate, working in conjunction with MI6. We at WICA will be involved in a supportive capacity.'

*Right. A capacity that takes all the risk and does all the work,* thought Glory. It put her back up, taking orders from the Inquisition. From the looks of it, the man from MI6 felt the same. Officially, the Inquisition had two main roles: to monitor law-abiding witches, and hunt down and punish the criminal kind. When it came to wider issues of national security, especially foreign intelligence, however, there was a feeling in the secret service that the Inquisition was going beyond its remit.

But Endor was a common enemy. Its fae-fanatics gave witchkind a bad name.

Glory fingered the gilt-trimmed pages of the prospectus. Going to boarding school wasn't exactly what she had in mind when she signed up to be a secret agent. But neither were verb tables and data analysis. Espionage in the Alps was bound to provide some sort of action, especially if she would be working undercover. Maybe she'd get to pose as somebody rich and glitzy.

Unfortunately, Rawdon's next words ruled this out.

'The big advantage is that you can go more or less as yourselves. Lucas, as the son of a government advisor and ex-High-Inquisitor, would be a natural fit for Wildings in any case. And you, Glory, will go back to your roots. The story is you've been getting into trouble with the authorities, and so your Morgan relations have decided to get you out of the country until things blow over and they can find a suitable place for you in the coven.'

Guy Carmichael had already begun to hand out a stack of files from the box by his feet. They bulged with briefings and data reports.

'When do we go?' Glory asked him.

'The end of next week.'

# CHAPTER 6

Lucas found the preparations for enrolling at Wildings much more straightforward than when he had infiltrated the Cooper Street Coven. His family had been told where he was going, though not why, and he would be able to have written contact with home. After a couple of weeks at the academy, he would even be allowed visitors. His would be an agent from MI6, posing as his godfather. Their meeting would allow Lucas to make a full progress report.

A farewell family dinner was held the night before he was due to fly to Zurich. Family meals had been an ordeal for some time now, composed of long interludes where only the chink of silver cutlery on good china disturbed the silence. Thursday's gathering was different. It almost had a festive atmosphere.

This was mostly due to his stepmother. A gracious hostess and formidable networker, Marisa had married a High Inquisitor in expectation of sharing all the prestige of her husband's position. Having a witch for a stepson was not part of the plan. But with Lucas's embarrassing condition under wraps – covered by the Official Secrets Act, no less! – the family's standing was secure. Even better, Ashton's new government post meant he might still be in reach of a knighthood . . .

And now Lucas was off to boarding school, just like she'd proposed from the start. Marisa's good spirits danced over the dining table.

'Switzerland is a lovely country,' she remarked as she passed Lucas the petits fours. 'So civilised. I wonder if you'll still be there for the ski season?'

'He's not going on holiday, darling,' said Ashton.

'Well, no, but it would be a pity not to make the most of his travels. Perhaps you could bring us back some of that wonderful chocolate, Lucas. Or cheese. It would be such a treat.'

Philomena yawned. 'No wonder Swiss bankers get fat.'

'Don't worry, Philly,' Lucas told her. 'I'll be sure to find you a slimline cuckoo clock.'

'If we could put the souvenir requests aside,' said Ashton, with heavy patience, 'perhaps we might take a moment to reflect on Lucas's new venture, and why we should applaud it.'

'Dad . . .' Lucas looked down at his plate, embarrassed. Marisa pursed her lips. Philomena got ready to roll her eyes, saw Ashton's expression, and thought better of it.

'It's true I had reservations about you joining the agency, Lucas. I still do. That is a parent's prerogative. But serving one's country has always been the Stearne way, and though it's not an easy path to take, it is – I believe – the best and bravest one.'

Lucas tried to speak, but the words wouldn't come.

'To Lucas,' Ashton said, and raised his glass.

'To Lucas,' the others obediently chorused.

Glory kept picking up her passport and turning it over in her hands. She hadn't travelled more than a few miles outside London before, let alone got on an aeroplane. Until recently, she wouldn't have been able to find Switzerland on a map.

Witches had special passports in addition to their ID cards. They had to apply for permits to go abroad and register with the Inquisition of the country they were visiting. Because Lucas and Glory were acting the part of unregistered witches, however, they had been issued with standard British Citizen passports. They could come and go as they pleased.

It was an intoxicating idea. Glory thought of her mother and grandmother, roaming the continent from one adventure to the next, crossing borders in search of new horizons, restless and free . . .

Yet now the time had come, she didn't feel ready for it. She was a Londoner born and bred. Its grime and grit were knitted into her bones, close as the fae. And although its streets teemed with the sights and sounds of other nations, she struggled to imagine herself as a foreigner; the person who couldn't read signs or follow instructions, who made the wrong gestures and got overcharged buying the wrong stuff. What if nobody understood her accent? What if she didn't like the food? Even the electricity was different abroad. She'd had to get special plugs.

Part of the anxiety was not knowing how long she'd be away. Wildings Academy was open all year round; its students stayed on campus until their graduation. Glory's lip curled at the thought of them – a bunch of snots who'd prefer to pose as delinquents rather than face up to being witchkind. Pathetic.

Patrick had been told where she was going but not why. The official story was she'd won a place on a charitable study abroad programme for inner-city teens. He had taken the news of her departure quietly. At odd moments, Glory would go into her room and find an offering left on her bed: an inflatable travel pillow, a tin of sweets, a pair of Union Jack socks.

On her last night, he came in and watched her pack. He'd spent the afternoon with Rolf, a fellow gaming enthusiast he'd recently met through the Computer Club. Rolf was very tall and very fat, and as chatty as Patrick was quiet. They made an odd pair, Glory thought, but she was pleased Patrick had someone else to hang out with apart from Peggy.

He seemed more puzzled than worried by her departure. 'I never liked travelling,' he said. 'Too much fuss. Your mum was different. She would have liked to get out of town, gone exploring . . . Well.' He smiled ruefully. 'I was never the adventurous type.'

Glory gave him a hug. 'You made Mum happy,' she told him. 'I know it. That's what counts.'

'*You*'d make her happy. She'd be ever so proud.'

'Would she? I wish I'd some proper memories of her. Mine are all from other people's stories. I ain't got none of my own.'

'Your mum's a part of you, Glory. But it's your own self that makes you special. Don't forget that.'

'Is – is Mum still a part of you? After so long?'

'Yes.' Her dad nodded slowly. 'Yes, I think she'll always be. But not like a real person, more like an idea of one. A nice idea too. No painful thoughts.' He patted her hand. 'As you said, it's been a long time. You don't have to worry.'

It was true that in spite of his shambolic air, her father was self-sufficient as well as solitary. But the Cooper Street Coven had been a family as well as a business, and however dysfunctional that family was, it had offered security and support. Looking at her father now, Glory was suddenly glad of Peggy's presence. She would get Troy to keep an eye on him too.

Glory had left a letter for her father with Zoey Connor, one of the few agents she was friendly with at WICA. She had been determined to make the letter everything Edie's fragment of farewell was not. It was a surprise to find the words came quite easily. Afterwards, she felt relief and also optimism. It was like insurance – once it was taken out, you forgot about it. Besides, the idea of failure was inconceivable. She was Gloriana Starling Wilde. She always achieved what she set out to do, whatever it took.

However, there was something else Glory had to cross off her list before she left. It involved a consultation with Troy.

When they arranged to meet in a greasy spoon near Tower Bridge, she had looked forward to being evasive and mysterious. Even if she couldn't namecheck Endor, she planned to drop dark hints about the mission ahead. Unfortunately, at the first mention of boarding school, Troy nearly fell off his chair laughing. 'Jolly hockey sticks! Cold

showers and double Latin! It'll be the making of you, girl.'
The only thing he took seriously was her request to check up on Patrick.

'There's something else,' she said. 'Rose Merle. Have you made any progress?'

Rose was the seventeen-year-old daughter of Lady Serena Merle, a bridled witch who had died in a fire she had set herself. Rose, left brain-damaged after a botched operation to remove her fae, had been put in the care of a private hospital. Her memory had gone; she couldn't hold a thought or feel an emotion. Glory had met her briefly and couldn't think of her blank and frozen face without a shudder.

Lady Merle had been married to one of Silas Paterson's co-conspirators. She had also been an informant for the Wednesday Coven. But Glory and Troy had discovered her relationship with the coven was more than just business. When Serena Merle had been an aspiring young actress, and before she turned witchkind, she'd had a fling with Vince Morgan. Rose was therefore Lily Starling's grand-daughter and Troy's cousin. Troy had been trying to track her down for some weeks now.

He grimaced in response to Glory's question. 'Yeah, and it's not good news. She's been discharged from hospital. It took a hefty sweetener before I could get the nurse to talk. She said Rose was collected by a Mr S. Evans – her uncle, allegedly. The thing is, I've done some research, and Serena didn't have a brother. Nor did Lord M.'

Glory fiddled with a sugar packet. 'You don't reckon . . . it couldn't have been Vince, could it? If he found out about Rose, and –'

'No,' said Troy firmly. 'If that was the case, I'd know about it. Besides, this bloke was a Yank according to the nurse. Bit of a smoothie, she said.'

Glory thought about Vince Morgan; the wild red hair and the beaten-up face, the scars and tattoos. He had a way of looking at you that made you think the back of your neck would crack. How had he charmed Serena Merle, so polished and fragrant, with her dewy eyes and pearly skin? With those two for parents, Rose would have made a formidable witch.

'How would Vince take it, d'you reckon?'

'A long-lost kid is one thing,' said Troy, shrugging. 'A kid with mush for brains is another. And Uncle Vince isn't exactly the paternal sort. He was quite the ladykiller in his younger days – in more ways than one.' He gave a humourless laugh. 'Could be there's a whole litter of mini-Morgans we don't know about.'

'Still . . . he's gotta find out about her someday. I mean, if the coven takes Rose in, people'll want to know why.'

'We'll cross that bridge when we come to it. I'll keep searching for her, of course. I'll keep asking questions. But for now, I'm afraid it looks as if we've hit a dead end.'

# CHAPTER 7

Peggy had offered to drive Glory and Patrick to the airport. Glory said that she'd prefer to go on her own. It was true she'd prefer not to go with Peggy, but she had no wish to bring her dad along either. He wasn't good in crowds, or noisy and unfamiliar places.

Glory almost regretted refusing the lift as she battled across London on public transport with her bags. The airport was thronged and echoing; wherever she looked, inquisitorial guards were on patrol. She had an irrational fear somebody would pinch her passport, and she grew hot and harassed working out which signs to follow and where to go.

She caught sight of Lucas after checking-in. They were supposed to be strangers, as part of their cover, but his family were with him and Glory would have kept out of his way in any case. She retreated behind an information desk to observe. The elegant blonde must be his stepmother, talking to the stepsister with the stupid name. The girl's face looked stupid too. Lucas was standing next to his father.

Glory had seen Stearne Senior once before, when he'd

stormed into the basement where Lucas was held captive. Her memory of him was confused by the other images of that night. Now she could really see how alike he and Lucas were. Tall, imposing, assured. Ashton Stearne could be flipping burgers in a fast-food joint, or scrubbing the airport floor, and he'd still look a High Inquisitor to the bone.

He put his arm round his son. They were posing for a photograph taken by the blonde. The girl threw back her glossy hair with the practised ease of someone in a shampoo commercial. Lucas said something, and they all laughed. There were other families all around them, saying other goodbyes, but the Stearnes stood out from the rest. So attractive and prosperous, so absolutely sure of their place in the world. Even Glory was dazzled. She screwed up her face.

'Glory!'

Now it was her turn to be looked at. Even the Stearnes paused. 'Glory!' called Troy Morgan again, striding towards her. His breadth and height made it easy for him to pick her up from the floor, crush her against his chest and whirl her round.

'How – what –' She was pink and breathless with surprise. Troy was never demonstrative, let alone theatrical.

'You didn't think I'd let you go without a proper goodbye, did you?' he said, finally setting her down. He glanced towards the Stearnes, and straightened out his suit in a satisfied sort of way.

Glory laughed. 'So where's me red carpet and the brass band?'

'I'm saving them for when you get back. Got everything you need?'

'Should do.' She felt suddenly shy. 'I hope things go OK for you while I'm gone.'

'Stay lucky, Gloriana Starling.' Troy touched her, lightly, on the cheek. He glanced again towards the Stearnes. 'Remember who you are.'

From near the airport security area, Lucas watched as Troy Morgan swept Glory up into an embrace. There was a lot of laughter.

Ashton frowned. 'An unfortunate association.'

'Wait, *that's* the coven girl?' Philomena stared at the hooped earrings, the low-cut red top, the bottle-blonde hair. She sniggered. 'Chavtastic.'

'Enough of that,' said Ashton sharply. 'Our family, and indeed the country at large, owes that young woman a great deal.'

Marisa gave a little cough. 'Darling, it's time Lucas went through security. We mustn't delay him any longer.' She took Lucas's hands in hers, before daintily swooping in for a farewell kiss. 'I'm sure everything will work out for the best. You're bound to do *splendidly*.'

Philomena bumped briefly against him in what passed for a hug. His father clapped him on the back. 'Be safe,' Ashton told him. 'Be strong.'

Glory had joined the queue to screen hand luggage. Lucas turned back for a final look at his family. Troy Morgan was standing behind them, hands in his pockets, watching. Lucas could almost feel the force of that hard green stare.

He passed the fingerprint test and iris scan, and walked through the metal arch hung with iron bells. Arches like this were placed at all stages of the arrival and departure process, to give warning of witches who were trying to hex a bane. Glory was not far ahead, but once in the terminal, they were careful to keep out of each other's way, even though their flight turned out to be delayed for over an hour.

It was only after Lucas had boarded the plane that he allowed himself to look for her. She was in her seat, chewing gum loudly, and absorbed in a stash of gossip magazines. A tinny beat rustled from her earphones. Her neighbour already had a long-suffering air.

Lucas settled into his seat and tried to relax. This proved impossible. Instead, he tried to collect his thoughts by going over the plans they'd made and the research they'd done. Names, faces and statistics scrolled through his head.

Wildings' membership was a closely kept secret and MI6 had gone to considerable trouble to identify the five other students already enrolled. The eldest was Jenna White, aged seventeen, from California. Her father was an IT entrepreneur and dot-com millionaire. The photograph in the file had been taken at her school prom, and was a vision of tanned limbs, white teeth and big blue eyes. She'd joined Wildings three weeks ago, some time after the rumours of Endor infiltration emerged. Still, although a cheerleader-turned-terrorist was unlikely, it wasn't impossible. Appearances were particularly deceptive when witchkind were involved.

Yuri Polzin certainly looked like trouble. According to his mugshot, the sixteen-year-old heir of a Russian oil tycoon had a scowling face, shaven head and stony glare.

Yuri had joined Wildings at the same time as fourteen-year-old Anjuli Verma. Anjuli was an orphan, who had been brought up by her older sister, a successful Bollywood actress. The notes said she had previously been hospitalised with mental problems. The final girl was Mei-fen Zhou, the daughter of a senior official in China's ruling party, who was the youngest student at thirteen.

It was Raphael Almagro, though, who had been the focal point of Lucas's and Glory's briefing. Aged sixteen, Raphael had been at Wildings for nearly eight months. His father was the Chief of Police in Cordoba, a small republic on the northern coast of South America. In the 1960s, a witchkind-backed revolutionary movement had overthrown a brutal dictatorship, and broken up the Cordoban Inquisition. The rebels were subsequently overthrown in turn by a military junta, but the Inquisition was never reinstated.

Times were changing, however. The upcoming presidential election was widely expected to be won by Senator Benito Vargas, who was riding high in the polls on an anti-witchkind, anti-corruption ticket. Vargas was on record for calling the police as criminal as the covens, and supported the use of private militias to hunt witches. No wonder Raphael's family wanted him out of the way . . . or that WICA and its partners had marked him out as of special interest.

Wildings' staff were almost as varied as its students. Three of them were ex-inquisitors: the head of security, the matron and the academy's principal, Emil Lazovic. Lazovic was a Serbian national, but had worked all over the world in his former job in the diplomatic corps of the United Council of Inquisitors. Lucas found it hard to understand why former inquisitors would seek employment in such a place. Maybe they genuinely believed Wildings offered a necessary resource. Or maybe they were just unprincipled opportunists.

The curriculum followed the International Baccalaureate. In order to cater for the age range and abilities of the students, much of the teaching was one-on-one, though such a tiny school only required a handful of teachers. They were supported by a fitness instructor, a psychoanalyst and an assortment of housekeeping staff and security guards. The latter were all Swiss and mostly local. They too signed a confidentiality clause before joining the Wildings. They too were under suspicion. Once Lucas and Glory were at the academy, the only people they could trust were each other.

# PART 2

# CHAPTER 8

Compared to sky-leaping, flying in an aeroplane was no
big deal, Glory thought dismissively. Where was the thrill?
But she was still relieved to return to the solid ground of
Zurich airport.

In the arrivals hall, a short muscular woman in a black
trouser suit was holding up a sign with her name on it. A
good distance apart, a man held up one for 'L. Stearne'. Lucas
was some way behind; he was still waiting for his bag to be
unloaded when she left the collection point. Now it seemed
they'd be driven to the academy separately. Wildings'
authorities didn't want their witch-kids getting friendly
without proper supervision.

Glory's driver curtly introduced herself as Elga, then
lapsed into a silence that lasted for most of the two-hour
drive. The car was a gleaming hulk with blacked-out
windows, and when Elga opened the boot, Glory noticed a
telltale bulge in the woman's jacket. Not just a chauffeur,
then, but a member of Wildings' armed security team – the
so-called 'school guardians'.

She decided not to waste energy on worrying what it

would take for Elga to draw her gun. Here, finally, was Abroad, and she wanted to see as much of it as possible. Although the car's tinted windows leached the colour from the view, she could tell the late-afternoon sky was as blue, the sun as golden, as the tourist information websites had promised. They sped past rolling green hills, silver lakes, snow-dusted mountains, toytown villages. Everything was like a child's picture book, clean and bright.

As evening drew in, the mountains loomed larger, their lines more jagged. Signs appeared for *Swiss National Park*. Elga, though, turned off at a small unmarked road that wound up to a narrow valley.

There was a village at its head; a huddle of houses with high-pitched roofs, white walls and exposed beams. Every balcony was hung with flowers, every window twinkled with light. There were people strolling in the cobbled lanes. Just for a moment, Glory was able to imagine herself on holiday too. But the car sped swiftly through, leaving the lights and people behind, moving up the valley towards the mass of pine.

The countryside was as alien to Glory as Abroad. In the fading light, she saw how different this landscape was to the neat meadows and rolling hills they'd passed earlier; a true wilderness. Uneasily, she peered out of the back window, looking in vain for Lucas's car.

The road became a track, leading to a high wire fence and a gate with a checkpoint. *Private Property* signs in English and several other languages were prominently displayed as well as *Danger!* warnings.

'The locals don't go in here. Nor do tourists,' said Elga,

after presenting her pass for inspection and exchanging a few clipped words with the sentry. 'There are wild animals in this forest. Wolves, bears. And stories that the place is haunted too.'

Glory didn't believe in ghosts. There'd been no mention of Swiss wolves or bears in her research. But anything could be hiding in those trees, so thick and dark and silent.

Elga looked at her in the mirror. 'Don't fear. The fence is electrified. There are patrols. You will be very safe.'

Her smile had an ironical slant. Glory understood. The fence was to keep her in, as well as danger out.

After a mile or so the trees began to thin and they reached a stretch of grassland, sloping up to a hill. It was crowned by a small castle in the Gothic style, its walls high and palely gleaming in the dusk. A place of dreams, and fae-tales. But in the fae-tales, the witches were mostly wicked, putting poor princesses under a bane until a prince came to the rescue.

The car came to a halt by the steps up to a wide stone terrace. Glory got out stiffly. For a moment, she had the sensation that the mountains, trees and sky were closing in on her. How ridiculous to feel claustrophobic in the country-side! Yet she had a homesick craving for concrete. For fumes and noise. Her nose twitched at the cool green smell of pines and earth.

'Hello, my dear, and welcome to Wildings.' A dumpy woman in twinset and pearls was coming down the steps. She had a round, cosy face, but Glory watched her warily. She remembered from the files that Mrs Heggie, the school matron, was an ex-inquisitor.

'I *do* hope your journey wasn't too tiring. *Such* a pretty drive, isn't it? Now, I'm sure you're *longing* to take a look around, but before you get settled, Principal Lazovic was hoping to have a quick word. You won't mind, will you, popping in to say hello? *Splendid.* Don't worry about your bags – we'll have someone take them up to your room.'

The entrance hall was like the lobby of a posh hotel, with antique rugs over polished flagstones and flower displays so luxuriant they looked fake. The principal's study was much the same. There were no school trophies, photos or certificates on display, just lots of tasteful watercolours of the local countryside.

The head of Wildings Academy came to shake Glory's hand. He was a small man with an alert, pointed face and neat speckled beard. 'Emil Lazovic. It's a pleasure to meet you.'

'Glory,' she muttered.

'Ah,' he said. 'Yes. Of course. Glory . . . for Gloriana. Such an evocative name. So many, er, *interesting* associations.'

He smiled at her engagingly. She knew that by 'evocative' he meant 'provocative' – Gloriana had been the informal title of Elizabeth I, the so-called Fae Queen. Glory wasn't sure how to react. Her brief at Wildings was to be troublesome enough to attract attention, but not so obnoxious that she'd be thrown out. She settled on a sulky shrug, and put some gum in her mouth to soothe her nerves.

Principal Lazovic invited her to sit in one of the overstuffed armchairs and perched opposite. 'Well, Glory, I'm pleased to say you're not our only new arrival. One of your compatriots will be joining us shortly. Before then, I'd like to take the opportunity to have a little chat.

Just the two of us.' He gave another impish smile. 'As you know, the students at Wildings are a very select, very specialist group –'

'Right,' said Glory with a snort. 'Special Needs.'

The principal tutted in a way that was humorous as well as disapproving. He held up a copy of the school prospectus and began to read aloud. *'By removing troubled young people from the pressures of their home environment and relationships, Wildings Academy provides a safe haven where they can explore the reckless and deviant behaviours arising from their condition. At Wildings, they will learn to accept their place in the wider community, and find positive solutions for the challenges ahead . . .'* He gave a neat little laugh. 'This is the language of Wildings, you see. The vocabulary of your "condition"; the terms of your "trouble". Do you understand?'

'I understand why I gotta be here,' Glory said grudgingly, 'if that's what you mean. Don't mean I have to like it.'

'Nobody at Wildings is held against their will. If we fail to meet your needs, you are free to leave.'

'And go where? I ain't exactly flavour of the month back home.'

'Then I'm sure you'll learn to make the most of your stay here.' Principal Lazovic nodded and smiled. 'It is true your background is somewhat . . . unconventional. This is not something that worries me, but some of your classmates might be a little less open-minded.' His eyebrows waggled mischievously. 'So it might be an idea to keep the details of your family, ahem, business to yourself.'

'I know when to keep my gob shut, all right? I won't cause no trouble as long as no one comes troubling me.'

'In that case, I trust your time here will be a very peaceful one.' There was a knock at the door. 'Aha! Our other new arrival. Come in, come in.'

As Lucas entered the room, it was hard for Glory to conceal a rush of relief. Remembering the first time they met, Glory folded her arms protectively across her chest, chewing her gum loudly. Lucas winced, exactly like he had before.

'Gloriana, meet Lucas,' Principal Lazovic said.

'Hello,' Lucas said with frigid politeness.

Principal Lazovic invited him to take a seat. 'I've been having a little chat with Glory, telling her something of what Wildings is about. Naturally, this is a difficult time for you both. We at Wildings will do everything in our power to help, but it's important for you to appreciate the constraints we work under. *Everything* here is done within the law. All of us – staff and students – have a duty to uphold it. Any hint of deviancy and you'll be out. There are no second chances.'

The principal's tone was grave. Yet all the while, there was a glimmer of a twinkle in his eyes.

'Your privacy and protection are of the utmost importance. That means, I'm afraid, a certain amount of isolation. Matron will inform your families of your safe arrival, but I must ask you to hand over your mobile phones and any other sources of communication you have brought with you. In the meantime, you can write and email, subject to supervision. Your families can also arrange to visit. Although most of your time will be spent on campus, you can apply for permission to visit the local village. One of our guardians will accompany you there.

'While we take our academic programme very seriously, your personal well-being is our priority. For this reason, we have a trained counsellor on our staff. Your meetings with her will soon become a normal part of your school routine. When the time comes for you to leave the academy, you will be well prepared for the challenges ahead.'

There was a short pause. Then Principal Lazovic clapped his hands together with a comical sigh of relief. 'I think that's *quite* enough lecturing for one evening! You've had a tiring journey, and it's getting late. Perhaps you would like to have supper in your rooms? Yes? The tour and assessments can wait until tomorrow – nothing to worry about, I promise.' He twinkled merrily at them. 'Especially after a good night's sleep. Everyone sleeps well at Wildings. It's the fresh mountain air, you see.' He got up and shook their hands again. 'Really, we are so *very* pleased to have you!'

Lucas and Glory were collected by two of Wildings's black-clad guardians. Before being shown to their rooms their clothes were searched. They had already handed over their passports, wallets and phones. 'It's for your own security,' Glory's guardian – a taller, thinner version of Elga – told her blandly. Glory didn't risk looking at Lucas as he was led away. The girls' and boys' accommodation were in opposite wings of the castle.

Glory was taken through a succession of long empty corridors and past ranks of closed doors, with iron bells set across every threshold. Thick stone walls kept the place cool and silent. It was easy to imagine being here in winter; banks of snow heaped against walls and windows, blocking out the world. Her footfall on the plush carpet hardly made a sound. Where *was* everyone? Bed already? It was only half past nine.

'Yours is the only room in use on this corridor,' the guardian told her, as she pushed through a heavy set of double doors. 'One of the maids will bring you your supper. Lights go out at ten thirty. The wake-up bell is set for seven.'

'*Seven?*' Glory didn't have to fake her outrage. 'Bleeding hell. I thought the whole point of boarding school was being able to roll straight outta bed and into class.'

The guardian pursed her lips. 'Principal Lazovic believes that early morning is the most productive part of the day.'

Glory's bedroom was furnished in varying shades of beige. Like in a hotel, there was a kettle with tea and coffee supplies, and a miniature set of toiletries laid out in the gleaming ensuite bathroom. There was even a vase of white flowers on the bedside table. The bars over the window were the only discordant note. Then she discovered there was no lock on either the bedroom or bathroom door.

Her suitcase was nowhere to be seen. Someone had already unpacked for her and put everything neatly away. No doubt they'd taken the opportunity to search through her belongings for signs of witchwork and other deviancies. Pinned to the noticeboard was a long list of school rules. The timetable next to it was almost as depressing.

The big white-painted desk was equipped with station-ery and a laptop. Glory knew that emails had to be sent from a special Wildings account, and then only to previously approved recipients. All correspondence was checked by academy staff. But thanks to the MI6 geek-squad, Glory wasn't without resources. Her favourite gadget was a lock-picking set: fourteen stainless-steel blades fitted into the barrel of a pen, whose pocket clip doubled as a tension tool. Then there was a tiny spy-cam disguised as a button and a bug-detecting device disguised as a lipstick. She also had a spare passport sewn into the lining of her washbag, together with a wad of Swiss francs and a debit card for a WICA-run account.

Witchwork was supposed to be a last resort. Glory frowned when she remembered the MI6 techie's words. 'Who needs to grub around with mud and spit and such, now that nanotechnology gets things done far better?' He had given a cheery laugh. 'You lot'll be out of a job before long.'

Still, Glory had no intention of cutting off her nose to spite her face. She unscrewed the base of her 'lipstick' and switched on the bug detector. It was a tiny electronic scanner that swept the room for radio frequencies of the kind given off by hidden cameras and audio feeds. So far, so good.

There was a knock on the door and she put the device in her pocket in a guilty rush. A maid came in with a tray of food. 'Please put it outside the room when you are finished,' she said softly.

There was a chicken and rice casserole, fruit salad and a bottle of mineral water. Nothing too weird or foreign. Still, it was strange to eat in solitary silence, and Glory gulped her meal down without really tasting anything.

After taking a shower, she remembered she was supposed to leave the tray outside the door. The corridor was dark and lifeless; presumably the accommodation was designed to keep students in as solitary a confinement as possible. Back in her room, Glory pulled faces at herself in the wardrobe mirror. 'I board, yah,' she said aloud, making her voice rich and drawling, like Lucas's. 'This *frightfly* nice little place in the country. Going private keeps the scum out of the classrooms, don't yew know. It's *super* fun.'

Suddenly, the room was plunged into darkness. A power cut? Groping, she stumbled towards the bed and found a switch. She thought it might connect to a night light above the headboard. Although she didn't really expect it to work, the bulb glowed into dim life; just enough for her to check her watch. It was ten thirty. So lights out really did mean lights out!

Starlight glimmered through the window. Glory closed the shutters with a bang. Who would have thought she'd miss the sickly orange haze of a London night? In bed, the foreign darkness closed around her. She touched the Devil's Kiss beneath her collarbone, thinking of Lucas, somewhere in the depths of the building in a room just like this. Her mind reached out for him. Fae to fae, witch to witch. But this was a castle of witches. Neither of them was special here.

# CHAPTER 9

Lucas was woken by a harmonious rippling of strings. Alpine music was being piped into his room as a wake-up call. At least it wasn't yodelling.

As Lazovic had promised, he'd slept deeply, but he didn't feel refreshed by it, just slow and sluggish. He was brushing his teeth when he heard the door to his room open. It must be the maid. But when he came out of the bathroom he found a boy of about his own age, lounging in his chair and noisily chomping on a piece of toast. Lucas's toast, presumably. A rummaged-through breakfast tray was on the floor.

'Hola,' his visitor said through a mouthful of jam. He was dark and pudgy, with spiky hair. But the main thing Lucas noticed were his jeans, which were very tight and a startling shade of green.

'Hi . . . I'm Lucas.'

'And I am Raffi.' He belched. 'You are *inglés*, no?'

'That's right.'

'Cool.' Raphael Almagro stroked above his lip, where a few straggling hairs were failing to form a moustache. He was studying Lucas with open curiosity. 'And your family? They are government? Business? Celebrity?'

'I thought we weren't supposed to talk about –'

Raffi laughed. 'Please. All that hush-hush is just for show. There are not many secrets at Wildings – you will see.' He ambled over to the open window and lit a cigarette, before offering the pack to Lucas.

'No thanks. Look, I don't mean to be . . . but, well. Isn't that against the rules too?'

'Amigo, you need to relax. Seriously. OK, they hit you with all these rules and crap when you arrive. Boom! Keeps you scared and the parents happy, yes? But they don't want to piss you off too bad. Else you might do some deviancy and get yourself expelled. Then they lose their big fat school fees.'

Raffi wandered around the room, looking at the photos Lucas had put up, and the books on the shelves. 'Some rules you can bend. Some you can't. It's all compromise. This is how we do things in my country of Cordoba.'

'Yeah. I'd heard Cordoba was quite . . . tolerant.'

'Cordobans just want to have good times. Live and let live. No Inquisition, even. We threw it out. Ha!' Raffi took a drag on his cigarette and his face darkened. 'But now is not so good. There is this crazy bastardo running for president. He is making a lot of hot air, lot of commotion, about witch-villains. He says these wicked witch-villains are destroying our happy society . . . on and on. So, my papá, he decides until this stupid man is gone it's safer for me to be out of the way.' He sighed. 'Soon I hope to return. Cordoba is like a heaven, believe me. Great beaches, great bars, great babes.

And when we are talking of babes . . . there is a girl who came with you, yes? A new girl here?'

'She was on the same flight as me. I don't know her.'

'Is she hot?'

Lucas thought of Glory's bright hair, whipped up by the wind over London's rooftops, how her eyes were black in some lights, softening to brown in others. The snap and crackle of her. He shrugged. 'Flashy,' he said. 'Bit cheap-looking.'

Raffi grinned. 'Cheap! Ha. I like this very much. That is the good thing with our trouble, you know? More girls than guys. At least, that is what I thought. I thought when I came here there would be many, many ladies. But, *amigo*, I have to say the lady situation here is not so cool. There is an American who is a cheerleader. She has the most –'

A bell rang. No alpine chimes this time. It was shrill and summoning. Five minutes till school assembly.

Raffi stubbed out his cigarette in a guilty rush that rather undermined his airy talk about rule-bending. 'I must run for it now. If a guardian is collecting you – well. We are not supposed to go visiting in this time.'

'How did you even know I was here?' Lucas asked as Raffi opened the door. He was remembering the maze of halls and stairways that separated his room from the rest of the building.

'I know many things in this place.' Raffi tapped his finger solemnly on the side of his nose. 'You stick with me, and I will show you the ropes.'

Lucas didn't know what to make of this. Raphael Almagro was high on the list of Endor suspects, and it seemed odd that he had confided so much about himself so quickly. It could be a tactic to get Lucas to reveal his own secrets in turn. Or maybe Raffi was simply bored and nosy. In a place like this, any new arrival must be a big deal.

Shortly after Raffi left, the guardian who had taken Lucas to his room the night before arrived to show him the way to the assembly. His name was Ivan and, like all of the guardians, he had a military bearing and brusque manner. Still, he was polite enough. He asked Lucas if he'd slept well and didn't mention the cigarette stink.

Assemblies took place in the castle's former ballroom. It was a high bare room hung with mirrors, its walls lined with faded primrose silk, its floor a vast expanse of polished wood. The group of chairs arranged in front of the dais at one end was the only furniture.

Raffi had moved his seat next to Jenna White's in an attempt to engage her in conversation. She was twirling the end of her treacle-brown ponytail with a vacant expression. Next to her was the Bollywood star's sister. Anjuli was painfully thin and hunched, her features hidden by a curtain of lank black hair. The little Chinese girl, Mei-fen, was sitting quietly, hands folded neatly on her lap, overshadowed in every way by her neighbour, Yuri. The Russian's tank top revealed a menacing bulge of muscles.

As the double doors swung shut behind Lucas, Raffi abruptly stopped chattering and everyone else turned and stared. Lucas gave an awkward nod of greeting and slid into one of the two remaining seats. Silence fell, but not for long.

Glory came in with a crash, banging the doors behind her, high heels clattering across the floor.

She flounced into the chair next to him and he started to smile. Her hostile glare stopped him in his tracks. And the next moment, Principal Lazovic came in, followed by the matron and the other senior staff. They lined up behind the dais. Two guardians took their position by the doors.

The principal greeted everyone with his customary good humour, and announced that he was delighted to welcome two new members into 'our little community'. Introductions over, post was distributed, followed by a run-down of the day's schedule. The assembly finished with a short reading from Plato's *Republic*, on the education of philosopher-kings.

The education of witches followed. But while their classmates went to their lessons, Lucas and Glory were shown into another reception room to take tests in English, maths and verbal reasoning. At the end of it was a 'wellness questionnaire'. It was taken for granted that all Wildings' inmates suffered from the stress of their condition, and so therapy sessions had always been part of the school curriculum. After all, nobody wants a witch in the middle of a mental breakdown.

*How does your condition make you feel?*
*Please rank in order of relevance, with 1 being the most relevant, and 8 the least.*
    *a) Afraid*
    *b) Angry*

c) *Embarrassed*
d) *Disgusted*
e) *Depressed*
f) *Excited*
g) *Dangerous*
h) *Powerful*

*How do you think your friends would react to your condition?*
*Please rank in order of likelihood, with 1 being the most likely, and 5 the least.*
    a) *Afraid*
    b) *Embarrassed*
    c) *Disgusted*
    d) *Pitying*
    e) *Supportive*

*If your enemies found out about your condition, would they be more likely to:*
a) *Fear your capabilities*
*or*
b) *Rejoice at your disability?*

And so on. Assessments complete, Glory was taken off for her meeting with the therapist, while Lucas went on a campus tour.

'Whatever your interests,' Lucas was told, 'we do our best to accommodate them.' But none of the facilities looked as if they saw much use. His route took in the science lab, art studio, library, music suite, cinema, gym, swimming pool and tennis courts . . . All this for a mere seven students, when the building could have accommodated seventy.

He rejoined the others for lunch in the dining room, where a single table was set up in the middle of a cavernous wood-panelled hall. The food was good, accessorised with silver cutlery and served by maids. But the meal was a subdued one.

Mrs Heggie, the matron, presided at the head of the table and chivvied her neighbours into making stilted small talk. Lucas managed to make eye contact with Glory once, when she passed the salt. He would have been glad to finish the meal, except for the fact that his psychological assessment came afterwards.

Dr Flavia Caron had been working at Wildings for two years. She was a forty-something French-Canadian with a neat brown bob and a long, rather melancholy face. Her clothes were plain and her only adornment was a large tarnished ring on her left hand. Lucas expected her tower room to be similarly austere. However, there were modern-art posters on the wall, and a bunch of wild flowers brightened the mantelpiece.

Lucas sat down on the chair set out for him. There was a small table next to the chair, with a plastic tray of sand on it.

'Have you ever had any kind of therapy before?' Dr Caron asked him, after the introductions were over. Behind her unfashionable spectacles, her eyes were large and mild.

'No.'

'Do you know what to expect?'

' "The talking cure" – isn't that what you call it?' Lucas's tone was dismissive. He was careful to sit upright, not relax into his chair.

'Pyschoanalysis is a cooperative process. It should be a journey of discovery between therapist and client. I don't look on you as a patient with disabilities to treat.'

He almost laughed. 'But I *do* have a disability. A disability I'm not allowed to talk about – that's the whole reason I've been sent to this place. So you can understand,' he said with exaggerated politeness, 'why I don't quite see the point of our meetings.'

'These sessions are about tackling blocks to your personal development, whatever their origin or cause. Your condition is only one part of who you are.' Dr Caron looked at him enquiringly. 'Or do you, in fact, believe it defines you?'

'It defines my life choices. Or lack of them.'

'You have the choice here to talk about whatever you want.'

'What if I chose to say nothing?'

She smiled a little. 'Then we can sit in silence for the next hour.'

Lucas mustn't be too obstructive, however. Glory was the designated troublemaker. He was supposed to be the dutiful one. *Just be yourselves*, Rawdon had told them. *No cover could be more convincing.*

'All right. What's the sand for?'

'Well, talk therapy isn't for everyone. Sandplay is an alternative therapeutic technique. I invite my clients to use the sand however they wish. Some people like to dig, others to build. Some create landscapes, others abstract patterns.

Either way, the world that a person makes in the tray can represent aspects of their feelings and experiences. It's a tool for self-expression that doesn't require speech.'

Lucas touched the sand experimentally. It was granular like sugar, but cool and slightly damp. 'You don't have to do anything with it if you don't want to,' Dr Caron told him. 'It's relaxing just to fiddle about with.'

He noticed she had a disability of sorts too. The top joint of her right index finger was missing. She saw him looking. 'I was in a car accident last year,' she said. 'It took several months in hospital before I recovered.'

'Oh. Um . . . I'm sorry to hear that.'

'Healing the mind is no easier than healing the body. Both processes take time, and patience.'

He sighed. 'OK. Fine. Where do you want me to start? Should I dredge up a childhood trauma or something?'

'Do you consider your childhood traumatic?'

'Not at all. It was a very happy one.' He wondered about the file she'd been given, and what it said about his mother. Idly, he began to trail his fingers through the sand.

'You must miss your family.'

'Obviously. But I have to accept I'm here for my own good.'

'Is that what your father told you? He's an inquisitor, I gather.'

'He used to be. Now he works in government.'

'You don't have a problem with the work he does or has done?'

'Why would I? It's important. Admirable.'

'So you are proud of him.'

'Yes.'

'And is he proud of you?'

'Yes,' Lucas told Dr Caron. 'Yes, he is.' But he couldn't quite meet her eye.

# CHAPTER 10

The session with the shrink was every bit as bogus as Glory expected. Dr Caron droned on about new pathways and positive thinking – the sort of junk you'd find in a third-rate horoscope. Invited to play with the sand, Glory amused herself with writing rude words and sculpting even ruder body parts.

'I know I ain't disabled,' she told the therapist. 'Or wrong in the head. And nothing you can say will make me think different.'

'I can understand why the terminology used at Wildings would make you uncomfortable,' Dr Caron said tranquilly. 'The other students I see often choose to give their disability a name, as if it were an actual person. This allows them to address the issue, while keeping within the rules.'

'I don't get it.'

'Well, if you were to call your condition "Anna", for example, then we could talk about the effect "she" has on your life. What your family and friends think of "her" and so on.'

Glory considered this. 'All right. But I ain't going for a lame name like Anna. How about Esmerelda Thunderpants?'

Dr Caron pursed her lips.

Good. If the nosy cow was recruiting for Endor, then so much the better.

After being shown the academy sights, Glory was told she had an hour's free time before supper. Her guardian left her at the door to the student common room – not that there was anything common about it. Dark wooden arches converged in the centre of the ceiling, and giant leather armchairs were set out on acres of rugs. The only person there was Mei-fen, playing solitaire. Dwarfed by her over-size surroundings, she looked tinier than ever. She glanced at Glory with indifference before returning to her game. Maybe Glory should have stuck around, casually interrogated the kid, but she wanted to find Lucas.

Glory set off in what she thought was the direction of Dr Caron's lair, hoping she'd meet Lucas on his way back. However, the plush hallways and stairwells were confusingly alike. Most of the doors she tried were locked. She knew the outer ones were alarmed. If you wanted to go outside – to walk in the gardens or use the sports facilities – you had to get one of the guardians to escort you. Similarly, if you wanted to use the art studio or library or whatever, a member of staff had to open it up for you first.

'Hey, are you lost?'

It was the American, Jenna. Even in the dimly lit corridor she seemed to glow. Shiny teeth, shiny eyes, shiny hair.

'Sorta. I was having a nose about. Trying to get me bearings.'

'It's crazy, right? I keep expecting to bump into Frankenstein's Monster on the stairs.' Jenna looked down at the cardboard box she was carrying. 'Look . . . my mom's sent me a care package. You wanna hang out, help me eat some candy?'

In the normal course of things, there was no way a girl like Jenna White would come within spitting distance of a girl like Glory Wilde. Not in the ordinary world. But here they were, outcasts alike. Glory sized Jenna up, wondering about the strength of her fae, and what, if anything, she'd done with it. Where the Devil had left his mark.

'OK,' she said.

Jenna's room had the same basic furnishings as Glory's, but there the similarity ended. There was a Stars and Stripes flag on the wall, a fluffy pink carpet on the floor and a butterfly mobile dangling from the ceiling. Posters of American athletes and celebrities jostled with snapshots of Jenna and her friends at football games, parties and on the beach. It appeared Jenna was one of those girls who photograph better than they look in the flesh. Not that she wasn't pretty, with her big blue eyes, perky nose and swinging hair. But the photographic version was even brighter than life.

'You been in Brat Camp for a while, then?' Glory asked.

'Brat –? Oh, I get it. *Too* funny! I've only been here a few weeks, actually.' Jenna opened her package and began to rummage through its contents. 'Here,' she said, tossing Glory a bag of chocolate drops. 'I figure there isn't much else to do in this place but get fat.'

Glory obediently ate some chalky-tasting chocolate.

What were they going to do next? Brush each other's hair and paint their nails? At school, Glory had been at the centre of an admiring crowd, but there was nobody she was particularly close to. The Starling name, her coven home and connections with the Morgans meant that other kids were a little wary of her. She realised she wasn't quite sure how to get the whole girly bonding thing started.

Jenna sat on the bed, hugging a heart-shaped cushion to her chest. 'So,' she said. 'You're from England, huh?'

'Yeah. London.'

'Awesome.'

'You've been?'

'No, but I *love* all that ye olde England stuff. Cucumber sandwiches, the Royal family, James Bond ... and the accents, of course. Are you a cockney?' Jenna didn't wait for an answer, immediately launching into, 'Cor blimey, me old china. Lor luvva duck!'

Glory cracked a smile. 'I should've brought some jellied eels.'

Jenna clearly didn't get the reference, but laughed anyway. 'I don't know why it's so hot when English guys talk snobby. Like that boy who came with you – Luke or whatever.'

'Yeah, Lucas is from the cream of society, all right. Rich and thick ... What about the rest of the gang here?'

Jenna wrinkled her snub little nose. 'Freaks and geeks, mostly. I don't know if that's because of their – our – trouble, or if it's because they're, like, foreign. The South American, Raffi? *Total* sleaze. And the Russian boy's just plain scary.

'Anjuli's sister is some kinda actress, but in India, so it's not like she's a real celebrity. Anyways. Anjuli's got this whole weird eating issue thing going on. I reckon she'd be in rehab, and Yuri'd be in juvie, if they weren't here. Mei's sweet, though. She's been in this place since she was, like, ten. It's practically home.'

Interesting. That hadn't been in the file. Teenage witches were rare, child witches almost unheard of. Mei-fen was potentially very powerful.

Aware that her expression had perhaps turned a little too serious, Glory turned to the photographic display. A bronzed hunk loomed large in the nearest one. 'Who's the talent?'

'That's my boyfriend. Ex-boyfriend, I guess. He thinks I've gone to Europe to learn French.'

'So he don't know?'

'No *way*. He'd totally freak out. I wouldn't blame him either. The whole thing . . . it's just . . . it's *so gross*.' Jenna gave an exaggerated shudder. 'And what about you?'

'What about me?'

'Any boys pining for you back home?'

'Hundreds,' she said airily. 'I'm glad to be rid of 'em.' Growing up in a coven, Glory was used to male attention of all kinds, good and bad. She knew how to turn on the charm, if it was going to be useful to her, but romance to her was Lily Starling sashaying into a smoky bar to the sound of low whistles and drawn-in breaths. Or Cora, caught by a policeman in the act of stealing a mink coat, and knocking him dead with a wink of her wicked black eyes.

'Well, how 'bout your family and friends? Won't they start to wonder what's become of you?'

'Tell the truth, this ain't my first disappearing act. And it ain't the only "trouble" I've gotten into neither.'

Jenna widened her already wide blue eyes. 'No kidding.'

Glory shrugged insouciantly. 'There's more than one reason I'm best off here, not home. Still, I'll have to go back eventually. Face the music.'

'Yeah . . . I'm hoping my dad'll have fixed something up by the time I graduate.' Jenna lowered her voice. 'He's got, like, contacts. I mean, there's always another option, right? Look at this place.'

True enough. The rich and powerful had many ways of getting out of trouble. But Endor had special contacts too.

As soon as Glory got to her room, she went to her desk and opened her laptop.

She dashed off a holiday-postcard-style email to her dad, and an equally brief, but jokier, message for Troy. Her update to WICA was sent to a fake email account for a fake friend called Christy. All messages would be read by Wildings staff before being released from quarantine in the academy's server, but she was able to use an arrangement of code words and phrasing to convey that, so far, things were going to plan.

Afterwards, she stared at the empty inbox. *All my family and friends.* She was down to two now – not that her original collection was much to boast of. The hangers-on and toadies at school. Patch and Earl, the Cooper Street old-timers who'd taught her how to hot-wire a car and cheat at cards. Her coven rival, Nate, and his two dim-witted sidekicks. Auntie Angel. Patron, protector, traitor.

Glory had many messages in her head, but none that she could send.

*Dear Mum –*
*How are you?*
*Where are you?*

I wish you were here.

# CHAPTER 11

Lucas and Glory didn't have any real communication until towards the end of their second day. But on the way out of morning assembly, Lucas managed to brush his arm against Glory's, and her heart jumped.

'How're you doing?' he asked under his breath.

'Super-bloody-duper.'

'Yeah.' He smiled crookedly. 'Me too.'

Later, they managed to have an actual conversation during their art class. The teacher, a thin and watery woman who described herself as a 'creative enabler', encouraged, 'free expression'.

'I want you to imagine a safe place,' she told them, turning on the stereo and flooding the studio with the sound of pan pipes. 'I want you to visualise yourself in it. Then I want you to make that vision of refuge real. Craft it! Shape it! Make it your own!'

After a decent pause, Glory wandered over to the table where Lucas was attempting a wigwam construction out of coloured twigs. For several minutes they talked together, as strangers, wary and stiff. Yet both felt the comfort of their shared secret. *Whatever else I've lost,* Glory told herself after-wards, I *am not alone.*

During the next week, they began to settle into Wildings' routine. They soon discovered that Principal Lazovic's cheerful wink-wink, nudge-nudge attitude to the fae was not the academy norm. When the other staff referenced a student's 'trouble' or 'deviancy', they did so with deadly seri-ousness, though none of them seemed to take a special interest in any of their charges. If there was an Endor agent among them, he or she was keeping their distance.

There was the double enclosure of the wire fence and forest, the patrolling guardians, CCTV, curfew, lights out and locked doors. Yet Lazovic was right to say no one was held at Wildings against their will. His charges knew that this place was their best chance to delay public exposure until adulthood. In the meantime, the academy protected them and their families from the kind of people who might try to take advantage of their condition – whether professional or personal enemies, government forces or criminal ones.

Even if Wildings' inmates did not rebel against their confinement, they still showed signs of strain. Raphael chain-smoked. Yuri spent most of his free time pumping iron in the gym. Anjuli had an obsessive relationship with food. Mei-fen was smiling but silent, covering rolls of paper with incredibly small and intricate labyrinth designs. Jenna, meanwhile, took refuge in denial. After her initial conversation with Glory, she never referred – directly or indirectly – to her 'trouble' again. She prattled on about her boyfriend, plans for college and hopes for a modelling career as if she really were on an extended European holiday. Any attempt to challenge this was met by a look of blank incomprehension.

It was a surprise to find that witchkind studies was a feature of the curriculum. In normal schools, these classes would involve discussing the best methods for detecting witchwork and protecting oneself against it. Students would look at inquisitorial practices, and study the history of witchkind, including the persecutions of the Burning Times. However, Wildings' approach was more old-fashioned – or 'a load of pyro-fascist brainwashing', as Glory put it.

In the first lesson she and Lucas attended, the subject was witchworked plagues. In the second, they studied the casting of banes to induce madness. Stroking the small silver crucifix around her neck, Senora Theresa Ramirez described how witches rotted their victims' bodies with infected air, and their brains with visions of demons. The message was that the fae was not just a disability, but a disease; something that corrupted everything it came into contact with.

The other students had clearly heard it all before. They sat in blank silence, letting Senora Ramirez's rasping voice wash over them. Lucas kept his eyes fixed on his desk. Glory's attempts at challenge were immediately quashed. The Senora had both the look and manner of an inquisitor, with her black dress, and gaunt, haughty face.

For Lucas and Glory's third lesson, which came towards the end of their second week, the class gathered in the academy's film theatre. Their teacher announced she was going to show them the methods by which a witch-criminal was identified. First off: the exposure of the Devil's Kiss through witch-ducking. To fully understand the procedure, they were going to watch a documentary film.

Glory was two seats down from Lucas so she couldn't see how he reacted to the news. As the screen crackled into life, she found she had tensed up on his behalf. The setting was a concrete bunker. Puddles on the floor, rusting manacles on the wall. Foreign voices could be heard off-screen. It was somewhere in Eastern Europe, perhaps. Moments later, three men in military uniform dragged in a fourth, dressed in prison garb. The camera swung round to an iron tank of ice-water and the ducking-stool.

The prisoner was tied into the leather straps. He was trying to fight his captors, cursing and thrashing, his voice hoarse. Glory saw that Lucas was gripping the arms of his chair so hard the knuckles had turned white. The camera honed in on the witch's face. Lucas's was strained, and sweating.

As the witch crashed backwards into the ice-water, his muffled scream turned to choked gurgles. Lucas got up abruptly and blundered out of the auditorium. Senora Ramirez didn't try to stop him, but watched him go with a tight little smile. Glory burned with rage and helplessness. But she couldn't go after him. It would draw the wrong kind of attention to them both. And in any case, she didn't know what to say.

'I gather there was an unfortunate episode in Senora Ramirez's class today,' said Dr Caron, later that afternoon. Her tower room was warm with sunshine and the smell of fresh coffee. Lucas kept his eyes on the sand-tray. He was building London's rooftops, trying to fill his head with images of a pale primrose morning, as he shaped the chimneys and smoothed the slopes.

'You must have spies everywhere.'

'Senora Ramirez was concerned.'

'Funny. I got the impression she was enjoying herself.'

'The Senora takes pride in her vocation. She spent many years working in a charity for the rehabilitation of witch-criminals. As a result, her methods can be, perhaps, a little extreme.' Dr Caron's brow creased regretfully. 'It is possible she went too far on this occasion.'

'Must be an occupational hazard. When dealing with witches, I mean.' The icy pressure had returned, squeezing his lungs.

'Do you object to the Inquisition and its techniques?'

He had to wait until his breath came back to him. Damp sand clung to his fist. 'Not when they're conducted correctly.'

Dr Caron's voice was gentle. 'Then what was it that particularly disturbed you about the film?'

He shrugged.

'Are you afraid you might find yourself in a similar situation to the prisoner you saw?'

'Well, presumably that would only happen if I did something wrong. Illegal.'

Gideon Hale's face flashed before his eyes. *Look at you . . . Look at the dirty hag.* Glancing at his hands, Lucas almost expected to see the inky witch-stain bleeding from under his fingertips.

'So you're saying it is an irrational fear?'

'I don't know. My "trouble" is irrational too.'

'In what way?'

It was an unexpected relief to say the words out loud. He was already sick of *Don't Ask, Don't Tell.* 'Nothing about it makes sense. How it works . . . why it happens . . . who it happens to.' His hand swept over the sand rooftops, crumbling the parapets and chimneys together, turning London into a desert waste.

Dr Caron nodded. 'This is why you feel constricted, yes? You are a victim of circumstances beyond your control.'

'I suppose.'

'Yet some might say you have more options, now. A different kind of control. A different kind of power.'

'But it's not something . . . that is . . . I don't always feel in control. Of it. Of myself.'

'And how does that make you feel?'

The cold sweat was still on his brow. He couldn't answer.

On his way out, Lucas passed Dr Caron's next patient, Yuri, waiting at the foot of the stairs. The hulking Russian was bouncing a tennis ball against the opposite wall with repetitive and ferocious force. *Thud, thud, thud.*

'The head-shrink is ready for me?' Yuri asked.

'Yeah.'

'It is she who is the crazy one. She talks to herself – I have seen.' He tapped his head. 'Everyone crazy here, but most of all the teachers.'

If Endor was in fact recruiting at this school, Lucas

thought, then Yuri would be the perfect target; not a doubting, dithery witch like himself. The trouble was, he had wanted to talk. Unburden himself.

The castle walls closed in around him. He had nowhere to go, nothing to do. Pausing on a landing, he became aware of music floating down the corridor. It sounded like Mozart. He went down a flight of stairs and found Mei-fen at the piano in one of the music studios. She was so small her feet barely touched the floor. Aged thirteen, she could almost pass for eight, if it wasn't for the look of absolute concentration on her face. It gave her an air of maturity far beyond her years.

After a while she became aware he was standing in the doorway and stopped.

'Sorry. Am I bothering you?'

'Not at all,' she said.

'You're very good.'

She smiled faintly. 'I have had a lot of time to practise.' Till now, Lucas had never heard her speak more than a couple of words at a time; the fluency of her English was a surprise. 'That is the stereotype of Chinese people, is it not?' she continued. 'Industrious, obedient.' She played a little trill on the keys. 'I was not like that as a child at home. I was very spoilt.'

'It must have been a shock coming here.'

'My family was afraid that if the Party found out about my trouble, they would put me to work.'

China's official line was that it didn't have any witches at all. But, as everyone knew, if its witches weren't imprisoned in the labour camps, they were engaged in government espionage.

'And why are you here, Lucas?'

'Because – because my dad's an inquisitor.'

'That must be difficult,' she said gravely. 'He is angry with you?'

'He's worried.'

Mei-fen idly fingered one, two, three notes. 'My father is afraid for me. I am his only child. But he underestimates me too.' The notes became a scale, up and down. 'That is why I practise, why I study hard. When I leave here, I need to be as strong and clever as I can be.'

'And what will you do then?'

Her neat little fingers danced over the keys. 'I will find new things to practise, and new kinds of work.' The music came effortlessly now, loops and ripples of melody. 'And when I do, I will be the very best.'

None of Lucas's classmates referred to his abrupt exit from the witch-ducking film, at least not in his hearing. But he wasn't the only student to have an 'episode' that week.

On Saturday, the school was taken on an alpine trek, accompanied by three guardians and led by the sports instructor, a meaty slab of a man named Brett Peters, who'd been in the US Marines and liked everyone to know it. The morning was grey and misty as they set off through the pines, following a winding trail up the mountainside.

As the day wore on, the mist burned off and the weather became blue and blazing. The scenery was magnificent, but they were not given much time to enjoy it. Peters discouraged idling. The guardians discouraged conversation. Soon, everyone was too hot and breathless to talk, even if they'd wanted to.

Anjuli in particular was suffering. She always wore baggy layers of clothes, perhaps to disguise her painfully thin frame. For the walk, she was wearing a waterproof coat, now tied round her waist, and a fleece jumper. Under her protective curtain of hair, her face had an unhealthy sheen, and her breath rasped painfully. She began to fall behind.

'Julie,' barked Peters, coming to a halt. 'You're going to get heat exhaustion. Take off that jumper.'

Anjuli shook her head.

One of the guardians, Elga, made an impatient noise. 'Don't be stupid, girl. You've got a T-shirt on underneath, haven't you?'

'No . . . no . . . I am fine,' Anjuli whispered. 'Please.' She was swaying on her feet.

'Aw, give her a break,' said Glory. 'Give us *all* a break, in fact.' She sat defiantly down on a boulder and fanned her sweaty face. She was already fed up of alpine scenery. *Bloody countryside*, she thought.

Peters ignored her. 'Take off that jumper,' he growled at Anjuli. 'At once. You're slowing us down, and endangering your own health.'

Slowly, reluctantly, Anjuli began to peel off her sweat-soaked jumper.

She was wearing a black T-shirt underneath. But now that her arms were bare, they could see for the first time the ugly white splotches that disfigured her right arm. Cigarette burns.

'There,' said Peters. 'That wasn't so hard, was it?'

But Anjuli had begun to cry, tears rolling slowly down her face as she futilely tried to cover the scars with her hands. Peters smirked. Everyone else looked at the ground.

Everyone except for Yuri, that is. He'd already stripped down to a vest; now he took off the cotton shirt he'd tied around his waist and draped it round Anjuli's shoulders, as a kind of shawl. She clutched at it gratefully. '*Svoloch*,' he spat in Peters' direction. '*Sukin syn*.'

For a moment, Peters looked as if he was going to make something of it. The guards moved closer too. But Yuri stared them down. 'We are tired,' he growled. 'It is time to go back.'

And so they did. As soon as they returned to the academy, Anjuli fled to her room.

Rather than go after her, Glory caught up with Yuri. The others tended to keep out of his way, but he wasn't that different from the boys on the Rockwood Estate, and she knew how to handle them.

'It were good what you did for Anjuli,' she told him. 'Peters is a pig.'

Yuri looked at her warily. 'Pig. Yes. He knew about the marks.'

'How'd she get them, d'you think? The Inquisition?'

'No,' said Yuri reluctantly. 'It was the sister.'

'But . . . but why?'

'She was angry. She think a witch-sister, she will stop movie career.'

Glory wondered how Yuri knew about this . . . until the next morning, when he and Anjuli turned up to assembly hand in hand. Anjuli had tucked her hair behind her ears; in spite of the dull skin and hollow cheeks, it could be seen that her eyes were every bit as large and lustrous as her famous sister's. Yuri's scowl was now accessorised by a swagger.

'Love's young dream,' Jenna said, curling her lip.

'Yeah,' said Glory. 'And Lazovic's worst nightmare.'

It was evident the guardians had been told to keep an extra close eye on the pair. Their classmates too were riveted. In the morning's art class, where they were supposed to be creating 'mood diaries' of their emotions in swirls of coloured paint, very little painting was being done because everyone was watching Anjuli and Yuri instead. The lovebirds were mixing colours in a corner, with much whispering.

'The Russian is a clever snake to make the moves so quick,' Raffi lamented. He put his hand to his heart. 'Ah, is even more a pity the red girl is no here.'

'Who was that?' Lucas asked.

'Inglés student, like you. Rosa. Very hot.'

'She was unhappy to be here,' said Mei-fen in her small, precise voice. 'She cried. All the time.'

Glory and Lucas didn't need to look at each other to share the jolt of recognition. They already knew about a beautiful, red-headed English witch. And now they knew Rose Merle had been at Wildings.

# CHAPTER 12

Glory and Lucas didn't have a chance to confer until after lunch. Sunday afternoons were free time and so the two of them booked a tennis court, on the pretext that Lucas was teaching Glory how to play.

'We might have guessed Rose would have come here,' Lucas said, testing Glory's racquet strings. 'Rich relations, high profile.'

'The timings fit,' she agreed. 'Mei says Rose left just over eight months ago. That's about one month before her brain got fried.'

He demonstrated a few strokes: backhand, forehand, slice, lob. 'You think there's a connection?'

'Anything's possible. The American bloke who collected Rose from the clinic? He said he was her uncle, but he weren't family, that's for sure. Maybe he was someone from here.' Glory batted a few balls over the net.

'Rose isn't our concern,' Lucas said, as they ambled over to pick them up. 'We can't get sidetracked.'

'From what? It's not like we got anything else to go on.'

Glory glanced at a patrolling guardian, who had

stopped to watch them play. She took up the position to serve. She couldn't compete with Lucas's years of coaching at the tennis club, but she was a quick learner. They played a short rally, then once the coast was clear, drew nearer to the net to confer.

'OK, so I'm thinking we should take a peek at the files,' she said.

'Which ones?'

'The student ones, of course. What Lazovic's got in his study.'

He gaped at her. Taking advantage of his distraction, she moved back and got in a sneaky kick serve. Lucas lunged, and missed. 'Hex.'

'Ooooh! Language!'

Lucas moved round to Glory's side of the net and took her arm, under the pretext of correcting her grip on the racquet.

'That's moving on from "observe and report". That's breaking and entering.'

'I know. It'll probably need witchwork too,' she said airily.

'If we get caught, all hell will break loose.'

'And if we find a smoking gun, we'll be the heroes of the hour.' She turned to face him properly. 'C'mon,' she whispered coaxingly. 'Don't it drive you crazy, not using your fae? Mab Almighty – if I don't get to do something soon, I'll go *mad*.'

Lucas had to lean in close to hear her. The sun had brought out a dusting of freckles on her cheek. Underneath her collarbone, he could see what looked like a darker freckle. The pinprick mark of her Devil's Kiss. He remembered how it waxed and waned with the fae, the inky bloom of it. Now, it seemed as if he could brush it away with just a fingertip.

Out of the corner of his eye, he saw the guardian was walking past again. He gave a warning cough. 'Better show me your backhand.'

What Glory lacked in technique, she made up for in bloody-mindedness. She lunged, sliced and swiped, with whoops of triumph or howls of frustration.

Grey turrets against a blue sky, pine breeze, mountain shadow. And he, Lucas Stearne, playing tennis in a Swiss castle with a coven witch. Mab Almighty . . .

'What's so funny?' Glory demanded, pausing mid-serve. 'Are you taking the piss?'

He shook his head, unable to explain the joke, but filled with an unexpected happiness all the same. Maybe it was catching, for suddenly Glory started to laugh too.

'Hey, guys. Wanna play doubles?'

It was Jenna, immaculate in tennis whites, her ponytail as perky as her smile. Raffi was with her, in tight red shorts, and grinning broadly. Glory and Lucas exchanged glances. But the guardian was still watching, and it would be rude not to say yes.

It turned out that Lucas and Jenna were evenly matched. Raffi was more experienced than Glory, but his smoking habit and lack of fitness meant that they were at about the same level too. They played three sets before the bell rang for afternoon tea.

This was a Sunday institution, served on the front lawn,

and hosted by Principal Lazovic. It was one of several rituals designed to create the illusion that life at the academy wasn't all that different to a holiday at a grand hotel. As the tennis players made their way over to the tea tables, Jenna came over to Glory and linked arms.

Jenna was one of those people who never seemed to break into a sweat. Her whites were still daisy-fresh, unlike Glory's vest top and tracksuit bottoms. 'So,' she said. 'That was *fun*.'

'Yeah.'

'You and Lucas looked good together. On court,' she explained. 'I was watching you kid around.'

Glory tried to remember if they'd said or done anything that might give them away. She shrugged. 'He's not quite as square as he looks.'

They paused to survey the party. Lucas was offering a plate of biscuits to Mei. After two weeks in the sun, his English pallor had almost gone. Glory noticed his eyes looked even bluer, against the tan.

'Cute too,' Jenna observed.

'Bit young for you, I'd've thought.'

'Hey – are you calling me a cougar?' Jenna gave her a playful slap. 'I'm seventeen, not seventy.' Then, confidingly, she added, 'Not that I'd, like, get in your *way*, or anything. If, y'know, you and him . . .'

'I told you,' said Glory through gritted teeth. 'Not my type.'

The ponytail swished. 'If you say so.'


It wasn't just the witchwork ban that was making Glory prickly. It was the stifling atmosphere of the place. All the cream teas in the world couldn't alter the fact that they were fenced in with wire and guarded with guns. In her blacker moods, she wondered if the whole Endor business was a scam on WICA's part, just to get rid of them. But despite her best efforts, Lucas continued to oppose direct action. They needed to work on building relationships with the other students and staff, he said. Breaking into the principal's office should be a last resort.

Typical Lucas, the teacher's pet. He'd already got footage of all the students and staff on his spy-cam, and continued to email coded updates to WICA. Glory wondered what on earth he found to write about. It was even a struggle with her dad. *I've made friends with an American named Jenna. I'm learning how to play tennis. We went on a walk yesterday and saw an eagle.* Patrick's reply was mostly devoted to describing how he and Rolf had cracked Level Six of *Inquisitor's Creed*, their latest computer game obsession. Glory wondered what the censors had made of it.

Her correspondence with Troy was already petering out, though she'd tried to get Rose into her last message: *Apparently there used to be another English girl here, called Rose.* She doubted Troy was in a position to do anything with the information, even if it got past the censors. Still, she couldn't get the girl out of her head. In their brief encounter, Rose had seemed like an apparition from a fae-tale. Hair like fire, skin like snow, eyes the colour of violets . . . A girl like that belonged in a castle like this. But Rose was now imprisoned by her own body, not by stone walls and electric fences.

Glory knew she mustn't allow herself to get distracted. Her priority had to be the students who were actually present. So far, she was making the most progress with Raffi. When he wasn't being a sleaze, he could be amusing company, and had a cheerful disrespect for the academy – and authority in general – that she could relate to. On the Thursday of their third week, she even had the opportunity to talk to him about Endor.

Although TV at Wildings was strictly rationed, an exception was made for the news. So when reports came in that the Chief Prosecutor of the Italian Inquisition had been assassinated, lessons were suspended to allow students to watch the news on the BBC World Service. Alessandra Giordani had been killed on her way to the trial of the head-witch of a notorious Sicilian coven. It was said she'd been hexed into slitting her own wrists, sitting tranced in an empty field as she waited to die.

Afterwards, Glory sloped off to join Raffi for a fag outside the gym. Glory was not a smoker, having had her first cig-arette at the age of eight. Nate had given it to her, and then laughed when she threw up afterwards. The taste still made her nauseous. But she felt a sneaky puff now and then was appropriate for her Wildings persona. Also, she knew Lucas disliked it, and she was annoyed with Lucas at the moment.

'Well,' she said, lighting up next to Raffi. 'There's one less inquisitor in the world, at least.'

'Poor lady, even so. It was a wicked thing.'

'Who's to say it weren't an actual suicide?' Glory inhaled, trying not to retch. 'Anything bad happens, it's witches what get blamed. Journalists, politicians, police – they're all in it together.'

'In Cordoba, it is different. There the police and the

covens are often friends.' Raffi winked at her through the smoke.

'Oh? And what about Endor – do they have mates in Cordoba too?'

Glory had kept her tone light, but Raffi looked at her askance. 'With the covens, you can do business. But with the terrorists, there are no deals. No rules. It's very bad for business. Bad, too, for the good life.'

'I dunno about that. Endor want witches on top, calling the shots. Running the show. That ain't so terrible.'

Raffi, though, was shaking his head. 'Glory, seriously, you don't know what you say.' He ground out his cigarette beneath his heel. 'Endor is for crazy people. They bring only fire and blood.'

Dr Caron and Lucas were also discussing the headlines. It was Lucas's twelfth session with the psychoanalyst, as new students had to attend four sessions a week. Glory filled the time by making up incredibly complicated, incredibly graphic dream sequences, all starring Esmerelda Thunderpants. Lucas was trying a different kind of game. He turned question-and-answer into hide-and-seek; his camouflage a blend of truth, lies and evasions.

'What was your first reaction when you heard of the assassination?' Dr Caron asked.

*Truth*: 'I thought of my father.'

'But not your mother?'

*Lie*: 'No.'

'Even though she was murdered in similar circumstances?'

*Evasion*: 'I never knew her. I was a baby when she died.'

Alessandra Giordani had been a mother of two, celebrated in the press for her love of designer clothes as well as her dazzling legal career. Lucas wondered if there had been any chance for her mind to fight the invader's, as the assassin's fae snaked into her brain. He wondered for how long afterwards she had waited and watched as her life seeped out in scarlet streams. In the final moments, he hoped the witch had the mercy to leave her mind a blank. He hoped this was true for his mother too.

'I gather your godfather will be coming to see you,' said the therapist, in an apparent change of tack.

'Er, yeah.' Lucas's godfather was, in fact, the man from MI6.

'Are you close?'

'We get on pretty well. But he doesn't know about my condition. He thinks I'm here for behavioural issues.'

'It is a pity your father could not visit.'

Lucas stared down at the sand. It was all wiggles today, a knot of lines and curves.

'He's . . . he's very busy with his new job.'

'Do you think he misses his old one?'

'I don't know. Maybe. Probably.'

'He put many witch-criminals away. And sent some to the Burning Court, I believe. You know, there is a theory that witchkind are naturally criminal. That the fae is predisposed to cause harm. What do you think?'

'I think there's always a choice. Whether to follow an urge, or fight it.'

'So you do feel an impulse?' Dr Caron was looking at him with new kind of concentration. 'An urge to harm?'

Lucas touched the thread of grey in his hair. He reminded himself that he didn't know what the doctor wanted from him, or what she might be looking for. Truth, lie or evasion?

He took a deep breath. 'Yes,' he said. 'Sometimes I do.'

# CHAPTER 13

On the Saturday of their fourth week, Principal Lazovic told Lucas he'd been granted an afternoon pass to Blumenwald. 'Consider it a reward for good behaviour,' he said.

Lucas had already visited the village once. There were a couple of gift shops, an outdoor pursuits store, a small hotel and a café. That was pretty much it. But wherever Lucas chose to go, a plain-clothed guardian came too. It wasn't clear if this was for Lucas's protection or Blumenwald's. The villagers might take Wildings' money, but that didn't mean they liked living in its shadow. Everywhere he went, Lucas felt eyes on his back. On his last visit, he was pretty sure a mother had picked up her child and crossed the street just to avoid him. It seemed these people had their own extra sense for sniffing witches out.

Nonetheless, he was pleased to get out of the academy. He hoped a change of scene might help him get some perspective on the place before his meeting with the MI6 agent. He was beginning to think Glory was right, and that unless they did something drastic, they'd have nothing to show for their time here. Maybe there really was nothing untoward going on at Wildings. Maybe the intelligence chatter was just that: meaningless noise.

After inspecting the gift shop's selection of cowbells and snow globes, all the while shadowed by Ivan, the guardian, Lucas ran out of things to do. The cobbled street outside the café was crowded with happy families eating honey cakes in the sun. Rather than endure the stares and whispers his presence would provoke, he took refuge in the hotel. The only other customer in the dining room was a whiskery old gent snoozing over his newspaper. It might have been cosy here in winter, with a log fire and snow falling outside. In summer, the abundance of carved wood was overbearingly gloomy. Lucas ordered coffee as Ivan took up position two tables away.

'Hello, Lucas.'

He looked up to see Dr Caron.

'Oh. Er, hello.'

The therapist gave one of her melancholy smiles. 'I hope I am not disturbing you. Ivan messaged me to say you were here. You see, there is someone I would like you to meet.'

'Another therapist? I didn't realise I was such a hopeless case.'

'Another kind of doctor. Please,' she said. 'It's nothing to worry about. I have arranged a consultation, that is all.'

Lucas's heart began to thump. His instincts told him something was about to happen, something important. After only a slight hesitation he got up and followed Dr Caron. This was his chance, and he had to take it.

They went upstairs into a small private dining room.

Ivan waited outside the door. The rustic wooden beams and floral drapes seemed an unlikely setting for an act of violence, yet Lucas braced himself all the same. There was a man in a suit at the table. He had a blandly handsome face, square-jawed and cleft-chinned. Spray-tanned too by the looks of it. As he got up, Lucas thought of Gideon, taking out the syringe from his inquisitor's cloak, advancing with a smile . . . But the man only wanted to shake hands. 'I'm Dr Claude.' His accent was American. 'Great to meet you.'

'How do you do,' Lucas said automatically.

Dr Caron and Lucas took their seats. For a few moments they waited in silence. The way the therapist was fiddling with her ring suggested she wasn't quite as composed as she appeared. 'Lucas, I have been working with young people with your condition for many years. I believe I have made progress with all my patients, but some have been easier to help than others. More . . . rewarding. That's why I've taken a special interest in you, even though, in some ways, you are the most problematic of the students at Wildings.'

He frowned. Really? More problematic than Anjuli, who didn't eat, and Yuri, who liked to hit things?

'You are expert at suppressing your feelings, Lucas. Yet compared to the other students, you are the least reconciled to your condition. In the wellness questionnaire you completed on your first day here, you ranked being "angry", "dangerous" and "powerful" at the top of the list of reactions to your condition. In our sessions, however, you have talked of fear . . . of being at the mercy of destructive impulses.'

She took out a folded piece of paper from her pocket and passed it over to him. It was a page from the mood diary he'd been doing in art class; a splurge of red and black swirls, jagged yellow scribbles.

'What does this represent?'

He tried to laugh. 'Nothing good, by the look of it.'

He remembered doing it, of course. It was when he and Glory had discovered Rose Merle had been at Wildings. He had been thinking of Rose's mother's death in the burning attic. And of his mother, in the burning car.

Lucas glanced at the other doctor, who nodded encouragingly. He decided to take the cue.

'I suppose it's true I'm, er . . . conflicted. But I thought I was making progress.'

'Indeed you are. That's why I have brought you here today. I've seen how you have begun to let your guard down, and your vulnerabilities show. Some patients with your condition have no desire to open up, no real motivation to alter their behaviour and attitudes. But you, I think, want to change.'

'My behaviour?' He didn't need to pretend to be confused. This was not where he expected the conversation to be going.

Dr Caron gave him one of her measuring looks. 'Adam.'

Self-consciously, Lucas touched the grey in his hair. 'Adam' was the name they had agreed to use in the therapy sessions when talking about his fae. 'Adam's' arrival had been very unexpected. 'Adam' caused a lot of trouble for Lucas's family, and his father disapproved of 'him'. And so on. But Lucas was tired of codewords and evasions.

'There's nothing I can do about my fae.'

'Ah,' said Dr Claude, leaning forward, 'but *we* can.'

\* \* \*

The breath rushed out of Lucas's body. All of a sudden he knew what this was about. It was about what had been done to Rose Merle. These people wanted to cut the Seventh Sense out of his brain.

He forced himself to keep calm. All the signs indicated this was a sales pitch, not an ambush, and he needed to play along. At least it was no effort to appear confused. 'I – I don't understand.'

'You believe your fae is an aberration, something inexplicable and uncontrollable. Yes?' Dr Caron asked.

He nodded.

'Well,' said Dr Claude easily, 'I'm here to tell you that's not true. The Seventh Sense is a physiological, not supernatural, condition, which can be mapped to regions of the brain.'

'You're a brain surgeon?' Lucas tried to keep the scepticism out of his voice. Dr Claude looked like he'd walked straight off the set of one of those American hospital soaps.

'A neuroscientist.' He gave a modest yet manly smile. 'I work for a company called Cambion, which specialises in neural technology. Our brain-imaging systems have identified the neural network responsible for the Seventh Sense, or rather, the range of symptoms ascribed to the Seventh Sense. In witches, the neurons in this network form inappropriate connections – faulty brainwaves.'

Lucas looked at his therapist. 'So witches are mentally ill?'

'We aren't questioning your sanity,' she said mildly. 'Certainly, not all the fae's attributes are negative. Some probably had an evolutionary advantage, before the technological advancements of the modern age. This particular technology simply aims to help those who feel their condition is a burden, rather than a gift.'

'What's the treatment?'

'Something called a deep brain stimulation implant,' Dr Claude replied. 'It's an electrical device that is set to block the signals emitted by the dysfunctional area of the brain.'

'Sounds a bit sci-fi.'

'Not at all. DBS implants have been in use since the 1990s to treat conditions such as dystonia, Parkinson's disease and epilepsy. The device we use is similar to a cardiac pacemaker, and made of nanoscale carbon fibres. In size, it's no larger than a grain of rice. Once in place, it delivers minute electrical impulses to block the impulses producing the fae – the technique is known as intra-abdominal vagal blocking. Simply put, the instinct to commit witchwork as well as the ability is suppressed. The mark known as the Devil's Kiss fades within an hour of the procedure.'

His delivery was plausible and practised. The faint lines around his eyes and sprinkling of grey at his temples seemed to have been expertly applied – just enough to convey gravitas. Lucas remembered what Glory had told him about the man who'd collected Rose from her clinic, the smooth American.

He risked a frown. 'OK, but how come I haven't heard of this before? I mean, this is a major medical breakthrough. It could change . . . everything.'

The gravitas intensified. 'Exactly. If the procedure was to be made public, it would arouse a storm of controversy. Witchkind Rights organisations would be sure to campaign against our work, or even attempt sabotage. Then there's the danger that some authorities might force people into wearing the implants, whether they wanted to or not. The fact is, many powerful organisations are prepared to go to any lengths to possess Cambion's research and technology.

'For this reason, I'm not at liberty to tell you where our clinic is based until you and your family have formally committed to the procedure. To all intents and purposes, Cambion and its staff do not officially exist.'

*I'll bet*, thought Lucas. That way, the moment the medical malpractice suits arrive, you'll vanish in a puff of smoke. 'How many people have already undergone this procedure?'

Dr Claude smiled reassuringly. 'A wide range. The outcomes have been consistently successful – I can show you many personal testimonies in support of our claims. Of course, you must have plenty more questions, and I will be happy to answer them. But for now, I'm sure you'd like to have some time to reflect on what we have told you. There's a lot to take in.'

'I know your godfather is coming to see you on Wednesday,' Dr Caron put in, 'but this is something you need to discuss with your father. If you wish, I can arrange for you to make a private telephone call. He will doubtless want to meet with us too. But it is of the highest importance you talk to no one else about this, either at the academy or anywhere else. If you do, I'm afraid the opportunity will be withdrawn.'

'And you won't have it again.' Dr Claude shook his head regretfully. 'Cambion knows how to guard its privacy. I assure you, we will be impossible to find.'

Dr Caron reached out and put her hand on Lucas's. Her eyes were large and gentle behind the frumpy glasses.

'Unlike your classmates, there are no instances of witchkind in your ancestry. For you to get the fae was a particularly cruel twist of fate. There is no shame in admitting this is something you would like to change. The fae isn't a part of who you are. Not if you don't want it to be.'

Lucas remembered the moment of discovery; how he'd crouched naked in his bathroom, stabbing a needle through the black blot on his shoulder blade. The Devil's Kiss could not bleed, but the rest of him had. Briefly, he closed his eyes, and saw bright red flecks spot the darkness.

If he hadn't gone to WICA . . . if he hadn't met Glory . . . if he didn't know about Rose . . .

Of course he'd be tempted. Of course he would.

# CHAPTER 14

'The perfect scam,' was Glory's verdict that evening. 'And the perfect mark: a load of pissed-off teenagers who want their lives back. How much does it cost?'

'I didn't ask,' Lucas admitted.

She gave him a look. *Typical rich boy*, it said.

They were in one of the music practice rooms. Mei-fen, as Wildings' longest-serving inmate, had been granted a key so that she could play the piano when she wished. She had lent it to Lucas, no questions asked, and Glory had checked the place for bugs. The only place they had found them so far was in the common room. But better safe than sorry.

'There wasn't much opportunity for questions,' Lucas explained, a little defensively. 'Just lots of scientific jargon.'

'I'll bet – razzle-dazzle you with fancy words. It was the same when Patch was flogging this balding cure cream down Talbot Market. Made a packet for the coven, he did.'

'Rubbing snake oil into your scalp isn't the same as drilling into someone's skull.'

'No,' said Glory soberly. 'Well, we know we ain't dealing

with Endor at least. It's not like they'd want to cut down the number of witch-kids in the world.'

'Lady Merle said the procedure worked at first, didn't she?'

'Oh yeah. Rose's fae was gone, all right. Then a coupla days after she got home, she had some sort of fit and woke up doolally.'

It wasn't the first time Lucas had heard the theory that the fae could be traced to abnormalities in the brain structure. Cambion's claims possibly had a legitimate scientific basis. But without registered clinical trials, let alone a medical licence, Dr Claude and his friends were essentially using witches as human guinea pigs.

However, Lucas was sure that if Cambion were able to get past the experimental phase of development, they'd take their technology mainstream and sell the licence to the highest bidder.

'We can't be sure if Rose was just unlucky,' he said, 'or if that's the fate of everyone who has the implant. It could happen to one in three, or one in a hundred. We don't even know how many people have undergone the procedure.'

'Huh. They must pick their victims carefully – people desperate enough to try anything, but who can be trusted not to blab. Which is where the dodgy shrink comes in. Bet she gets a nice fat commission from sending business the brain-cutters' way.' Glory looked at him curiously. 'What do you talk about in your sessions, anyhow?'

'Oh, the usual rubbish. Whatever I think she wants to hear.' But Lucas knew that he hadn't needed to fake being aggressive and fearful when he talked about his fae with the therapist. No wonder she thought he was an ideal candidate for its removal.

'Well, she might have made out you was a special case, but it could be there's others here who've been approached. So it's not Principal Lazovic's files we need to break into. It's the doc's.'

'Shouldn't we hold off until Wednesday and wait for instructions?' Wednesday was when the MI6 man was due to arrive. 'This isn't what we were sent here to investigate.'

'Yeah, and up till now we've turned up nothing but dead ends. We gotta have *something* to show for ourselves, and if we wait for Wednesday, it might be too late. From what you said, these creeps are a paranoid bunch. They could up sticks any moment.'

Lucas wasn't convinced, but he thought he understood where Glory was coming from. She must be frustrated that he was the one to make the breakthrough. Neither of them wanted to go home empty-handed, but Glory had more to prove than him.

She pressed on. ''Sides, this might be my only chance to get a lead on Rose. I reckon whoever broke her out of that clinic was connected to Cambi-whatnot. She's living proof of what crooks they are. What if they've decided to get rid of the evidence?' Her voice swelled. 'Rose is *family*, remember. I got a responsibility for her.'

'All right,' he said at last, defeated. 'Fine. If you come up with a feasible plan for breaking into Dr Caron's office, then I'll go along with it. Deal?'

'Deal.' Glory spat on her palm and made as if to shake his hand, before looking at his horrified expression and bursting into laughter.

With a proper job to do, Glory felt her prospects brighten. And she'd spoken the truth when she said she had a responsibility for Rose. Her faith in Starling Girl solidarity had been shaken by her Great-Aunt Angeline, but that only made it all the more important that she did things right by Lily's granddaughter.

Dr Caron did not live on campus, but commuted from one of the larger towns in the east. Since Sundays and Mondays were her days off, Glory decided to spend Sunday on planning and preparation, and stage the break-in the following night.

She knew the therapist's office was protected by a keypad on the door as well as a sturdy lock. The windows were iron-shuttered. However, there was a small toilet adjoining the office, with an old-fashioned skylight in the ceiling. If she and Lucas could sky-leap on to the roof of the tower, her lock-picking skills should get them inside.

The problem was where to sky-leap from. The windows in their bedrooms were barred, and the attics out of bounds. Trying to break into them would be an unnecessary complication. Instead, Glory had chosen a top-floor window that looked into the smaller of the castle's two interior courtyards. It had a decent ledge and was overshadowed by the eaves. Once on the roof, the castle's towers and turrets should shield the sky-leapers from view.

The biggest challenge, however, was avoiding the

interior security patrols. A pair of guardians made the rounds four times a night, but kept their timings deliberately irregular. The situation was further complicated by the fact that she and Lucas would be coming from different directions.

On Monday after lights-out, Glory waited in her room. She was sitting on a chair opposite the window, hands resting on her thighs, with five threads of cotton strung loosely between each finger. She had worn the threads looped around her wrist all day, and that evening run them between her hands, damp with spit, as she worked her fae into the cotton. Then she'd cut the cotton in half, and laid five of the ten pieces along the route from her room to the exit window. The castle's luxurious carpeting was an advantage, for she had nestled the lines of cotton so deep in the plush they were virtually invisible.

Back in her room, she'd run the other five threads through her hands again, and licked them too, before tying them to her fingers. She kept her breath slow and steady, visualising the darkly shimmering thread of fae that bound those laid on stairways and thresholds to those knotted to her fingertips. In his own room, Lucas would be doing the same. Her eyes were fixed on the window.

After over an hour's wait, the glass suddenly bloomed with mist, as if a ghost had breathed on to the pane. The ghost's invisible hand wrote a tick mark into the mist, which quickly faded away. It meant the patrol had passed by Lucas's quarters first, and was now headed in her direction.

A faintly smeared handprint was still visible on the window pane. Lucas had put it there, making a furtive dash into her room after morning assembly. Communicating between windows or mirrors was one of the more useful tricks they'd learned at WICA, but for it to work, both witches had to have laid their palms on both panes of glass. Glory smiled a little, remembering how she had bumped into Matron on the way back from a reciprocal visit. 'These are the boys' quarters, Gloriana,' Mrs Heggie had told her, frowning. 'Did you take a wrong turn?'

Glory intensified her focus on the threads she held. Her fingers felt cramped and stiff. Finally, almost twenty minutes after Lucas's message, the line of cotton between her thumbs twitched and tightened. It was a sign that someone had crossed over its other half, which she had laid under their exit window. The patrol must be heading to the stairs down to her floor. Sure enough, about five minutes later, the thread between her forefingers snapped straight, and Glory knew the patrol had passed by the door at the end of her corridor. A third, and they'd turned right. A fourth, and they'd reached the main staircase. A fifth – much weaker, since the thread was at a considerable distance from her room – told her the guardians were on their way back to their station in the north tower.

With a sigh of relief, Glory disentangled the cotton, rolled it into a small clump and flicked it out of the window. The talisman only worked once, and the importance of cleaning up after witchwork had been drummed into her time and time again. She would get rid of as many of the remaining threads as possible while on her way out.

First, though, she laid her left hand over the smudge left by Lucas's handprint on the window. Glory breathed deeply on to the glass next to the print, feeling her fae swell within her, a silvery second breath. Her right forefinger tingled as it traced a slightly wobbly tick in the condensation. Time to go.

They had calculated they'd have at least forty-five minutes before another patrol was due to make the rounds. In all likelihood, they'd have considerably longer, but it wouldn't do to take any chances. At her bedroom door, Glory pulled down a wool beanie to hide her face. She was wearing a navy tracksuit and plimsolls and had her lock-picking set in her left pocket. In her right was the pine cone she would be using as a lodestone. A pebble might clatter too noisily, though it would be easier to throw.

It was near midnight: the witching hour. The illuminated dial of Glory's wristwatch – another MI6 gadget – provided the only light outside her room. They needed to keep witchwork to a minimum in case they got caught. That way, it would be easier to pass off their exploits as a prank.

Lucas was already by the window, his face a pale smudge under his hooded top. Good gear to go robbing in, said Auntie Angel's voice approvingly in Glory's head, and she almost laughed. She squeezed Lucas's hand, partly in greeting, partly in celebration of the fae fizzing through her, and he pulled back a little, startled.

She undid the window latch. The sash moved up smoothly. There was only one outside light in the narrow courtyard, set over the door five steep storeys below. Glory rolled the pine cone between her palms, feeling the bark scratch pleasantly against her skin. She propped it on the sill, summoned it, and climbed on to the ledge, eyes fixed on her chosen landing spot. It was the other side of the court-yard, to the left of the gable opposite, meaning she would need to leap upwards on the diagonal. She could sense Lucas tensing up behind her, and took a deep breath, not to calm her nerves, but to settle her excitement. The thrill of witch-working was like champagne bubbles in the blood.

Glory expelled the lodestone in a fluid arc, listening for the faint tap of its landing. There was a half-second of suspense, then the tug of fae jolted up through her body and into the air, and she soared after it: easily, sweetly, naturally. In the blink of an eye, her hand closed on the pine cone, and her feet found purchase on the stone.

Lucas's turn. It was hard to see in the darkness, but he looked uncharacteristically lumpen and awkward as he shifted about on the ledge. *Come on*, she thought. *Just do it.* When he finally made his move, however, his aim was true, and landing steady.

'All right?' she whispered as he straightened up. His teeth gleamed in a smile.

The castle's rooftops were a forest of stone, bristling with parapets and peaks and pinnacles. The black, murmur-ing sea of pine heaved below. Ragged clouds scudded over the sky, parting briefly to expose a scoop of moon, a smatter of stars. Glory felt immortal, invincible. She wanted to sing and dance and shout. To leap with the wind.

But they had a job to do.

The skylight they were going to target was on the north side of Dr Caron's tower. The wall was straight and sheer, the roof pitched. Glory waited until a particularly thick bank of cloud obscured the moon, then did a running sky-leap on to the stone gutter at the edge of the roof, leaning her weight against its slate slope. From there, she was able to reach the skylight's frame. With the lodestone back in her pocket, she pulled on a pair of black gloves and got out her lock-picking set. Lucas had one too but she'd had more practice. The half-diamond, the short hook, the snake rake and single-sided pick were old friends. She'd had her first introduction to them aged ten, back in Cooper Street. Her nimble fingers eased the blades into the lock, feeling for the click.

The skylight hadn't been opened for a long while and creaked in protest. Glory turned the cog at the side of her watch to increase the light in its dial, and directed the beam into the bathroom below. She braced her arms on either side of the window frame and, grimacing, lowered herself down to the point at which she was able get a foothold on the handbasin. Lucas was not far behind. They opened the door, and slipped through into the adjoining office.

The best source of information would be the computer. Unfortunately, the witchwork method for getting past password protection would leave too much of a mess.

'I'll take the filing cabinet,' Glory whispered, getting out her lock-picks again. 'And you go for the desk. Remember: we're after anything connected to Cambion, brain surgery or Rose.'

At first, it looked like she'd struck lucky. The student files went back three years, and Rose's was right where it should be, under M for Merle. But it seemed the majority of documents relating to ex-students were archived elsewhere. Glory flipped through copies of Rose's old school reports and medical records to get to Dr Caron's notes, only to find nothing but a copy of the quiz that she and Lucas had filled in on their first day. (For *How does your condition make you feel?* Rose had ranked Disgusted, Depressed and Embarrassed at the top of the list.) The only other items of interest were two well-thumbed photographs, one a close-up of Rose's neck and the small inky blot that was her Devil's Kiss, and one a black-and-white shot of her chatting on a mobile in a street. Although Glory had only seen Rose as an invalid, she would have known those luminously perfect features anywhere.

'You got something?' Lucas asked.

'Not really. Just a photo of Rose before her brain got fried.'

Lucas peered at it. 'But there's a date stamp. See: it was taken last month. It looks like a surveillance shot.'

'Then it's a glamour. Someone's witchworked themselves to look like Rose, all bright-eyed and bushy-tailed. Maybe they was planning for her to meet you, tell you lies about what a success her op's been.'

'OK. Well, let's keep looking.'

Lucas started going through the books on the shelves, shaking them out in case anything was concealed in their pages. A locked cupboard revealed nothing more exciting than a stack of neatly bagged-up sand-trays. Glory checked the backs of the posters and framed certificates on the walls, before returning to the student files. It occurred to her that it would be useful to get a bit of background on Wildings' alumni. She had just pulled open the top drawer when an alarm started to ring.

Glory swore. 'What the –? That can't be 'cause of us, can it?'

It wasn't in their part of the building, but although not particularly loud, the noise was horribly insistent.

'Doesn't matter,' said Lucas tersely. 'Any minute now, the whole place will be swarming with guardians. We've got to get out of here.'

With trembling hands, Glory relocked the filing cabinet and desk. They had tried to put everything back in place as they went along, but it was still a scramble to remove every last sign of their presence. When it came to getting out, the scramble intensified. Lucas roughly pushed Glory up from the basin to the skylight, then she pulled him after her. It was a perilous business, jostling for space on the gutter, backs against the roof, as they attempted to summon and then throw their lodestones.

The rooftop jumble flashed past in a blur. When they got to the courtyard, both felt a crashing sense of relief that their window was still open, and the corridor behind it was still dark. Even so, they weren't home and dry. Glory forgot to position her lodestone with her mind as well as her throw, so that the pine cone fell through the window on to the floor, tugging her in a headlong tumble after it. Lucas's landing was even worse. He jumped on to the sill, but failed to get his balance right, and swayed dangerously on the ledge. If Glory had not been there to grab his arms, he might have fallen.

The alarm was louder now they were inside. As she closed the window, Glory saw that lights were being turned on across the way. Whoever or whatever had set off the alarm, it meant they had little chance of getting back to their rooms undetected. 'C'mon,' she hissed, beckoning Lucas round the corner and down the corridor. 'In here.'

She'd found the place on her previous scout of the territory. When not in use, most of the castle's rooms were locked, but the door handle on this one was broken. It wasn't much of a hideout, but it was all they had.

# CHAPTER 15

Lucas was furious. He couldn't think why he'd let himself be persuaded – bullied – into this pointless stunt. Glory was cocky and reckless, just like Commander Hughes said. And now he was paying the price.

Still shaking slightly from his near-fall, he peeled off his gloves and thrust them down the back of the radiator. He crushed his pine cone to dust under his heel. Glory was doing the same. Her wool beanie had got lost en route, but she was able to get rid of the lock-picking set by stuffing it down a crack in the floorboards. Getting caught would be bad enough, but getting caught with evidence of witchwork and espionage didn't bear thinking about.

They crouched in the corner furthest from the door. An after-echo of fae thrummed through Lucas's body. If Dr Caron could feel it for herself – the hunger, the intoxication – would she be more anxious to cut it out, or less?

The alarm had been turned off, at least, so the only sound was their own breathing. Glory's eyes glittered in the dark. Lucas remembered her on the rooftops, triumphant as an angel, wild as wind. Dauntless. He felt anger again, and envy, and despite himself, relief that she was there.

They waited in silence, for their hearts to stop hammering and their breath to slow. There were no sounds of pursuit. Maybe, just maybe, they'd get away with it. Lucas was about to suggest they take a look at the corridor, when they heard something. Footsteps, murmurs . . . the testing of door handles.

'Hex,' Glory muttered. And then, 'Quick,' she breathed in his ear. 'If they think – if we –'

She pulled him towards her. Her mouth was on his, soft and warm and yielding. Her heart was beating wildly, or maybe it was his. Caught off guard, he fell back a little, clutching at her. She clutched back. His fingers went up and met in her hair. We have to make it look real, he thought confusedly, as the door swung open with a crash.

They sprang apart, flushed and tumbled. It didn't matter that the interruption was expected. The moment was still uniquely shaming. Mrs Heggie and Brett Peters were standing in the doorway, shining a torch into their hot faces.

'*What* is the meaning of this?' the matron demanded.

'All too obvious, ma'm,' growled Peters.

It should have been funny. But it wasn't. They clumsily got to their feet, resolutely not looking at each other.

'You ought to be ashamed of yourselves.' There wasn't anything cosy about Mrs Heggie now. Her mouth was puckered in disgust. 'Such behaviour is grossly inappropriate, not to say irresponsible.'

Peters nodded importantly. 'The curfew's in place for your own security. There's been an intrud–'

Mrs Heggie gave a warning cough, and he fell silent. 'Naturally,' she said, 'Principal Lazovic will be informed. He will decide on the appropriate disciplinary action in the morning. In the meantime, I want you back where you belong. And *out of my sight.*'

A guardian in the corridor muttered into a radio, then hustled Glory away. Lucas was escorted by Brett Peters. The man's huge hand clamped down on his shoulder, grinding the bone. Lucas almost welcomed it. He was in need of something to steady him.

After Glory was pushed into her room, the door slamming behind her, she began to laugh. They'd actually got away with it! It was a safe bet the authorities would be too preoccupied with the mystery intruder to focus on her and Lucas's escapade. A pair of teens who'd snuck out for a midnight hook-up . . . why suspect them of anything else?

In the dim glow of the nightlight, however, her triumph began to fade. It wasn't as if the night's work had been a success. All that risk, and no reward. She wondered if Lucas blamed her. She wondered what he thought of her and the kiss; if anything had changed.

But she dismissed this as girly silliness of the worst sort. They were professionals. Of course they wouldn't speak of it again.

Glory went to the window and stared into the night, trying to remember how she'd felt on the rooftops. Immortal. Invincible. Free. And when breath bloomed on the pane, the lurch inside her was like a sky-leap.

Into the mist, Lucas's distant hand wrote, *You* OK?

She breathed back. Her finger, tingling, traced, *Yes.* The letters were smudged and ragged, dissolving into fae-silvered condensation almost as soon as they appeared. The witchwork wouldn't last past morning. *You?*

*Fine. Goodnight.*

Warm hand on cold glass. Warm breath, cold stars.

*Goodnight.*

# CHAPTER 16

The next morning, Senora Ramirez took the assembly, while Principal Lazovic interviewed Glory and Lucas separately in his study. 'You are on probation here. You haven't just broken our rules, but violated our trust . . .' Lucas tried to look suitably guilt-ridden. A list of sanctions followed: trips to Blumenwald were suspended, meals would be taken in isolation, and they were both required to attend extra sessions with Dr Caron until further notice.

The real ordeal was the man to man chat that followed the lecture. Principal Lazovic was 'not unsympathetic to the pressures young people were under or the temptations they faced'. But Lucas had a condition to manage. That was what he must focus his energies on. Whatever Gloriana's attractions, Lucas should bear in mind they were two very different people, from very different worlds. 'Imagine what your family would say, hm?'

Lucas pictured Marisa and Glory doing battle over the petits fours, and had to bite his tongue to stop the laughter. Still, he could see there were advantages to pretending to be together. They'd come under more scrutiny from the staff, but it would also seem natural for them to spend time with each other. They could be like Anjuli and Yuri, whispering in corners, strolling hand in hand.

On his way to class, Lucas bumped into Raffi. News of his exploits must have spread, as Raffi greeted him with a broad grin and a slap on the back.

'Seriously, *amigo*, you are the dude of all time! How far did you get, before the busting?'

It turned out Raffi had his own cause for celebration. The political situation in Cordoba had changed, and his father had summoned him home. Right now, he was going to his room to pack. Lucas expressed appropriate envy and congratulations.

'Ah, but this place will be party-party for you now,' Raffi said consolingly. 'I think the American might be hot for you also. She watches you – I have seen.'

Lucas didn't pay any attention to this. However, he did speculate about the reason for Raffi's abrupt departure. Was it possible he was the other person creeping around last night? Maybe the Cordoban was in need of a speedy getaway.

One way and another, there was plenty to distract him during the morning's lessons. And at break-time he was waylaid by Jenna, who'd been loitering in the corridor.

'Can I have a minute?'

'Um, sure.'

She drew closer. 'I'd like for us to meet later, in the afternoon recess. There's something you need to know. Do you know where the laundry room is?'

'Yes. But what –'

'I'll see you there.' Jenna looked him in the eye. No

fluttering lashes, no bubbly giggle. 'Don't tell anyone, not even Glory. It's important, 'K?'

She sauntered off, ponytail swinging.

Lucas didn't know what to make of the encounter, but it unsettled him. When he got to the common room, where Glory was sitting with Anjuli and Mei, he saw that she too looked tense and preoccupied. He stood in the doorway, willing her to look up. When she did, and her expression lightened, it felt like a small victory. The other girls exchanged glances.

Glory came to join him in the hall. The music pumping out of the stereo – one of Yuri's Russian thrash metal bands – was hard on the ears, but a good cover for conversation.

'Hey.'

'Hey.'

There was a rather breathless pause.

'How did it go with Lazovic?'

'Like water off a duck's arse.' She grinned. 'I've been yelled at by a lot of teachers in my time.'

'Look . . . I thought you should know . . . Jenna asked to meet me later. In private.'

Glory folded her arms across her chest, amused. 'Carry on like this, and you'll start to get a reputation.'

Lucas felt himself flush. 'She has something to tell me,' he said, more haughtily than he intended. 'It sounded important. Serious. We're going to meet in the laundry room.'

'Hm. What with all these secret conferences you're being whisked off to, I'm starting to feel a bit of a spare part.'

'Well, you shouldn't. This could be about anything or

nothing. Or maybe Jenna just has the hots for me.' He stopped. 'That was a joke. Because she doesn't, obviously. And it's not as if I'd . . . um . . .'

'Right,' she said blankly.

'I'll tell you everything that happens.'

Glory smiled at that. 'You'd better. Partners, remember?'

'Of course. Always.'

He smiled back at her. There was another pause, a waiting one. It took both of them an effort to look away.


The basement was a cramped and dingy warren. Lucas walked towards the thrum of machinery, and into the warm fug of the laundry room.

Jenna was waiting by a rank of tumble dryers.

'Thanks for coming. You sure nobody knows you're here?'

'I'm sure.' He looked around him and shut the door. 'Shouldn't there be a maid or something?'

'I've taken care of it. Anyways, we've got bigger problems to worry about.'

He stared at her in confusion.

'You were careless,' she said. 'You left evidence behind you last night. The guardians found a hat on the roof: a black wool beanie. They know someone's been sky-leaping.'

Glory's hat. Damn. It took a moment to steady himself. 'I don't see why you should think that's anything to do with me. Someone broke in last night; I heard Peters say.'

Jenna gave a small humourless laugh. 'That someone was me. And I sure as heck wasn't sky-leaping. I wasn't careless either – just unlucky. There was a motion sensor in Lazovic's office I didn't know about. But thanks to you and your woolly accessory, they now think witchwork was involved. And that makes life more complicated for all of us.'

Lucas was struggling to keep up. 'It was *you*?'

'S7 Agent White. Nice to meet you. I hear July's a good month for alpine flowers, even though there's still snow on the mountainside.'

It was the code phrasing Lucas had been told to expect from the MI6 agent who was visiting him tomorrow. So he wasn't being waylaid by an amorous cheerleader. Section Seven – S7 – was the American equivalent of WICA. The US Inquisition, based in Salem, Massachusetts, was called the Witchkind Security Agency, or WSA.

Jenna leaned back against the dryers. Her girlish features had hardened, and her voice had lost its sugary drawl. Lucas wondered how old she really was. 'OK, so here's how it is. My team have had this place under surveillance for a while. That's how we can be sure of being undisturbed down here, by the way – we've got an asset in the domestic staff. But two agencies running two operations in the same joint is only ever going to end in tears. So my guys have spoken to your guys . . . and everyone's agreed it's time to talk.'

'Fine,' said Lucas. 'You first.' He resented her superior tone.

'Then I'll start with Chase Randolph Parker III.'

'Quite a name.'

'Quite a guy. Son of a Supreme Court judge, heir to an

oilfield. A little birdie told the WSA he'd got the fae aged seventeen. The informant even supplied a snapshot of the Devil's Kiss, on the kid's ankle bone. But before anything could be done about it, hey presto, Chase was whisked off to Wildings. So far, so predictable – until he came home after graduation, that is.'

She spoke quickly and quietly, with an offhand sort of impatience.

'The WSA was over him like a rash, but he and his family stuck to their guns: he wasn't a witch, never had been, never would be. So the investigating officer bided his time. He figured the impulse to use the fae would prove irresistible. Sure enough, and sooner rather than later, Chase Parker was found in the neighbourhood of a minor witchcrime.

'The boy was immediately taken in and witch-swum. Nothing. Witch-pricked too. Nothing. The mark on his ankle was gone. He really was just an innocent bystander – fae-free.'

Lucas bit his lip. 'And he's normal in every way? In good health?'

'Apparently so.'

'OK, maybe your original information was wrong. It could have been a malicious accusation.'

'It could. But we don't reckon it was.' She looked at him shrewdly. 'You got any other explanation for a kid who's a witch one day, and not the next?'

Lucas hesitated. He hadn't had a chance to pass on his findings to WICA yet. He didn't know how open Jenna was really being. But in the circumstances, he had to give her something. Briefly, he described his dealings with doctors

Caron and Claude, but without going into the specifics of the procedure, or mentioning the name of the company. He kept Rose Merle out of it too.

'Hm.' She drummed her fingers on the top of the dryer. 'Interesting. We've heard the rumours, but never managed to follow them up. Sounds like it's time to start joining the dots.'

'So what now? We team up?'

Jenna paused. 'Look . . . I've had my instructions. And, yeah, inter-agency cooperation is all the rage these days. But the fact is, there's a lot of unease at Control. We don't get what Glory's doing here.'

'What do you mean? She's my partner.'

'She's got criminal associations.'

'That's in the past. Glory's left the covens behind.'

'It's not just the covens, though, is it? It's Endor.'

Lucas felt a premonitory tremor of alarm. 'I don't know what you mean.'

'Nice try.' Jenna shook her head. 'We both know that your Inquisition coerced Edie Starling into joining Endor as a double agent. She fed them chicken feed for a year or two, then vanished. If she's still alive, then odds are, she's been turned.'

'Edie's activities are nothing to do with Glory.' The words grated in his throat. 'She doesn't even know about the Endor connection.'

'I'm sure she doesn't.' Jenna raised her brows. 'Or that a certain Ashton Stearne was part of the clique who forced Edie undercover in the first place. But either way, Glory Starling's a liability. Damaged goods.'

There was a noise from outside. They both stiffened. Lucas knew what it was: breaking glass. Too late, he saw the tumbler on the floor behind a pile of laundry bags. Too late, he looked in the doorway to see Glory standing there. She was holding a shard of glass in a bloody fist. It was the shattered remains of the other half of a listening talisman. Her face was so white and pinched the bones seemed ready to poke out of the skin.

'Oops,' said Jenna.

There was a rushing and beating inside Lucas's head. 'Glory. Glory, I –'

He put out his hand towards her, and she jerked violently away.

'Liar. Traitor. Get away from me.'

'It's not what you think.'

'I think I've been played for a fool. And that you went along with it, every step of the way.'

'I'm sorry. I hated not being able to tell you. They told me if I did, I'd get thrown out of the service. They threatened me with prosecution.' It sounded pathetic, even as he said it.

'"*They*" all knew, did they? Rawdon, Jonah, Zoey, Carmel . . . Everyone but me. Christ!' She spat on the floor. 'What was the master plan, then, Lucas? To use me like your dad used my mum? As some kind of *bait*?'

'No, of course not. Listen, it's complicated –'

'*Don't hexing patronise me.*' Glory drew a ragged breath. 'I should've known. Like father, like son. I was a fool to ever think you was different. A fool to trust you, to think that you – that we –'

Her mouth quirked bitterly. Then she turned on her heel and ran.

A heavy-faced man in a cleaner's uniform was standing at the foot of the stairs. As Glory shouldered him aside, he looked at Jenna quizzically. Jenna shook her head, and when Lucas moved forward, dug her shiny pink nails into his arm.

'Calm down. You'll only make this a bigger mess than it already is. You've got a job to do, remember.'

Lucas wrenched himself free, but when he reached the top of the stairs, Glory had gone.

# CHAPTER 17

Glory stormed blindly through the castle. Harsh and unfamiliar tears rose in her eyes. She struck them angrily away.

She had decided to snoop on the meeting on a whim. Last night's witchwork had reinvigorated her; that afternoon, all she wanted was to indulge her curiosity and make some mischief. When she'd sneaked down to the basement, waiting for the chance to pick the lock on the caretaker's cupboard and position herself among the cleaning supplies, she hadn't even expected the stunt to work. The laundry room the other side of the wall was noisy with machines, and a listening talisman was hard to manage at the best of times. As her finger had circled the rim of the tumbler in her hand, calling to the fae vibrating through the glass she'd placed next door, the thread of sound that stretched between them was almost too thin and colourless to hear.

Yet the words still came, and with them, Glory's every nerve underwent a separate hammer blow of shock. She didn't remember breaking the glass. Either she'd gripped it too hard, or she'd lost control of the fae buzzing through her body. Her fingers were still smeared with blood. She regretted it was hers. She wanted to cause some damage.

Edie looked very young in the photograph Glory had always kept by her bed. Her expression was ill at ease. Perhaps when the picture was taken, she was already preparing to go. And what had Glory been left with? Her lovely, useless, defeated Dad. Charlie Morgan, with his shark-tooth grin. Bitter old Angeline – another person who'd lied to and betrayed her, and manipulated her for her own ends . . .

*I love you, but it's better if I go. Forgive me.* No wonder the note had been so short. Edie had been blackmailed, perhaps with threats against her husband and child. And yet the prickers had got their claws into her daughter all the same. Twelve years later, here she was, doing their dirty work.

Well. Not any more.

Rounding a corner, Glory nearly ran smack into Raffi. He was dragging an enormous suitcase behind him and the guardian escorting him was carrying another. 'There you are, Glory! I was looking to say *adios*. Have you seen where is Lucas?'

She was about to shake him off, then stopped. 'Wait for me,' she said, with an urgency that made him blink. 'Five minutes. Wait.'

Glory raced back up the stairs, through the passage-ways and into her room, where she threw a few essentials into a shoulder bag. She tore the spare passport out of its hiding place, and pounded downstairs and out on to the castle forecourt. Raffi was standing by the side of a white limousine. Cordoban rap was pumping out of the sound system and his driver was loading the boot, resplendent in aviator sunglasses and a tight white suit. A small group of students and staff had assembled on the steps to say goodbye. Jenna and Lucas were there too.

Glory skidded up to Raffi. 'Can I have a lift?'

'You are *leaving*? Why?'

She shrugged, and hitched her bag over her shoulder. 'Need a change of scene.' Then, under her breath, 'Get me outta here. Please.'

Raffi grinned. 'OK, sure. Jailbreak . . . road trip. Whatever!'

Lucas moved out of the knot of onlookers. He looked ill. 'Glory, please don't do this.'

'Shut up,' she hissed. 'Shut up, else I'll only make it worse for you. *Both* of you.' She shot a glance in Jenna's direction. Poisonous bitch. 'Don't you get it? I'll burn before I see or speak to you again.'

'Gloriana!' Principal Lazovic was marching down the steps, Mrs Heggie at his side. His neat little face was twitching with anger. 'You cannot leave on a whim. Your family must be consulted, the proper procedures followed.'

'Besides,' said the matron righteously, 'you have no resources. Without the necessary paperwork –'

'I got all I need.' Glory waved her passport at them. 'No one's kept here against their will; that's what you said. You can't stop me.'

'You are here for your own protection,' the principal said. 'We have a duty of care –'

Glory flung her back her head. 'WITCH!' she howled. 'I'm a WITCH! Hecate's Little Helper! Mab's Handmaiden! A hexing harpy HAG! There.' She gave the finger to the gaggle of shocked faces. 'Consider me expelled.'

This time nobody tried to stop her. She jerked open the passenger door and got into the limo. Raffi came and sat beside her, speechless for once. The car moved on, past the guardians, past the checkpoint and wire fence. The castle was swallowed up by trees. Glory sat back against the leather seat and closed her eyes. A terrible, wordless loneliness descended.

Lucas followed the others back into the academy. There was no other choice. He could feel Jenna's eyes on him but kept his face stonily blank. He was furious with her, and even more furious with himself.

And because Dr Caron was the last thing he wanted to deal with, there she was, waiting in the hall. 'Ah, Lucas. We have an appointment now. I hope you didn't forget?'

It was even worse when he sat down in her office. He tried not to look at the bathroom door. He tried not to think of the giddy rooftop swoops, the scramble on the ledge . . . Glory's eyes, black and bright . . . his hands in her hair . . .

The therapist pushed her oversize glasses up her nose. 'I had not realised you and the coven girl were so close.'

He didn't respond.

'I heard about what happened last night.'

'It didn't mean anything.'

She tapped her finger on the desk. It was the one with the missing joint; the skin was yellow and puckered at the end.

'People are gossiping. About you and Gloriana. You and Jenna too.'

'I don't pay attention to gossip.'

'Lucas. I know you are confused. And bored, and lonely. But to form an intense attachment in such a short space of time, and to such a girl . . . Gloriana is crude, aggressive. I confess I do not see what someone like you would see in her.'

'Why?' he asked, goaded. 'Because she's not browbeaten by this place? Because she's proud of what she is?'

Dr Caron's face grew sharp and watchful. 'And you admire that?'

At once, he realised his mistake. 'No. Not at all. It's just . . . well, it's different for someone like Glory. She's been brought up among criminals. She's used to – er – deviancy. That's why we quarrelled.'

'Did you discuss with her what we talked about in Blumenwald?'

'Of course not.' He swallowed. 'Anyway, she wouldn't be interested.'

Dr Caron's eyes travelled slowly round her office. Lucas began to sweat. What if he and Glory hadn't managed to completely cover their tracks? The woman must already know about the attempted break-in to Lazovic's office, and now there was evidence of sky-leaping too.

The silence stretched on. Finally, he said, 'I think I'm

ready to talk to my father now. About what we, er, discussed. Do you think you'll be able to set up the call?'

Dr Caron spread her hands out on the desk.

'I don't think that would be wise just now. You are overemotional. We do not want to overreach ourselves.'

The next morning, the school was informed that, for health reasons, the therapist had gone on indefinite leave.

'Hello? Hello?'

'It's me, Dad. Glory.' She could hear music and laughter in the background, and the chink of glasses. 'Are you at a *party*?'

'Oh, ah, well. Just a small gathering. The Residents' Association got the funds for the play centre, so me and Peggy thought a celebration was in order. Rolf's helping too.'

Glory leaned her forehead against the side of the service station phone box. She felt terribly tired.

'Sounds fun.'

'And how are you doing?'

'Fine. Mostly. That is – well, things ain't exactly gone to plan at the academy. We've hit a bit of a dead end. So I'm going to take a break. I thought I'd go travelling for a while. Maybe visit Cousin Candy.'

'On your own? What about money?' He coughed. 'Ahem. I'm not sure this sounds very, er, sensible.'

'I've enough funds to be getting by. And I'm with a friend.'

'Lucas?'

'No. Someone else from the school. Lucas . . . he's

staying on. Fact is, Dad, I might have made a mistake with this WICA business. I don't reckon the job's right for me after all.'

'I'm very sorry to hear that, love. I hope you're not in any difficulty.'

'I've always been free to walk. And I ain't done nothing wrong – don't let no one tell you otherwise. Don't let on what we've talked about neither. Any problems, you speak to Troy. I'll be in touch again soon.'

'Oh dear . . . well . . . I'm sure you know what you're doing. You're such a clever girl. But you will be careful, won't you?'

'Always. I love you.'

'Love you too.'

Glory put the phone down with a sigh. She knew she would have to broach the subject of Edie at some point, but her heart shrank from the prospect. At least Patrick was discreet. All those years in the coven hadn't been for nothing.

*Please, please pick up,* she begged silently as Troy's mobile, the one he used for personal calls, began to ring.

At the last minute, he answered with an irritable, 'Yes?'

'It's Glory, and I'm gonna have to be quick 'cause I'm on one of them phonecards and I ain't got much credit. But I thought you should know I've left the academy, and WICA, and the rest. You were right. More than right. I was a fool to trust them. I've been played.'

She worked hard to keep her voice strong.

There was a moment's pause. 'Exactly how much trouble are you in?'

'Hard to tell. I'm free to resign from the agency, I guess, but if I come home I'll be hauled in by the prickers for bridling and that. So I'm gonna lie low for a bit.'

'And go where?'

'Cordoba. I thought I might look up Candy.'

'Mab Almighty, girl – it's the back of beyond! Not to mention home to every kind of lowlife under the sun.'

She managed to laugh. 'Then I'll feel right at home. In any case, I got connections there. I won't be on me own.'

After some grumbling, Troy gave her Candice's address, which he'd got from one of the Wednesday Coven's contacts in San Jerico. At the moment, the only communication Candice's family had from her was the occasional email.

'Can't you tell me what happened?' he said afterwards. 'What they've done?'

'Later.' Glory gripped the phone tight to support herself. 'I need to get my head straight first. Keep an eye on Dad, OK, but don't worry about me. I'm a Starling girl, remember.'

'Not likely to forget, am I?' Troy said, softer now.

When Glory put the phone down, she saw Raffi waiting for her across the way, shovelling chips into his mouth.

'Sorry for the hold-up,' she said, as breezily as she could make it. 'I were just finalising my travel plans. Thought I might swing by Cordoba, as a matter of fact.'

'Seriously? This is totally excellent! San Jerico, my home town, is a very friendly place – good for us deviants, ha ha. We can party there.'

'Sounds fun. But I gotta keep my head down, till I sort stuff out.'

'You will be OK, though?'

'I'll be fine. I just . . . I just could do with a break.'

Raffi didn't respond immediately. His pudgy face was solemn.

'Lucas, he hurt you very badly, I think.'

The man from MI6 was tall and shambling and ruddy-faced. As he hovered in Lazovic's office, waiting to fill out the relevant paperwork, his eyes flicked about nervously, as if he expected an ambush of teenage delinquents at any moment.

'Ah, ahem, Lucas, m'boy. Jolly good.' He peered absent-mindedly at the view. 'Charming place . . . July's a good month for alpine flowers, they say, even though there's still snow on the mountainside.'

Lucas and his 'godfather' did not speak until they were several miles past Blumenwald, and their car pulled up in a deserted picnic spot. At once, the man from Six straightened up, became curt and shamble-free. 'Well,' he said, 'this is quite some situation we've got here. Care to explain how it all went tits up?'

It appeared that Jenna had lost no time in spreading the bad news, and cover her back in the process. Lucas kept his own story as concise and colourless as possible, while admitting that mistakes had been made at different stages by different people. The other agent heard him out in silence and without comment. Finally, Lucas ventured a question of his own. 'I don't understand where Section Seven got their intel. How did they discover we were WICA, and how did Jenna know about Operation Swan?'

'They knew about you and Glory because Commander

Hughes had a word with her opposite number at the WSA. As for Edie Starling . . . well, they have their sources. The UK Inquisition has been relatively slow to make use of witchkind intelligence, but Section Seven and the WSA have been collaborating for a good while. It's put them ahead of the game.'

'Not when it comes to Cambion,' Lucas pointed out. 'I didn't give Jenna the name of the company, or its connection to Rose Merle. Then there's Dr Caron. She might have backed off for now, but it's possible she'll still try to contact me. We've got a head start.'

'That may be true. However, it's not something that you should worry about.'

'How do you mean?'

The agent didn't answer him straight away. 'Frankly, I can't understand why you and Glory were ever paired up in the first place. It seems obvious there's too much personal history between you and your families for a professional distance to be maintained.'

'I wanted Glory to be told about her mother before we went on this assignment. I knew it was a mistake. I tried –' Lucas stopped, hearing the whine in his voice.

The other man drummed his fingers on the wheel. 'The long and short of it is, Section Seven thinks you're compromised, and I'm afraid our side is inclined to agree. So you're coming back to London with me. Tonight.'

The news was not unexpected, and yesterday Lucas would not have particularly cared. Today he seethed at the stupidity of it all: his own, and everyone else's. 'What about Glory?'

'We'll keep an eye on what she's up to. But she's not our priority. Or yours.' The agent's tone softened slightly. 'If I were you, kid, when it comes to the debrief, I'd lay the blame at her door. It's your best chance of walking away from this mess.'

# PART 3

# CHAPTER 18

At the airport, Glory changed her remaining Swiss francs into a mix of US dollars and Cordoban crescents, and used her WICA-funded debit card to buy a ticket to San Jerico. Ever since the introduction of biometric ID, it was a lot harder for witches and other criminal types to travel undetected. But although WICA could track her passport as well as her debit card, Cordoba was infamous for poor immigration controls and illegal border crossings. If things didn't work out, Glory hoped she'd be able to slip away elsewhere without too much trouble.

She was not able to get on the same flight as Raffi. It would be a twenty-hour journey with two stopovers, one in Paris and one in Rio de Janeiro, and she wouldn't arrive in Cordoba until eleven in the morning. Although she had thought she wanted to be alone, when she waved Raffi off, she felt a renewed sense of abandonment.

Before boarding, she bought a Cordoban guidebook. She needed to know what she was letting herself in for. And if her brain was stuffed full of facts and figures, maybe there wouldn't be room to think about anything else.

Dutifully, she read that Cordoba was the smallest sovereign state in South America. Its main economic activities were sugar-growing, gold-mining and shrimp-fishing. Most of the population lived in the lowland coastal area. Its southern border was mountainous. Two-thirds of the country was covered in forest. The climate was tropical. Blah de blah.

The historical background bit didn't tell her anything she didn't already know. During the Spanish and Portuguese invasion of South America, it had been the conquistadors' guns and diseases versus the natives' witch-priests. When these proved harder to defeat than expected, squads of witch-convicts from the Spanish Inquisition's cells were shipped over, and promised their freedom if they would use their powers against the 'savages'. Ever since, witchkind had been better integrated in South America than the rest of the world. Cordoba, though, was unique in that it currently had no Inquisition. Most forms of witchwork were officially illegal, yet formed the basis of a thriving black economy – something the guidebook failed to mention.

Eventually, Glory put the book away and fell into a thin doze. She dreamed of mining for golden shrimp, and fighting conquistadors in the jungle. Of Jenna, leaning over her skull with a drill. 'It won't hurt a bit . . .'

San Jerico's airport was everything Zurich's was not: noisy, ill-lit and disorderly. There were no inquisitorial guards; just a handful of bored policemen in dirty-looking brown uniforms. After being waved through immigration, Glory made her way to a bus station and found one going to *Centro*

*Ciudad.* Those Spanish lessons were going to come in handy after all.

She got off the bus in the city centre, a cramped square of broken cobblestones. The cathedral loomed overhead, looking like a crazed wedding cake, with its layers of sooty pink and white marble. It had just stopped raining; puddles winked in the sun. Traffic growled and honked. Glory sniffed the fume-laden air appreciatively.

At the beachfront, the water was a shimmering green, the promenades lined with palms and crammed with ranks of boutiques and bars. Many buildings were in the colonial style, with wrought-iron balconies and low-pitched clay roofs. Their plaster facades were pockmarked and stained, or else gaudy with gilded arcades and brash colours. Although there was plenty of wealth on display in the high-rise apartment blocks, the bronzed tourists and flash cars, much of it was ugly. Glory didn't mind. *I'm going to do all right here,* she thought.

She bought a map and a Spanish phrase book from a tourist shop, and fried fish-balls and iced tea from a pavement vendor. For the first time since getting on the plane, she allowed herself to wonder how Candice would react to her arrival. It wasn't as if they had ever been close. Candy and her younger sister Skye, raised in the lap of mobster luxury, had always sneered at their younger cousin's inferior clothes, accent and prospects. Glory had sneered back, dismissing them as a pair of spoilt airheads. She'd last seen Candy in November, just after her cousin had got the fae, and had embarked on the latest in a series of epic benders. Even Charlie, her doting dad, was forced to face the fact she was out of control.

Then there was the new boyfriend – some Yank TV actor Candy had met in rehab. Todd Lawson. How would he react to Glory showing up on his doorstep?

The immediate challenge was finding their villa. Glory peered determinedly at her map and bus timetable. She knew the moment she allowed herself to rest properly she'd be good for nothing, but for now adrenalin was still coursing through her veins. I *can do this*, she told herself, with a last slug of iced tea. I can do anything. Never look back.

San Jerico's rich either lived in swanky apartments by the beach, or in villas on the small rise – it was hardly a hill – in the south of the city. However, the second of the two buses that Glory took swung past a sprawl of tin shacks and dilapidated bungalows set along streets of mud. It was a different kind of poverty to the Rockwood Estate, but Glory recognised its surface layer of graffiti, broken bottles, car tyres and splintered boards. The same worn-down faces, the same defiant stares.

The bus soon moved on and up into the posh part of town. Most of the houses were hidden from view in gated compounds. Glory got off at what she hoped was the right point, and followed her map along a series of narrow paths shaded by high walls and dark foliage. Heat lay over her skin like a damp blanket; thunder rumbled overhead. Glory remembered from the guidebook that May to August was the rainy season. By the time she pushed open the rusting gate to Casa de la Armonia, the first fat drops had begun to fall.

The villa was smaller than she'd expected. Its pink plaster walls were flaking and the shutters sagged on their hinges. The garden was a wilderness of lush green weeds. Music thumped inside. It took a long time for the bell to be answered. If Glory had been a casual visitor, she'd probably have given up.

The man who finally came to the door had thinning fair hair and the beginnings of a paunch. Still, you could see he might be handsome, with a bit of effort. 'Yeah?'

Glory hoisted her bag over her shoulder. 'I'm here to see Candy. I'm her cousin.'

'Is that so, sweet-cheeks?' The man took a swig from his beer bottle and belched noisily.

'GLORY? Oh, my freakin' *Gawd*! Come here, kiddo, let's have a hug of you!'

Candice was very brown, very thin, very pouty. She had the red Morgan hair, grown nearly to her waist, but it was dyed fluorescent pink. The American accent she'd acquired since their last meeting was even faker.

'Um, hi.' Glory was squeezed breathless by Candy's hug. 'Sorry for the short notice. I hope you got Troy's email about me coming to town. And, er, maybe staying for a –'

'Hey, *mi casa es tu casa*, cuz!' Candice's bangles tinkled and clashed. She was wearing a diaphanous purple kaftan, and very little underneath. She turned to her boyfriend. 'Right, babe?'

Todd squinted at Glory. 'You a hag too?'

'Don't talk dirty, angel,' Candice pouted.

But Glory had reached a decision. She wasn't going to hide herself away any more. If her mother was going to find her, she needed to know what, as well as who, she was. 'Yeah, I'm a witch,' she said. 'Is that gonna be a problem?'

In the hallway, a miniature poodle was defecating on the carpet. Todd took another gulp of beer. 'Au *contraire*, sweet-cheeks. You'll make yourself very useful.'

At night, the centre of San Jerico was shaking. Every window and open doorway pulsed with heat and noise; ropes of coloured lights strung between the buildings added to the carnival atmosphere. The rain had been replaced by a warm breeze that smelled of fried fish and spices. Cars cruised up and down, honking horns, blasting music. Girls in towering heels and skimpy dresses tottered along in giggling groups. Packs of men pressed around them, whistled, yelled and moved on.

Glory and Candy got their fair share of attention. Candy was wearing a snakeskin-print playsuit; Glory a strapless red dress borrowed from her cousin. She'd slept for most of the afternoon and was feeling giddy with freedom. When was the last time she'd been out for a night on the tiles? *No more pointless essays or spelling tests for me*, she thought triumphantly, as Candy led the way to a beachfront bar.

'I've stopped the pills,' her cousin confided. 'They, like, totally mess with your head. And I don't do the whole binge thing any more. Just a tot of good ol' Cordoban rum now and then . . . well, a little of what you fancy does you good, right?'

Glory wasn't so sure. There was a tremor in Candice's hands, and her eyes never seemed to focus properly. She decided she'd stick with iced tea.

Todd was staying at home, to work on his screenplay. After he'd left his sci-fi TV show ('Creative differences,'

Candy explained), he'd decided to turn his disillusionment with showbiz and the American Dream into movie material. 'It's gonna be very dark, very *raw*,' he said. In the meantime, life at the villa was financed by Candy. She complained she was only receiving a pittance from home – Troy had dramatically reduced her allowance after she skipped rehab, and was apparently threatening to cut her off altogether unless she came back to the UK and cleaned up her act.

'He's turning into an even bigger grouch than Dad,' she grumbled. 'Throwing his weight around like you wouldn't believe. He might be boss of the coven goons, but he's not the boss of *me*.'

'I s'pose Troy's feeling the stress,' Glory said cautiously. 'It must be a right headache, keeping the business going with Charlie so ill.'

Candy took another swig of her rum and coconut water. Her fake American accent had started to slip, along with her high spirits. 'Poor old Dad. What a shocker. I cried *buckets* when I heard the news. That's why I thought it was better if I didn't come back and see him. Might set off a relapse, y'know? The counsellor at the centre, she said my family relations were very unhealthy, very *pressurised*.'

'D'you think you'll ever go back to the coven?'

'No chance. Soon as I do, Mum'll get her claws in me. She's still scheming to train me up, and she's almost as big a slave-driver as Troy. They're always ganging up on me . . . always *nagging*. You're lucky, Glor. Patrick's so dopey you've always been able to do whatever the hell you like.'

Glory had to turn away. Beyond the sands, the sea was

black and glistening. It was impossible to think of: a whole ocean between her and home.

But Candy was still complaining. 'Things would be different if I was some super-celeb witch. Like Granny and Great-Aunt Cora. As it is, my fae's just enough to be a pain in the arse, without any of the perks. It's *so unfair*.' She flicked back her hair. 'Though I should've known you'd turn harpy too. Aunt Edie was apparently quite the prodigy.'

'Yeah,' said Glory gruffly. 'So they say.' She hadn't told her cousin anything about Edie or her own involvement with WICA, only that the Inquisition was breathing down her neck and she needed to get out of London for a while. Luckily, Candy was far too full of her own affairs to ask awkward questions about Glory's.

'Well, prodigy or not, if you want to hang with me and Todd, you're gonna have to pay your own way. And round here, witchwork's your best chance of making a quick buck.'

'Good. I want to work.' She needed the cash, for one thing. But she also wanted to spread the word of who she was and what she could do too. San Jerico was the unofficial capital of the witchkind underworld. If Edie Starling was alive, she might well have contacts here.

'Aw, look at you. My baby cousin, all grown up!' Candy reached across and patted Glory's cheek. 'I'll take you to see Rona, then. She's the gal I work for – at the Carabosse Club. Seriously, Glor, you'll love it. Best show in town.'

The Carabosse Club was located just off the Plaza de la República. They headed there through a series of dingy backstreets whose walls were scrawled with graffiti. One bore a cartoon of a witch with the traditional pointy hat and crooked staff doing something obscene to a mustachioed man in a suit.

'That's Benny Vargas,' Candy said with a smirk. 'He's running for president in the election next month. De Aviles, the guy in charge at the moment, is on trial for stealing money and stuff. But people are scared Vargas is gonna bring back the Inquisition, so it's not like he's Mr Popular either.'

Glory saw there were spray-painted slogans in English and Spanish from both sides of the debate. *Inquisition Stay Out!* was next to *Hags Go Home.*

'What's that?' She pointed to a white feather that she'd seen painted on several doors and window shutters.

'It's the sign for some old witch-woman. La Bruja Blanca. She's kind of a local legend – like a lucky mascot, I guess.'

Candy moved on to more practical matters, explaining that she worked at the club five nights a week. All the waiters and waitresses at the Carabosse were witchkind, serving up an array of fae-tricks along with the drinks. Because of the high volume of foreign visitors, they had to be English-speaking. 'The pay's crap,' she said. 'It's the tips you work for.'

The club was in the vaults of the former Inquisition. Although the Inquisition had been kicked out of Cordoba in the 1960s, Glory looked up at the building's frowning, fortress-like walls with a reflexive shiver. The only sign of the club's presence was the letter C, lit up like a crescent moon above the basement door. A long queue was waiting outside.

Candy got them in through the staff entrance, though Glory would have preferred to take the main staircase down to the club – it was an extravagant spiral affair, every step inlaid with crystals. Bling, in fact, was everywhere. The vault's stone walls and floor had been overlaid with black marble, and tall mirrors threw back sequins of light from the giant silver glitterballs that hung from the arched ceiling. Purple velvet booths were dotted around the cavernous central space; behind a curtain of crystal beads, a row of cells had been converted into private party rooms.

The patrons were as varied in age and nationality as the revellers in the streets, but richer and sleeker. Candy had told Glory that the place was popular with politicians, celebrities and businessmen alike. Apparently two A-list Hollywood stars had visited last week.

Candy went to find the manager, leaving her cousin to wait by the bar. A colourful range of bottles shone from its mirrored shelves. Glory pretended to study the drinks menu – house specials included 'Inquisitor's Elixir' and 'The Hecate Headbanger' – while sizing up the staff. They were young and attractive and mostly female, wearing a uniform of silver cocktail dresses with slits up to the thigh. The men were in tight black trousers and shirts open to their waist.

Each table was allocated its own host or hostess. The fae they performed was small-scale but flashy. One girl was using a low-grade glamour to change the colour of her skin every time she went behind the bar, turning from orange to indigo, red to green. A waiter lit all six candles on a candelabra by rubbing a match between his hands. Some were mere conjuring tricks of the kind outlawed in most countries because of their resemblance to witchwork. Across the room, an older woman was pulling coins out of somebody's ear. No fae there, Glory thought contemptuously, just sleight of hand.

She didn't have as much time for people-watching as she would have liked before Candy beckoned her into the back office. The Carabosse's manager, Rona, was a tiny Native American woman with a long black plait hanging down the back of her pinstriped trouser suit. She looked Glory up and down appraisingly.

'How old?'

'Fifteen.'

The manager gave a bark of laughter. 'No. You are eighteen when anyone ask. But if you start this young, you are hot stuff, yes?'

'Yeah.'

Rona raised her strong black brows. 'Then show.'

Glory didn't need telling twice. She knew she would need an appropriately dazzling demo of her prowess, and as soon as she'd entered the office she'd looked round for materials she could use. Coolly, she selected a paper napkin from the bin, a bit of fern from a plant pot, a drawing pin, a newspaper and a can of air freshener.

Fascinations were always impressive. For this one, Glory decided she'd craft a rose. She pictured it in her head and let the fae suffuse the image until it was hyper-real, hyper-bright. A fascination needed to mimic the principal attributes of the object you were trying to create. Working quickly, fae tingling at her fingertips, she separated the white napkin into tissue-thin layers that she twisted into a rough blossom shape. She already had the rose's approximate colour and form, now she gave it a squirt of air freshener. It was a pine, not floral, fragrance, but she didn't think it would matter. The fern was a token of the natural world, while she fastened the drawing pin to the tissue paper to signify the rose's thorns. Attention to detail – that's what Auntie Angel always said made the difference between passable witchwork and perfection. Finally, Glory covered her creation in a piece of newspaper, which she gave to Rona to unwrap. A fascination could only be brought to life by another person's eyes.

The manager's face gave nothing away as she undid the bundle. Candice craned forward to watch. A single white rose was lying on the paper. Rona touched its thorny stem and sniffed the petals.

'Smells like Christmas,' she said, 'but still good. Still very good . . . How long to last?'

'Up to three hours,' said Glory, with justifiable pride.

Rona nodded briskly. 'OK. Enough. Training, you start tomorrow in morning at ten, then you work tomorrow night. Don't be late.'

Glory left the club with a swagger in her step. She thought of Dr Caron's bogus therapy talk and nearly laughed. Who needed the power of positive thinking when you had Esmerelda Thunderpants? But Candice was silent in the taxi back to the villa.

'So you're as good as my bro said you were,' she said at last.

'I have me moments.'

'I thought he was exaggerating. To wind me up.'

Glory shrugged.

Candice looked at her sidelong. 'He must be pissed you've given him the slip. If Troy shacked up with you, he'd be Mr Big and no mistake.'

Glory shrugged again. She felt uncomfortable. Candice had said she didn't want to work for the family coven; now she knew that even if she did, her place at the top table was no longer guaranteed. Glory's fae was the stronger. If she chose to ally herself with Troy, the Wednesday Coven heir, and leader in all but name, then Glory would be head-witch. Candice's boss.

Yes, the baby cousin was all grown up.

# CHAPTER 19

As soon as Lucas stepped off the plane at Heathrow, he was whisked away for a series of debriefs. The first one was the worst. Jack Rawdon looked grave, Guy Carmichael irritable, and Commander Hughes as if she'd swallowed a mouthful of wasps.

Although various people kept telling Lucas he wasn't in trouble, he still felt in disgrace. Over the following days, they took notes, and nodded thoughtfully, and asked questions in a quiet yet insistent manner. He was given very little opportunity to ask his own questions in return. He knew too how the process would end. His final interview with Rawdon confirmed this.

'I know this has been tough on you, Lucas. Since the Paterson business, you've barely had time to catch your breath. You've more than earned a holiday. I want you to take a month or two off, and get away from it all.'

Well, at least he wasn't getting kicked out of the service outright.

'But what about Glory?' he asked, for what felt like the thousandth time.

Rawdon looked at him carefully. 'You don't need to worry about her, Lucas. She's a resourceful and well-connected girl.'

'She's gone to Cordoba, hasn't she? What's she doing? Who's she with?' Then, when Rawdon didn't answer, 'Aren't you going to try and get her back?'

'Sadly, I think events have proved that Glory is not right for this agency, and we're not right for her. Not at this point in time. I regret how events have turned out, but what's done is done. Glory is free to live her own life. We won't intervene unless she gives us due cause.'

'Cause for what?'

'Alarm. If we were to suspect her of acting against the interests of this agency, for example. Or those of the nation.'

Lucas frowned. 'Glory wouldn't do that.'

'I'm sure you're right. But in any case, it shouldn't be your concern.' Rawdon's smile was as frank and warm as ever, backed up with the friendly clap on the back. 'Don't think you haven't done a good job. You've provided us with some very valuable information. Now it's time for you to rest up, and move on.'

Lucas got the message. Forget about Wildings and Cambion, Drs Caron and Claude. Forget about Glory.

He left WICA in a fog of exhaustion. At least the nature of his work meant he hadn't had any awkward questions to answer at home, though Philomena was sulking because he hadn't brought her a souvenir from his trip. In his brief encounters with his father – usually as one or other of them was on the way out – Ashton looked at him searchingly, as if on the brink of saying something important, but always seeming to think better of it.

In the three days Lucas had been back in the UK, he'd barely had time to unpack. Now he went to his bedroom and began pulling things out of his suitcase. Dr Lazovic had been informed that Lucas left the academy because his father had struck a deal with the Witchfinder General to keep his condition a secret. The principal had not taken the news well, and no wonder – he'd lost three students in two days.

A postcard fell out of a bundle of shirts. Raffi had pushed the card under Lucas's bedroom door before he'd left. He read the back of it idly. *Good luck! Stay strong! Your amigo, Raphael* ☺. There was a scribbled email address and phone number too.

Lucas turned the card over. *Hola from Cordoba!* was printed at the top. The subject was *La Catedral de San Jerico*. Incongruously, a babe in a bikini was posing on the steps. The pink-and-white baroque facade behind her was a maze of broken pediments, decorative shells and garland-draped columns. Something about it was familiar.

He closed his eyes and pressed his knuckles to them, so the darkness sparked. The building was flanked by two bell towers, and he'd seen one of them before. He was sure of it. That time, though, it had been in black and white. Suddenly it came to him. It had been in the background of the photograph of Rose Merle, or her witchworked double, that he and Glory had found in Dr Caron's office.

Lucas sat down on his bed. The fog in his head had gone; the air prickled with possibilities. If what he remembered was correct, he had just found a possible link between Cambion and Cordoba. He reached for his phone, then stopped. He was off the case. He didn't even know what WICA and their partners in the security services were going to do with the information he'd already provided. It was quite possible they'd hand it over to Section Seven, so Jenna White and Co could follow it up. And anyway, this wasn't evidence. Just a memory backed up by a hunch.

He looked at the other side of the postcard. Raffi had said he'd be welcome in Cordoba any time. Jack Rawdon had told him to take a break . . .

'Absolutely not,' his father said in the study later that night. 'You're staying at home, resting and catching up with your schoolwork.'

'I was told to go on holiday!'

'Cordoba is not a holiday destination. It's where you go if you're on the run from the Inquisition, or want to set up an international drug cartel.'

'Well, I have friends there.'

'You mean Glory.' Ashton's voice was steely. 'Don't think I don't know what this is about.'

'Then you should understand why I need to find her,' Lucas retorted. 'She's been chucked aside like a spare part that doesn't work any more.'

'She deserted her post.'

'Can you blame her? After what was done to Edie, to her family?'

The unspoken words bristled between them: *This is your fault.*

Ashton's manner remained steady. Infuriatingly so. 'You and Glory haven't known each other for very long. Your time together has been intense. Dramatic. She is very different to the other people you know. I can see how that would be . . . attractive. But you need to take into account that your feelings for her might be clouding your judgement.'

Lucas flushed angrily. 'This isn't about some stupid schoolboy crush. She's my partner.'

'If you want to be treated like a professional, then you have to act like one. Running off to some Third World hole out of a misguided sense of chivalry is not going to help. It could even mean the end of your career – have you thought about that? In WICA and anywhere else.'

So he'd be like Glory. A liability, as Jenna had put it. Damaged goods.

'I can't just stand back and do nothing.'

'And if I forbid you to go?'

Lucas didn't reply. *Then I'll go and see Troy Morgan,* he thought.

Lucas spent the next couple of days at home. If he gave his father and Rawdon any cause for concern, he was afraid he'd end up under house arrest, and maybe even bridled. He didn't have his passport in any case. WICA were 'looking after it', as well as the spare emergency one.

Lucas knew that he needed to do more than find Glory and persuade her to come home. She would still be in professional disgrace. So would he, probably. That was why the Cambion lead was so important. It gave him a chance of turning the Swiss failure into a Cordoban success. If Glory shared in that success – if it could be shown what a loyal and invaluable an agent she was – then everyone would win.

Ambition motivated him as well as loyalty. Lucas was not used to losing or giving up. It was one of the things he shared with Glory. He wanted to find out exactly what Cambion was up to, and take back control of the investigation from Jenna White.

It was no easy task to track Troy down. Finally, on Thursday, a week after returning to London, Lucas crafted an elusion and went to Glory's father for help. It was a big risk. But he knew that Glory didn't tell Patrick everything. It was his hope she hadn't shared the secrets of Edie Starling's double life, or Ashton Stearne's part in it.

As it happened, Patrick greeted Lucas warmly. He'd only seen Lucas without the disguise of a glamour once, but he recognised him immediately. He was less rambling, more animated, than Lucas remembered. Patrick gave nothing away about Glory's doings or whereabouts, but after some deliberation, went to make a series of telephone calls. He came back with an address, and the news that Troy would see Lucas there at five. Then he hesitated.

'Glory's a, er, strong-minded girl,' he said. 'A bit wilful at times. Her mum was like that too. But her heart's in the right place. It's just not as tough as the rest of her.'

Unsure how to respond, Lucas said his thanks and left as soon as possible.

Charlie Morgan's head office – Troy's for now – was attached to a wholesaler in East Hallam. Lucas was led through the dusty packing area by the kind of over-muscled thug he remembered from his time in the coven. The upstairs office, though, belonged to a different world. Brocade curtains brushed the parquet floor, a rosewood desk nestled on the Persian rug.

Lucas had always thought Troy had a lean, hungry sort of look. Wolfish, despite the designer suits and smooth veneer. But this afternoon, he looked sleek and relaxed. The heir to the empire, taking his ease on the family throne.

'Well, well. It's the Chief Pricker's kid,' he said. 'Still fighting for Truth, Justice and the Inquisitorial way?'

'I don't work for the Inquisition.'

Troy raised a mocking eyebrow. 'That's not what I heard.'

Although he hadn't been invited to, Lucas sat down. 'I presume Glory's talked to you, then. About Switzerland.'

'She told me some of it. She wasn't in a very conversational mood. All in all, I'm curious to hear your side of the story.'

Briefly, Lucas explained about Wildings and Cambion and Jenna White. Then he moved on to Edie Starling. He tried to describe what had happened as dispassionately as his father had.

Afterwards, Troy slowly shook his head. 'Christ. And they call *us* gangsters.'

'I'm not going to try and defend what went on –'

'That would be wise.'

Their eyes met. Troy's were shards of green ice. Not so long ago they'd been allies. Lucas couldn't imagine ever being friends with Troy. Yet it shook him, all the same, to think that they were bound – by family, careers, fate – to be enemies.

'My father and his colleagues acted wrongly. But I'm not responsible for the decisions they made.'

'Hm. "The sins of the father . . ."' Troy glanced at a photograph pushed to the edge of the desk. 'You don't believe they're visited on their sons?'

'No. My mistakes and regrets are my own. One of those mistakes – a bad one – was with Glory. I want to make amends.' He paused. 'And I'll need your help.'

Troy folded his arms across his chest. 'I'm touched. Really. Your starry-eyed selflessness is a joy to behold. But why would I want to coax Glory back to WICA? All things considered, I'd say she's made a smart decision. It would certainly make my life easier if she sticks to it.'

'So you think Cordoba is a good place for her? You think she'll be able to make a decent life out there?' Troy didn't reply. With renewed confidence, Lucas said, 'It's not as if she can just slip back into your coven either. She's a registered witch. As soon as she returns to the UK, the Inquisition will pounce. It will mean all kinds of harassment.'

'I do hope,' said Troy very softly, 'that isn't meant to be a threat.'

'No. Of course not. I'm just stating the facts. But this isn't only about Glory. I also need to talk about your other cousin: Rose.'

Lucas described Dr Caron's photograph and Raffi's postcard, managing to present the connection between Rose Merle, Cambion and San Jerico as fact rather than supposition. 'I think Cambion's dodgy brain surgery clinic is very likely to be in Cordoba. Where else would people be able to get away with something like this? I don't know exactly what's going on with Rose, or what she's doing over there. But it's too much of a coincidence to ignore.'

He added another small embellishment in support of his case. 'Glory aroused Dr Caron's suspicions when she left Wildings so abruptly. There were all sorts of rumours flying around. If Dr Caron thinks she's a spy, and then runs into her in Cordoba, Glory could be in serious trouble.'

'Serious trouble,' said Troy wearily, 'is what I've come to expect from the two of you. OK. What do you want?'

'Glory's contact details. A fake passport. And a smart-phone – the signal on mine can be traced. Money.'

'A coven loan!' Troy's mouth twitched. 'I hope you're prepared for our interest rates. Because I don't think Daddy Stearne would be best pleased if you lost your kneecaps.'

'I won't need much. I'm going to empty my current account before I go, but I can't access my savings without my father's say-so. And if I try and use my bank cards, WICA will be able to trace me. Then there's getting through immigration –'

'Shut up a moment and let me think.'

Troy swung round in his chair and regarded the scene outside. It was several long minutes before he turned back.

'OK. Fine. I'll get you what you need.'

'That's great. Thank you so m—'

'Truth is, I was already thinking of sending someone to San Jerico,' Troy said abruptly. 'My sister Candice is living there and my parents are increasingly anxious about her. I'd like to get a first-hand report of her welfare and activities, as well as Glory's, but for the moment I can't spare the staff.

Nor can I rely on my Cordoban contacts. This is a private family matter, and I want to keep it that way.'

'I understand.'

'Then here's something else you need to get into your head: whatever you find out there, whatever progress you make, you report it to me. Not WICA, not Daddy Stearne, definitely not the prickers.' Troy fixed Lucas in his cold green gaze. 'You're on my payroll now. Don't forget it.'

# CHAPTER 20

Before her first night's work at the Carabosse, Glory invested some of her dwindling cash in a trip to a hairdresser. She came out with her hair cut in a sixties-style bob, brown roots dyed a glossy platinum. With a picture of Granny Cora as her reference point, she bought some false eyelashes too. Her eyes were heavily rimmed in black and her lips were painted nude. If people were going to start talking about 'the Starling Girl', she wanted to look the part.

The job, though, proved to be a disappointment. It didn't take long for the novelty of performing witchwork in public to wear off, and there was none of the camaraderie she'd hoped for among her fellow witchworkers. Competition for tips and the preference of the regular punters was fierce. Inevitably, Glory's age and abilities caused resentment. Even Candice took to arriving for work separately, and turning a cold shoulder to her in public.

Glory's signature trick was the rose fascination. For the right price, she would craft a rose in the colour of her customer's choice. For her own amusement, she'd experiment with the scent, dousing her tissue-paper blossoms with a spritz of mint breath-freshening spray or lavender perfume or lemon hand-sanitiser. At the end of the evening, the fascination would fade and the buyer would be left with a crumpled ball of paper, leaf mould and drawing pins. Which was, of course, all part of the fun.

Glory would also spy in a scrying-bowl, and tell people what their friends were getting up to in other bars or hotels. A vanishing trick was equally popular. She would place a gentleman's watch or a lady's earrings on a pocket mirror, fogged with her own breath, which she proceeded to wrap in a black handkerchief and sprinkle with dust from the street. It was an amulet known as a shroud, because it 'buried' an object from view. Afterwards, she'd whip off the handkerchief to gasps of astonishment, as the customer prodded an object they could feel but couldn't see.

Most nights there was the additional entertainment of a cabaret singer or burlesque dancer. Only one witch ever took centre stage. This was a woman known as Sheba, whose handsome features suggested a mix of Amerindian and North African blood. She wore a costume of a silver leotard, and a decorative witch's bridle made out of diamanté that covered most of her face and neck. Her act centred on her familiar, a big black cat. She and the animal would dance together, and it would spell out answers to audience questions by picking out letters on coloured cards. Then it would go and collect banknotes in its mouth as tips. It was controlled by the ring Sheba wore on her right hand: a circlet of cat hair braided with her own, sealed with spit and the animal's blood.

Glory would watch their show whenever her duties allowed. She had always been told that using a familiar regularly was dangerous. If you merged your mind with an animal's too frequently, or didn't have strong enough fae, you were at risk of blurring the boundaries between human and beast. Sheba certainly had a cat-like look, with her wide cheekbones, snub nose and slanting eyes. Glory had never heard the woman speak, only yowl and hiss and purr. Once she'd seen her lick her hands clean, as if they were paws. Maybe it was all part of the performance, but it gave Glory the creeps.

The other creeps were the paying kind. Stag parties and businessmen out to celebrate a deal were the worst, and had to be told to keep their hands to themselves. Glory felt more comfortable with the gangsters; coven folk who weren't dazzled by witchwork and just wanted a pretty girl to serve the drinks.

Although Glory was soon making good tips, she had to give all her wages to Candy. As Glory was staying in her and Todd's home, it was difficult to object. But the villa wasn't much of a refuge. The little dogs ran wild, soiling the chipped marble floors wherever they felt like it, and the constant hip-hop shook the plaster from the walls. When Todd wasn't 'writing', he liked to play skittles with beer bottles in the hall. What with the smashing glass, pounding music and yapping dogs, Glory sometimes thought of Wildings' hushed hallways with regret.

'I know the real reason you came here,' Todd announced on the afternoon of her sixth day in Cordoba, when he came upon Glory slumped moodily in the lounge.

She tensed up in spite of herself. 'I told you. It were the pyros breathing down me neck.'

Todd pushed back his dark glasses with a smirk. 'You can't fool me. I've seen the way you mope around the place. Staring into space, heaving sighs, leaving your food . . . There's a boy, isn't there? Some heartbreaker you're pining for.'

'No,' said Glory, a little too quickly.

The way Todd stood posed in the doorway made it obvious that he was sucking in his gut. 'Plenty more *peces* in *el mar*, sweet-cheeks. Wait and see.'

Glory waited until he'd slouched off, then went to the patio doors. Purple storm clouds were already gathering over the city's haze of smog. A wine bottle and a couple of cigarette butts bobbed in the swimming pool. She breathed on the glass, traced her fingertip through the mist. *You* OK?

And though she knew she shouldn't, she closed her eyes, pressed her palm against the window.

Cold stars. Warm breath. His hands in her hair.

She was out of sorts for the rest of the afternoon. On her way in to work, the streets were as full of light and music and laughter as ever, but she was starting to notice different things. There was a group of beggars congregated on the steps of the cathedral. One of them had been hexed to think there were live insects crawling under his skin; his body was bloody and scabbed from constant scratching. Aunt Angeline had told Glory how to craft something similar. It was one of the black banes, the kind that could only be undone by the witch who inflicted it. She herself had threatened Silas Paterson with one.

There were bloodstains too on the Plaza de la República's cobblestones, along with broken glass and torn placards. It was the aftermath of a political rally, De Aviles's supporters versus the opposition, which had ended in a brawl. The number of *Hags Out!* slogans scrawled on the walls seemed to be increasing. So were the groups of private militiamen. Even the police got out of the way when they swaggered into view.

But once she arrived at the club, the sight of the spiral staircase lifted Glory's spirits again. Who knew who might come down those glittering crystal steps? That was the best thing about Cordoba, she reminded herself. Anything was possible.

It turned out to be a busy night. Just after ten a party of bankers arrived and specially requested Glory, keeping the tips flowing for the next hour. In the lull that followed, she waited by the bar, leaning against the wall in an attempt to ease the pinch of her high-heeled shoes. Then her eye was caught by a swish of dark red hair. A woman – girl – was descending the crystal staircase. She had a pale heart-shaped face and violet eyes.

The last time Glory had seen those eyes, they had been dull and unblinking; the face a frozen mask. The girl's movements had been stiff as a wind-up doll's. But Rose Merle was easing her way gracefully through the crowd towards a group of media types, where she was greeted like an old friend. She was dressed for the office in a tailored cream blouse and black pencil skirt. Her hair had been cut nearly as short as Glory's. She looked crisp, businesslike.

Was it truly Rose? Or some rent-a-witch, masquerading as her with a glamour? Glory felt giddy with anticipation.

She got hold of Ricki, the designated host for Rose's

table, and persuaded him to let her take his place. He only agreed after she promised him all her tips from the evening. Then before she could think better of it, she sashayed across the room and started taking orders. No fae-tricks were required, just waitressing.

'Inquisitor's Elixir for you, miss?' she asked Rose, who was deep in conversation in fluent Spanish with her neighbour.

'No, thank you. I think I'll have an orange juice –'

Rose turned around and started. A flash of recognition crossed her face, to be replaced with uncertainty.

'Hello again,' said Glory brightly. 'Rose, ain't it?'

'Oh . . . hello . . . have we met?' Her voice was cut-glass confident, not the slow, slurred speech that had followed Glory into her dreams. Glory's eyes flicked down to Rose's right hand, where the pearly skin was red and raised. One of the symptoms of Rose's condition was that she had lost all feeling in her body, and she'd scarred her hand by putting it into boiling water. If this was a glamour, then Glory had to approve of the attention to detail.

But the girl had definitely recognised her, and that was a good sign.

'It were back in England,' said Glory. 'I came to talk to your mum.'

Rose lowered her voice, smoothing her hair nervously. 'Back home when I was . . . ill?'

Glory didn't answer. To prove her identity, Rose needed to remember for herself. Only a handful of people knew about their encounter in Lord Merle's mansion. Lady Merle's murderous ambush of her husband and Silas

Paterson had been hushed up in the press. Just like Rose's brain injury – the result of a fall from a horse, according to official reports.

Rose's eyes filled with tears. 'It was, wasn't it? And Mummy was cross with you,' she whispered. 'Because it was the night – the night –'

'Go on.'

'It was the night of the party.' Rose looked down at her scarred hand. 'The night of the fire. And . . . everything else.'

Her face had become more as Glory remembered it: blank and glazed. 'You shouldn't have been there,' she said slowly. 'That's why Mummy was angry. I remember now. I – I used to forget everything, you see.'

'When you was ill?'

'Yes. Afterwards, most of my memories came back. Especially the ones I wish I could lose.' Rose gave a small strangled gasp. Her face was white and stricken. 'Why is this happening? Why?'

Glory wondered if she'd gone too far. One of Rose's neighbours had turned around. '*Te molesta esta muchacha?*' he asked, with a suspicious glance at Glory.

Rose blinked. At once, it was as if her outburst had never been. '*Estoy bien, gracias,*' she told the man. Her face and voice were bright. She turned back to Glory. 'On second thoughts, hold the orange juice. I'll have one of those Coven Dazzlers, please.'

Time for a strategic retreat. Obediently, Glory wrote down the order and made the rest of her rounds. She didn't make another attempt at contact until she saw Rose head in the direction of the ladies' toilets, and intercepted her by the door.

'Look, I don't want to cause upset or nothing. I just wanted –'

'It's the strangest thing,' Rose interrupted, 'but I feel like I know you already. I mean, I realise we've met before.' She put her head on one side. 'But there's more to it than that, don't you think? Something between us.'

This was encouraging. 'Sure. So . . . d'you think we could talk? There's some stuff I need to ask, about when you was ill and such . . .' She trailed off. Rose had that closed, vacant look on her face again. But then the girl gave a little shake, and smiled.

'Yes. Yes, it would be good to talk. How about tomorrow morning at nine? We could meet in the Café Grande.' She leaned in confidingly. 'They serve the best hot chocolate in Cordoba, you know.'

The Café Grande did not live up to its name. Its gilt basketwork chairs and cloudy mirrors had seen better days. Rain drummed against the windows, drowning out the old ladies mumbling over their coffee. The hot chocolate, though, was as good as Rose had promised, and rich with unfamiliar spices.

Glory had got to the café early to gather her thoughts, even though her shift had ended at 5 a.m. and she'd had very little sleep. She didn't know what to make of Rose, or what to expect from this second interview. But it wasn't surprising that Rose was a little odd, considering everything she'd been through.

And here she came now. Even in the pouring rain, heads turned as she hurried across the cobblestones and into the café.

'Ugh, this rain! Relentless!' she exclaimed. Droplets flew as she shook out her shining hair. 'Really, we might as well be in Wales.'

Glory waited as the waiter bustled up to take Rose's order. Once they were alone, she cleared her throat. 'Thanks for meeting me. I'm sorry I brought up all that stuff in the club. I was just surprised to see you. The last time . . . well. You was in a pretty bad way.'

'Ghastly,' Rose agreed, taking a sip of chocolate.

'I'm real sorry about what happened to your mum.'

'Poor Mummy was a very unhappy woman, I'm afraid. I hope she's at peace.'

Rose spoke as if her mother had been dead for years, instead of months. But, thought Glory, posh people weren't supposed to be good at showing emotion. She nodded sympathetically.

'Lady Merle told me what happened. About the surgery what you had to block the fae, and how it went wrong.'

'It was a virus, the doctors think.'

'A virus?'

'Inflammation of the brain. It set in after we got home. Then, just as suddenly, I sort of . . . well, snapped out of it.' She shrugged, then frowned. 'Why were you there that night, anyway?'

Glory gave a very brief rundown of the Paterson affair. She wasn't sure how much Rose knew of her mother's and stepfather's involvement. But in fact, Rose did not seem particularly interested. 'Mm. It all sounds very exciting. I'm afraid I haven't really kept up with things at home. Out of sight, out of mind, and all that.'

'Your mum said the operation worked at first. What about now?' Glory asked. 'Has your fae come back, along with your memory and feelings and such?'

'God no,' Rose said with a laugh. She lifted up her hair, and displayed the white skin of her neck. There was a faded mark there, pale lilac. 'That's where my Devil's Kiss appeared. I'm clean.'

Glory would have been sceptical if it wasn't for the photograph of the original mark that she'd seen back at Wildings, in Rose's student file. She raised her eyebrows. 'Clean? Does that mean I'm dirty?'

'Not at all,' Rose answered coolly. 'Being a witch is probably very useful for some people. I'm sure *you're* extremely talented at it. It was just wrong for me.'

'Wrong like how?'

'Like . . . a darkness.' She paused. 'A darkness inside me.' She rubbed her arms and shivered. Then she leaned forward, fixed Glory with her wide violet eyes. 'Eating me up. It's not wrong, is it, to want to be free? To be my own self again?'

''Course not,' said Glory soothingly, though she felt uncomfortable and confused.

'Good.' Rose sat back slowly. Her voice had steadied. 'At the clinic, they made very sure it was what I wanted. That's one of the few things I remember. I did a final piece of witchwork before the operation, and it was such a relief to know I'd never have to do it again.'

'What kind of witchwork?'

'Oh, something small and silly. I knew I'd never miss it. Mummy always said the fae had ruined her life. In the end, the pressure got too much for her and – well, you know. What if I'd turned out the same?' Rose was back to her brisk best. 'Even after everything that's happened, it all came right in the end. I mean, here I am, free to live my own life, just as Mummy always wanted.'

Glory was finding it increasingly hard to keep up with these abrupt changes of manner. 'OK. Why Cordoba?'

'Well, there's nothing for me back in England, is there? I thought I'd take an early gap year, have a bit of an adventure. My boyfriend helped get me a job at Benito Vargas's HQ. Only admin stuff, really, but it's still interesting.'

'But Vargas wants to bring back the Inquisition –'

Rose made an impatient gesture. 'And why's that so terrible? Liberal permissiveness is fine in theory, but it comes at a high price. Corruption, crime, social breakdown . . . Here,' she said, taking a brightly coloured leaflet out of her bag. 'Just read the Senator's mission statement, and you'll see. Our candidate is a man of real integrity. He wants to restore the rule of law in order to protect basic human rights – for witches and non-witches alike.'

Glory looked at the English language leaflet, and an airbrushed photograph of the Great Man. The slogan read, *Join in Security, Share in Prosperity*. Catchy.

'I guess he don't know you're an ex-harpy yourself.'

'Well, no. That might lead to awkward questions.' Rose frowned. 'I hope you're not going to make an issue of this.'

'My lips are sealed. But wouldn't your boss want to

know about Cambion? I'd have thought that something to limit the number of witches in the world would be right up his street. For example –'

Glory stopped. Rose was staring into middle distance, her teeth biting so hard into her lower lip that it was beaded with blood.

'Hello? Rose? Er, are you OK?'

Rose blinked. 'Sorry.' She massaged her forehead. 'I have these . . . blackouts sometimes. It's like being ill again, almost.'

''S'OK,' Glory said awkwardly. 'You've had a hard time. It's probably delayed shock and such.'

'I'm sure you're right. Yes. Quite right.' She dabbed her mouth delicately with a napkin. The polished smile had returned. 'I really should get going. I'm supposed to be meeting my boyfriend, and he gets so grumpy when I'm late . . . Tell you what, there's a party this evening, a fund-raiser, at Senator Vargas's place. Why don't you come along? I'll put your name on the list, and we can settle down to a *proper* talk.'

Tonight was Glory's night off. 'Um, OK. If you're sure it won't be a problem.'

'Do you have a phone?'

Glory had recently invested in a prepaid mobile. Numbers were exchanged.

'It's a date!' Rose swooped in for an air-kiss, and then she was gone.

# CHAPTER 21

Glory's curiosity had been piqued. There remained something a bit cold, a bit disconnected, about Rose. Perhaps it was a coping strategy, a cover for the trauma she'd gone through and could still be glimpsed in those flashes of emotional panic. Perhaps it was a side effect of losing her fae.

Then there was her work for the politician Vargas. Glory distrusted politicians on principle, and she was sure Vargas was just as shifty and greedy as the lot back home. Even so, she wasn't going to turn down the chance to freeload at his fundraiser.

The party was at the Senator's mansion, which was about five miles outside San Jerico. Rose had arranged to pick Glory up just after six. She arrived in a chauffeur-driven limo, from which she emerged in a cloud of perfume, wearing an emerald silk cocktail dress. Glory smoothed down her own outfit self-consciously. She'd nicked the least tarty dress from Candice's wardrobe, a polka dot halter-neck affair, but next to Rose, she felt underdressed.

'Here,' said Rose, presenting her with a security pass. It had Glory's photograph – by the look of it, it had been taken off the Carabosse website – but the name was Lorraine Stevens. 'The security at these events is always nightmare. Luckily for you, I've been helping with the invites. If anyone asks, you're a student journalist. Lorraine works on a local paper in London.'

'What if someone recognises me from the club?'

'Vargas supporters don't visit the Carabosse.'

'You did.'

'Ah, but I'm the exception.'

Towering walls lined with CCTV cameras enclosed the drive to Vargas's mansion. They had to pass through three checkpoints. At each, a soldier with a sub-machine gun peered into the limo. At the last one they had to get out of the car to be patted down, and the details on their passes were radioed ahead for checking at control.

Glory was feeling increasingly uneasy. She recognised the soldier's blood-red uniforms as belonging to the Red Knight Militia, the most thuggish of Cordoba's private security firms. Rose's next words didn't make her feel any better.

'All the staff in the house are ex-Inquisition. And all visitors, except close family, are bridled before they enter the living-quarters. With head-cages.'

'What? All of 'em?'

Rose nodded. 'Anyone over the age of twelve. It's because of Senator Vargas's little boy, Esteban. He's an only child and the mother's dead. There have been threats – witch-threats. Esteban's going to boarding school in England next year, when he turns seven. But for now he's a virtual prisoner.'

'That's . . . terrible.'

'It's what happens, when the state can't protect its own citizens. Vargas's child isn't the only one to be locked up this way. People are frightened.'

A section of wall swung open and the car turned off the road into a compound. The sweeping lawns were glaringly green, the house that crowned them glaringly white. A crowd of people were milling about. Smoke hovered over a huge barbecue pit on the far side of the building as young women in micro-minis sashayed back and forth with trays of drinks and canapés. On a bandstand in front of the ornamental pool, a folk band was going all out with a marimba, shakers and drums.

Rose beckoned over a waitress and got them both a glass of melon juice. 'Cheers!' she said, clinking her glass with Glory's. 'Isn't this *fun*?'

It occurred to Glory that the last time she'd infiltrated a fancy party like this, it had been at Lord Merle's mansion. 'Thanks for letting me gatecrash.'

'Oh, I'm grateful for the company. I'm not on any kind of official duty tonight, but my boyfriend's working. Really, you're doing me a favour.' Rose smiled and took her arm, leading the way to a bench among a stand of trees. 'You know I think there's a connection between us,' she said. 'I always follow my instincts. They're never wrong.'

So maybe Rose felt it too – the tug of Starling blood in her veins. And then there was the Morgan red in her hair, the strong line of her jaw. But Glory didn't feel ready to bring up Uncle Vince. Not directly.

'Actually, we got connections in more ways than you'd think,' she said. 'I even spent a few weeks at your old school

– Wildings, that is. My family sent me to keep me outta trouble.'

'And you escaped and came here? What an exciting life you lead!' Rose laughed admiringly. 'It's funny; I absolutely loathed the place, yet it proved my salvation. Wildings was where I first heard about Cambion.'

'But you didn't have the operation out in Switzerland, did you?'

'I honestly can't remember. The time immediately before my illness is mostly blank. I remember getting on the plane to go to the clinic with Mummy, but that's about it.'

'There was another hospital you stayed in, back in England. The one your mum arranged. Do you remember who checked you out?'

'I'm afraid I've forgotten that too.' She gave a wide, sweet smile, which Glory wasn't entirely convinced by. Maybe Rose wasn't sure how much she could trust Glory. Or maybe she was afraid what might happen if she spoke out.

'I can understand,' Glory said cautiously, 'Cambion don't want the wrong people taking advantage of their work. But it were a big risk you took, knowing so little about them. You was lucky to get over that brain-fever too. Could be there's patients that don't.'

Rose shrugged. 'No medical procedures are a hundred per cent safe. Of course, if I'd known what the stress of it all would do to Mummy . . .'

Glory decided to take a risk of her own. 'So what about your dad, then?' she asked, as offhandedly as she could make it. 'Your real dad, I mean. What's the story there?'

'Oh, *God*.' Rose pulled a face. 'It's all frightfully murky. He was some kind of two-bit gangster, apparently. Poor Mummy always did have bad taste in men.'

'You ain't curious about him?'

'No. I'm my own person.' She looked up into the rustling leaves, and frowned. 'That's important, isn't it? To know who you are. To stay . . . real.'

Glory nodded.

'But how does one *know*?' Rose continued, biting her lip. 'How can one be sure?'

'Sure of what?'

'Of who you are. What's real, what's – a – lie –'

She stopped speaking and covered her eyes with her hands. Her whole body trembled. Glory waited. Sure enough, the recovery, when it came, was swift. 'Goodness,' Rose exclaimed, getting to her feet. 'I think the speeches are about to start.' She smoothed out her skirt. 'Come on, we don't want to be late.'

A wooden stage had been set in front of the house, and decked with Cordoban flags and banners that read *Vargas para el Presidente!*. The man himself was small and plump with a sallow, melancholy face and tired eyes. When he took to the stage, they brightened, however, and his voice rang with determination.

Glory was more interested in people-watching than propaganda. She suspected at least two of the foreign guests were inquisitors; in contrast to rest of the gaily dressed crowd, they were in austere dark suits, each with a little crucifix pin on one lapel. One was a handsome Spaniard, the other a stocky, blunt-faced German. Both had a watchful air.

After the speeches were over, and the band had belted out a jazzed-up version of the Cordoban national anthem, Rose was beckoned over by a couple of elderly ladies in pearls. From there, several more guests claimed her attention. Time passed. Glory felt awkward and alone, sipping a sickly fruit punch, her heels sinking clumsily into the lawn. She could smell the roasting meat from the barbecue in her hair.

'There you are!' Rose hurried over, flushed and glowing. 'Sorry to desert you; if you've had enough, I can order a car. I just have one little errand to do first.' She flourished an envelope someone had given her. 'It means going into the house. Want to come?'

Glory glanced at the militiamen patrolling the grounds. 'Uh, I don't think that would be a good idea. The security . . .'

'Oh, don't worry about that. You're with me, remember.' Rose smiled mischievously. 'Surely you're not scared by the thought of a few ex-inquisitors.'

Despite her misgivings, Glory followed the other girl across the lawn and round to the back entrance of the low white mansion. It led straight into a cloakroom. Across one wall, a collection of differently sized iron muzzles hung from hooks.

The traditional witch's bridles had spiky prongs to place on the tongue, but these were a more user-friendly version. They were made of thin, polished iron bands; the widest circlet was designed to fit around the brow, with another that clipped around the throat. One slender hoop crossed the crown of the head, ear to ear; another went from the back of the neck to the centre of the forehead, dividing on either side of the nose. Glory put a hand out to the metal, already feeling the shiver of anticipatory sickness. The cold of the iron went through to her bones. It would be much worse if she was attempting witchwork; as it was, the contact flooded her with a wave of tiredness.

Rose pulled a commiserating face. 'Poor you. I remember how horrid the stuff used to make me feel.' She'd already selected her bridle, and was putting it over her head, briskly clipping the head and throat bands into place.

She opened the door leading to the hallway. At the end of it was an iron-enforced door to the main house, with a security guard stationed to one side. He obviously knew Rose, as he checked her security pass and turned the lock on the bridle with a good-humoured grin. 'Back in a minute,' Rose said, swiftly typing a code into the door's keypad.

Glory sat down to wait on a bench at the end of the hallway furthest from the guard. There was a table with flowers and magazines, like a posh doctor's waiting room. It was not one minute, but nearly fifteen, before Rose returned. She stood in the hallway, a little flustered, for a strand of hair was tangled in the neck-band's catch. The guard came to assist.

While his back was turned, the door behind him opened, and a little boy peeped out. 'Rosa! *Quiero venir a la fiesta!*'

'Esteban!' Rose exclaimed. 'How did you get here? N*iño travieso!*'

The boy giggled. He had his father's big dark eyes, though his were merry, not mournful. The guard swore

208

under his breath and tried to shoo him back through the door, but the child squirmed out of his way.

'He wants to go to the party, of course. Little monkey – he must have learned the door code.' Rose said something to the guard, then turned to Glory. 'I'll take him back to his room and explain to the nanny.'

The guard checked her bridle was still locked in position before Rose was allowed to take Esteban by the hand. He chattered away to her in Spanish like an old friend. As they went through the door, he waved at Glory. Surprised but charmed, she waved back.

When Rose returned for the second time, she was full of apologies for the delay. 'I've called our driver, so he should be waiting out front.'

'That Esteban's a cute kid,' Glory remarked, as they made their way to the car.

Rose's face lightened. 'Isn't he a darling? So much fun too.' But afterwards she fell into a distracted silence, which lasted throughout their journey home.

When their driver pulled up at the turning to Casa de la Armonia, Rose got out to say goodbye. 'Maybe,' she said, biting her lip, 'I shouldn't have brought you to the party. Maybe it was a mistake.'

'We got away with it, didn't we?'

'This time.' Rose's voice was scratchy and forced. 'But you mustn't go again. You could get into trouble.' A flash of pain crossed her face. She reached out and clenched Glory's arm, so her nails dug into her flesh. 'A *lot* of trouble, do you understand?'

'Thanks for the tip,' Glory said tersely. She wasn't sure

she had the energy to keep dealing with Rose's mood swings, whatever their cause. She walked off without saying goodbye. But later that night, Rose left a message on her phone.

'I'm sorry if I – well, if I was a bit rude or odd earlier. When we said goodbye, I mean. Maybe I'm not coping with things as well as I should.' There was a pause. 'Please, Glory. Don't give up on me.'

And Glory's memory lurched back to Serena Merle's final moments in the attic.

White skin, violet eyes; frenzy and flames.

# CHAPTER 22

The fake passport, debit card and smartphone from Troy took three days to arrive, and were left for Lucas in a locker in Euston station. It appeared Troy wasn't above making the most of the situation: the photograph of 'Wayne Bond' was of an acne-scarred teenager with long greasy hair and a receding chin. The passport came with a set of latex moulds to put on his fingers for the print check, and a pair of fake-iris contact lenses to fool the eye-scan. The final component was a small plastic bag containing a sprinkling of hairs, eyelashes and flakes of skin, to match the features in the photograph. A glamour didn't physically change a person's looks, but covered them up with somebody else's. It was like making a mask, with samples of bodily matter used as the basis of the illusion.

Of course, as soon as people realised Lucas was missing, they would guess where he had gone. If the authorities wanted to monitor his activities, they'd probably be able to track him down without too much difficulty. But he'd deal with that when the time came. For now, his priority was getting out of the country.

Lucas booked a Monday morning flight with 'Wayr debit card. Ashton was at work, Philomena was at scho and Marisa was embarking on her daily round of tenn. club, lunch, shopping and salon appointments. He had a ready-made elusion to get him to the airport and packed lightly, using a sports bag. There was a letter for his father, similar to the one he'd written before leaving for Wildings, which he intended to send by post. Everything was in place for a speedy getaway. But just as he headed towards the door, it opened, and his father came in.

'You're going after her,' Ashton said flatly.

Lucas knew the game was up. He didn't even attempt to bluff, just got a better grip on his bag.

'I have a lead. It's something I need to follow up. And though I can't tell you the details, I need you to trust me on this. Just like you trusted me before, when you let me join the secret service.' He paused. 'I'm not on my own either. I have help.'

'I suspect,' said Ashton with a bitter smile, 'that is something else I'm better off not knowing about. It seems nothing I do or say has any influence on you.'

'That's not true.'

'Isn't it?'

'For God's sake!' Lucas's voice sharpened with frustration. 'Duty, loyalty, Doing The Right Thing – isn't that supposed to be "the Stearne way"? Isn't that what you've always taught me? When I was alone with Gideon and Striker, Glory was the one who found me. And if she hadn't . . . if I'd been left . . . if . . .'

'I know,' his father said quietly. 'Don't think I'll ever

forget it.' He closed his eyes; when he opened them again he looked older, and greyer. 'I realise you're trying to do the right thing. That doesn't alter the fact I think you are acting wrongly. Recklessly.' Then, when Lucas was getting ready to argue again, he said, 'But I won't stand in your way. Is that enough?'

Lucas nodded. He had a choking feeling in his throat. He went to the door, and opened it, and Ashton didn't try to stop him.

But then his father put out his arms and drew him back, with unexpected strength. 'I'm proud of you,' he said. 'Come back to me. Come back soon.'

Lucas transformed into Wayne in an allotment shed. He began by sketching two portraits: one of himself, and one of the face on the passport photograph – spots, lank hair and all.

Glamours were more effective the closer they were to a person's real appearance. This meant that altering one's build was very difficult, disguising age even more so, and changing gender impossible. Whether Wayne Bond was a real person or a computer generated one, Lucas would have to work hard to recreate him convincingly.

With each stroke of the pencil, he felt his fae unfurl on to the paper. He burned the self-portrait on a mirror, watching his reflection dissolve, and mixed the resultant ash into a smatter of the physical ingredients. Spitting on his finger, he worked the mess into a paste. This was smeared on to the drawing of Wayne, which he then folded into a small square. He pressed it between his hands, visualising Wayne's features, saying his name. The next time he looked into the mirror, a stranger's face was reflected back.

Yet another alter ego. Perhaps Dr Caron had been on to something, referring to her patients' Seventh Sense as if it were an actual person. Lucas and Glory had laughed about it together. He'd christened his fae Adam, but she'd come up with something ridiculous for hers. What was it? It troubled him that he couldn't remember.

To restore his true appearance, he simply had to tear up the amulet. For somebody else to expose him would be more difficult. If they destroyed the amulet, they wouldn't immediately destroy its illusion, because the witchwork was prolonged by physical contact with the witch who crafted it. The longer Lucas carried the amulet around, the stronger the glamour would be.

Thanks to his WICA training, he already knew how to use the fake finger moulds and contact lenses. They and the black-market passport were as good as anything the secret service could provide; in spite of the lank hair, Lucas knew he had reason to be grateful to Troy. The journey to Cordoba went without a hitch.

He arrived in San Jerico at three o'clock in the morning, in a torrential downpour. The water spilling from the gutters was full of scum; the air stank of fumes and garbage. Blurred by rain, the city appeared a jumble of violently bright lights and colours. Even at this hour, the street parties were in full swing. He managed to find a taxi to take him to one of the budget hotels listed in his guidebook. The room was cramped and dingy, but he was past caring. He rolled into bed, and didn't wake up until four the next afternoon.

He'd slept for nearly thirteen hours but Wayne's reflection was still puffy and bleary-eyed. Lucas disliked hiding behind somebody else's face, yet he had to do so for a little longer. It was his best chance of surveying the set-up at Casa de la Armonia. Troy had heard nothing since a brief email from Glory to say that she'd arrived safely. Lucas needed to bear in mind that he was here for Candice Morgan too. He owed Troy a report on his sister's welfare. So, after a quick shower, he took a taxi up to the villa.

An overgrown but patchy hedge surrounded the back garden. The afternoon was warm, and there was a skinny young woman with bright pink hair and a bikini to match sunbathing by a pool. Candice, he presumed. Lucas watched from behind the hedge as she was joined by a man in swimming trunks and a Hawaiian shirt. That must be the no-good actor boyfriend he'd researched on the web. A lot of stomach-churning pawing and slobbering ensued.

Most of the windows in the villa had their shutters closed so he wasn't able to see if Glory was inside. He began to move deeper into the foliage, in the hope of some useful eavesdropping. He might have got away with it, if it weren't for two yapping dogs who suddenly appeared out of nowhere and hurled themselves noisily into the hedge. Lucas beat a hasty retreat back into the road.

'It's a freakin' *pervert!*' Candy squealed. 'Spying in the bushes! Watching me sunbathe! Urgh!'

Todd lumbered towards the hedge and shouted, '*Vaya! Vamos!*'

It was time for part two of Lucas's plan. He gasped excitedly.

'Todd? Todd Lawson?'

'What's it to you?'

'Everything! *Galaxy Combat* is my favourite TV show of all time. Well – until you left. I mean, you were the reason everyone watched it, right? And then I come here on holiday, and find out you're actually living in San Jerico! Unbelievable!'

'So he's a pervert *and* a stalker,' Candy huffed. Lucas suspected she was peeved she wasn't the object of his interest after all. 'Seriously, babe, we should call the police.'

Lucas interjected a note of hurt into his voice. 'I'm not a stalker; I'm a *fan*. I only came here to tell you how awesome you are. It's not just about your acting either. Because I heard you were writing a screenplay and that it's going to be *huge* –'

He didn't need to say anything more. He was immediately invited into the villa and supplied with an autograph. And a photo opportunity. And a very long, very boring monologue about the fascist conspiracy at the centre of the Screenwriters' Guild.

Lucas smiled and nodded, and did his best to look suitably overawed. Meanwhile, he took the opportunity to check the place out. The house was a mess, but it wasn't the crack den of Troy's fears. He was pretty sure Glory wasn't at home. There was a red cardigan on a chair, though, that he recognised as hers. And a sparkly hairclip lying on the floor. While Todd was mid-anecdote, Lucas scooped up the clip and put it in his pocket.

'Precious,' Candice said, reappearing at the door with a pout, 'I'm gonna have to get ready for work soon. Rona wants me in early tonight.'

'Are you an actor too?' Lucas asked.

Todd guffawed. 'She's a barmaid.'

'I'm a celebrity hostess,' Candice snapped. 'And me and Glor's wages are paying for that beer, remember.'

She flounced out. Todd just laughed again. 'She and her cousin work at the Carabosse,' he said. 'It's a freak show for hag-fanciers. Now, where were we? Oh yeah.' He repositioned his laptop. 'Here's a clip of me two years ago at Comic-Con . . .'

Lucas dutifully peered at the computer screen. He'd got what he needed, anyway. That night, he would go and find Glory at her club.


The Carabosse's door policy was highly selective, and punters required both cash and clout to gain admittance. Wayne Bond didn't look as if he had either, but Lucas Stearne did. He checked out of his hotel, and destroyed the glamour by tearing up the little paper amulet he carried with him at all times. Hidden in his bag were the materials to craft two more from scratch: one to get him out of the country, and one spare.

At the new hotel, a slightly less grotty establishment down the road, the receptionist tried to sell him a charm to protect him against witchwork. 'Best quality,' she assured him. 'Very safe, for all your holidays. All the tourists get them. Blessed by La Bruja Blanca herself!'

It was a clear plastic pouch to hang round his neck, containing a white feather, bits of dried leaves and hair and, for good measure, a tiny wire crucifix. Lucas doubted any witch had gone near it, though he'd seen quite a few people wearing similar things. Many houses had lucky talismans and bundles of amulets tied to their doorways, as well as the usual iron bells. Useless superstitious junk, for the most part. But with no Inquisition to protect them, what hope did ordinary citizens have?

At night, the city turned from seedy to sinister. Away from the glitzy boulevards, the backstreets were so narrow and crusted they seemed subterranean. The humid air made his shirt stick to his back. He thought the people – from the beggars squatting in doorways to the Eurotrash types stumbling out of bars – had the same kind of slippery, greedy look about them. The sooner he got Glory out of here the better.

He had no problems getting into the Carabosse. Rich foreign teenagers with more money than sense were always welcome. 'Is the Starling girl working tonight?' Lucas asked the woman in a pinstripe suit who was behind the ticket desk.

'Si. She'll be here at ten.'

'Good,' he said, in his most lordly manner. 'I'd like to request a private performance.'

The woman smiled slyly. 'Gloriana is very popular. For this, you pay top price.' She named a sum that made him inwardly wince, though he handed over a wad of US dollars without a murmur.

Lucas was shown to the row of cells that had been converted into a VIP area for private partying. The walls in his cell were padded in purple velvet and the ceiling was studded with fairy lights. It was small and claustrophobic. He tried not to think of the room's former use, but supposed that was meant to be part of its attraction. The illicit thrill.

The curtain over the doorway was pulled back and Lucas felt his heart speeding; a thin, dry buzz. But it was just a waiter, come to take his order. He asked for a Coke and tried to keep calm. He knew he would only have a few seconds to persuade Glory to hear him out. Already, he was wondering if he was right to have come. The noise from the main club – thuds of music, laughter, squeals – made it hard to concentrate.

The curtain twitched again, and he thought it was the waiter with his drink. It was Glory. She'd cut her hair and lost weight. Under the heavy sixties-style make-up, she looked tired, though her face was fixed with a professionally perky smile.

'Good evening, sir. And what can I –'

He leaned out of the shadows. 'It's me. Lucas.'

She went very still. 'You came after me,' she whispered with a soft incredulous breath. 'You –' Then her expression reordered itself, snapped into angry strength. 'You need to get outta here.'

'Please. Give me five minutes, at least. Just to talk.'

She looked back behind the curtain and he could tell she was thinking about calling for back-up. There were a lot of mean-looking bouncers in this place.

'Did WICA send you? Or the Inquisition?'

'Neither. I'm on my own.' He thought it better not to mention Troy for the moment. 'I'm AWOL, in fact. Like you.'

'You ain't *nothing* like me.'

But she sat down – cautiously, at the very edge of the seat, and tensed for flight. Her flimsy dress kept riding up her legs, and she pulled it down with an irritable twitch.

'I didn't come here to argue. I came to apologise and explain, if you'll let me. And – well, I need help, not for me, but for your cousin. For Rose.' He paused for effect. 'I have evidence she's in Cordoba.'

Glory didn't react as he'd expected. She looked, if anything, amused. 'Is that a fact?'

He explained what he'd deduced from Raffi's postcard. She listened without comment, her face an unimpressed blank. 'Cambion could be a real danger to witchkind,' he said, in a final attempt to rouse her. 'This is our best opportunity to find out what's going on, and maybe even put a stop to it.'

'So you, what, want us to join forces? Do some freelance detecting? "Starling & Stearne: No Witchcrime Too Large"?'

'There's no need to take the piss. I just thought you'd want something better to do than – well – this –' He gestured around the cell.

She narrowed her eyes. 'What's wrong with it?'

'C'mon. Performing fae-tricks for cash? You're better than this, Glory. You know you are.'

'I know I'm paying me own way. Earning a living at something I'm good at.'

'Well, you're certainly expensive . . .'

She stared at him disgustedly. 'And yet,' she said, 'you've gotta way of making me feel cheap.' She rose to her feet. 'I ain't some damsel in distress. I don't need you. I don't want you. So stay away from me and my family. You Stearnes have already damaged us enough.'

# CHAPTER 23

Lucas hated the thought of Glory in that trashy club, in that trashy outfit, being leered at by all those trashy people. Their encounter had ended badly, but he wasn't about to give up. He kept returning to her first reaction; that hushed, incredulous breath. *You came after me . . .*

As soon as he got back to his hotel, he emailed a report to Troy on where Glory was working and living. He concluded that while Todd might be a loser and an idiot, he was fairly harmless, and that Candice was managing to hold down a job. He finished by saying that Glory seemed well, and that he was 'making progress' with communications.

He was increasingly curious about how Glory was spending her free time, and who with. The trouble was, now she knew he was in town, she would be more than usually on her guard. There was no point going back to the Carabosse; it was a safe bet she'd have told the staff not to let him in.

He did, however, have a secret weapon: Glory's hairclip that he'd stolen from the villa. He could use it to spy on her in a scrying-bowl.

Scrying was dependent on a number of things. You needed a physical token of your target and it had to have been taken from them fairly recently. Within twenty-four hours was usually the limit for someone of Lucas's powers. It didn't work if the target was wearing an elusion, or was in an iron-proofed room. The greater the distance between you and your target, the poorer the result.

The next morning, Lucas got up early, put the Do Not Disturb sign on his door handle, and filled a glass bowl he'd bought with water. Glory's hairclip floated on the surface. He also crafted a second glamour for Wayne, so that there would be no delay in going after Glory once he'd found her.

Taking slow, steady breaths, he began to sway gently so the water started to swirl and the hairpin to sink, as the Devil's Kiss warmed his skin and his fae flowed into the bowl. He stirred the water with his forefinger, thinking of Glory. A stream of tiny bubbles began to form, rising to the surface in a silvery cloud. But there was nothing to be seen in them, and no corresponding image floated into his head.

He kept trying at half-hour intervals. At eleven thirty, the bubbles, pinprick small, began to rise and fall with renewed energy. Glory must have moved into his area of vision. Nothing could be seen in the water, though. That meant she was wearing an elusion. But since an elusion only lasted for a single journey, once Glory was at her destination the camouflaging effect of her witchwork would wear off. For the next twenty minutes, Lucas concentrated on the bowl, staring at the water until his eyes grew gritty and his head ached.

At last he got his reward. The silvery bubbles grew denser, forming blurred patterns. He closed his eyes, and a picture foamed into his head. A blonde sitting at a table. The people around her were indistinguishable and the image as a whole was watery, probably because the hairclip had been away from its owner for so long. But he was just able to make out some lettering behind her. *Café Grande*. It was enough.

Lucas opened his eyes and got to his feet, a little unsteadily. In moments, he had located the café on his smartphone, and was hurrying towards it, splashing through puddles left by the latest downpour. It would be too bad if, after all this effort, Glory had already moved on.

No, she was still there. Sitting in the sunshine, drinking hot chocolate, checking her watch. She must be meeting someone.

Damp and out of breath, Lucas positioned himself in the window of a neighbouring bar. Even disguised as Wayne, he had an irrational fear that Glory would see past the glamour. He ordered a coffee, pulled out his guidebook, and prepared to wait.

It didn't take long. Glory looked up and waved at a young woman walking across the square. The two embraced. Glory's friend's hair shone fire-bright in the sun, her face as pale and perfect as a princess's in a fae-tale. Rose Merle, in the flesh.

The impossible was true: the girl was cured. More than just healthy; radiant. No wonder Glory had been so unimpressed by his big reveal that Rose was in Cordoba! By the look of it, the two of them were already BFFs. He remembered her parting shot from last night: *stay away from me and my family.* She'd found her cousin, and she didn't want Lucas to – what? Intrude? Endanger? Investigate?

For the next forty minutes or so, the girls chatted together like old friends. Then Glory got up to say goodbye. Lucas wavered, unsure whether or not to go after her. For the moment, he was more curious about Rose. He thought of her mother; her fragile beauty and burning rage. At Wildings, Mei-fen had said that Rose cried all the time. She didn't look unhappy now.

And then, about ten minutes after Glory had left, Rose was joined by a new arrival: a tall, fair-haired young man who greeted her with a lingering kiss. The breath was violently knocked from Lucas's body. It was Gideon.

Gideon Hale. Tanned and debonair in a linen suit, sitting with his beautiful girlfriend, drinking hot chocolate in the sun. His laughter rang round the square. The last time Lucas had heard that sound, it had been in a basement cell. Rose laughed too, leaned her head on his shoulder.

Anger rolled inside Lucas with a terrible energy; it demanded action. Its force propelled him out of the bar and round the corner into a deserted alley, where he ripped Wayne's glamour in half. Suddenly, somehow, he was at the table where Gideon was sitting.

'Hello, Gideon. Small world.'

Gideon was more amused than shocked. 'Good Lord. It's Stearne minor.' He pushed back a flop of gilded hair; Lucas remembered the gesture, just as he remembered the narrowing of his light grey eyes. 'Rose, darling, this is my old school chum, Lucas. Lucas, meet Rose.'

'How do you do,' Rose said coolly.

There was an excruciating silence. The blood drummed through Lucas's head.

*Look at you. Look at the dirty hag . . .*

For the most part, Lucas had tried not to think about what might happen if he came face to face with Gideon again. Now the moment had come, he realised he didn't even know what he wanted to do – confront him? Accuse him? Cage him in iron and drown him in ice?

Gideon turned to Rose, who was nuzzling his ear. 'Lucas works for the British government. Maybe that's why he's looking so down at heel.'

It was true. Lucas was pale and haggard, in travel-stained clothes. He'd been skulking about in alleys and seedy hotel rooms, disguised in an even seedier glamour. He was AWOL from his job, subsisting on coven cash. Adrift and alone.

Whereas Gideon, a debarred and disgraced inquisitor, sadist, conspirator and criminal –

Gideon was clearly doing very nicely for himself.

'We can't all be on permanent leave.' With great effort, Lucas kept his voice steady. 'How's unemployment treating you?'

'Well, the Devil makes work for idle hands . . . and, as you know, I don't like to be idle.' He smiled. 'This place isn't called the New World for nothing. A land of sunshine and opportunity.'

'For criminals, maybe.'

'Oh, indeed. That's why private law enforcement is Cordoba's premier growth industry. Honest citizens are crying out for order, authority, discipline. And unlike their British counterparts, they're not squeamish about what it takes to provide it.'

So Gideon was a mercenary. It made perfect sense. The same powerful family connections that had kept him out of jail had no doubt helped ease his way into one of Cordoba's militias. He'd probably got a crisp new uniform and shiny new gun out of it too.

A waiter had arrived and was greeting Rose like an old friend. 'I wouldn't have thought she's your type,' Lucas hissed, while her attention was elsewhere. 'Playing with fire, isn't it – with her mother a witch?'

'It's not as if I'm planning to *breed* with her,' said Gideon, amused. He'd barely bothered to lower his voice. When the waiter moved on, he put his arm around Rose's waist. 'Lucas was just saying what an adorable couple we make.'

Rose smiled, then looked at Lucas doubtfully. 'Aren't you rather young, to be working for the government?'

'He's a child prodigy, darling. Whatever business he's doing here, it will be very hush-hush. A secret mission in the mean streets of San Jerico. Am I right?' Gideon held up a hand. 'No – wait. You'd tell me . . . but then you'd have to kill me!'

He laughed heartily. His eyes met Lucas's. They were as chill and pale as glass.

'You take care, Gideon.'

Somehow Lucas managed to walk away.

Icy bands squeezed his lungs. The breaths he took were bitter and choking. It was as if Gideon himself were a bane,

226

something twisted and unnatural, which made the air sicken around him.

Lucas had achieved nothing – Gideon's composure was as unshakeable as his arrogance. But Lucas couldn't waste time on regrets. His priority had to be finding out how Gideon, Rose and Glory were connected, and why.

However angry Glory was with Lucas, she would never knowingly consort with the likes of Gideon Hale. He embodied everything she most hated and feared about the Inquisition. So either she didn't know about Rose's boyfriend, or else Gideon was keeping his identity from her. It wouldn't be difficult: they hadn't previously met. And if that was the case, then Rose must be in on it too.

And if Glory thought she and Rose were friends, God knows what she might have told her; what secrets she'd confided or confessed.

Or how Gideon would make use of them . . .

And so one hour later, Lucas was standing outside the glittering high-rise that was home to Cordoba's Chief of Police.

'Welcome, welcome my friend!' Raffi's grin was as irrepressible as ever. 'You are here for Glory, yes?' He flung out his arms dramatically. 'You are come to declaim your *amor* and do the grovel on her feet!'

'No grovelling,' said Lucas drily. 'Or declaiming either. But I think Glory's in trouble, and she needs our help.'

# CHAPTER 24

Glory had enjoyed her second café-rendezvous with Rose. San Jerico was lonelier than Glory liked to admit, and getting to know Rose had given her a sense of purpose. But now it was becoming a distraction. She decided it would be better if she began to keep her distance.

Finding out what had happened to her mother was Glory's priority. But she wasn't naive. She knew there was a good chance Edie Starling was dead. She'd give it her best shot, and if nothing came of it, well . . . she'd be no worse off than she'd been a few months ago.

The obvious thing to do was to use the contacts she'd made at the Carabosse to get introduced to the Cordoban covens. Perhaps she'd hear about her mother that way. There would always be opportunities for a witch with her gifts. She was smart and talented. A good job in a strong coven was all she'd wanted, once.

But then she thought of the bleeding beggar on the cathedral steps, the frightened citizens clutching their charms and saying their prayers, the little boy locked away behind iron doors. A life of witchcrime . . . Did she even have the stomach for it any more?

Much as she hated to admit it, Lucas was right to say that working at the Carabosse was beneath her. She scowled at the thought of him lounging back on the purple velvet, looking down his aristocratic nose, curling his aristocratic lip. Judging her. As if she was some fallen woman in need of rescue!

She had been training herself not to think of him. She needed to believe they wouldn't meet again. Yet that first moment, when he'd leaned out of the shadows ... Her insides still turned over at the thought of it. A deep, hot shiver of recognition.

Glory thumped her pillow in annoyance. She was trying to have an afternoon nap, but couldn't relax enough to drop off. She kept wondering how Lucas had tracked her down. It was possible WICA had somebody following her. Or, worse, the UK Inquisition. Not that any of them could touch her, not out here ... The house throbbed with the sound of the TV blaring, dogs yapping, raised voices. Close her eyes, and she could almost be back in Cooper Street.

Amid the racket, she heard her name. Todd was shouting for her from downstairs.

'WHAT?' she yelled back.

'VISITOR!'

*Lucas*, she thought, and her insides gave another jolt.

She swung out of bed and reached for something to wear. A moment later the door to her room was pushed open by Todd.

'Don't you knock?' she growled, wrapping her dressing gown round her even more tightly.

'Don't you listen? You've got someone to see you.'

'I know. I heard. I'm coming –'

'Seems like your pal needs a shoulder to cry on. And I'd be happy to lend one . . . she's hot, for a ginger chick.'

So it was Rose then. With dragging feet, Glory went downstairs.

Rose did indeed look as if she'd been crying. Her face was blotched and her hands were shaking.

'Oh, Glory,' she gasped, drawing her outside the front door. 'Thank God you're here. Something – something terrible's happened.'

'What's wrong? Are you hurt?'

'Not me. It's Esteban. Esteban Vargas. The little boy – we – you – saw at the party yesterday –'

'Has he had an accident?' But even as she asked, she knew the answer.

Rose spoke in a frightened whisper. 'It's witchwork. He's been got at. We don't know how. They called the doctor at first. And then a fae-healer, from one of the private hospitals. But neither of them can do anything. And then I thought of you. You're powerful, aren't you, Glory? And experienced. I thought – if you could just – just come –'

'The kid's been hexed?' Glory sucked her teeth. 'I ain't got skills in that sorta thing.'

But that wasn't quite true. Auntie Angel had taught her banes. And WICA had taught her how to undo them.

'Please. If you could just *try*. If you could see him . . . it's so horrible . . .' Rose's eyes were welling with tears. 'Vargas – he's desperate, frantic. We all are. But I know I can trust you.'

Glory had only seen Esteban for a few moments, but she had liked the kid. To inflict a bane on a child would be taboo for any witch that she could think of, criminal or not.

'OK,' she said. 'I'll come and see.'

There was another limousine waiting to take her to the mansion. The closer they got to their destination, the more distressed Rose became. 'He's just an innocent,' she kept saying. 'I don't understand.' She rocked back and forth. 'Such darkness. It's like I can feel it . . . feel it spreading . . .'

They passed through the same three checkpoints, the militiamen even more hatchet-faced than before. Rose said that nobody knew how the security had been breached. No bells had rung or alarms been activated; there was nothing untoward on CCTV. Disaster had struck at midday, when Esteban was in his playroom. He had pointed at the floor, and said there was a snake. His nanny could see nothing. Almost immediately afterwards, the boy had started banging his head against the wall. When he was forcibly stopped, he fell into a trance.

This time, Glory was brought through the mansion's main entrance, but there was little opportunity to take in her surroundings. Accompanied by three soldiers and with Rose at her side, she was taken up to Esteban's bedroom. It was large and well-lit, despite the iron shutters covering the windows, and should have been a cheerful place; the colourful walls were lined with books, the floor littered with toys. Now it was hot, noisy and crowded with frightened people. A group of servants and family members took up most of the space; muttering and weeping, clutching charms. A doctor in a white coat and a woman in a green striped uniform, who was presumably the fae-healer, were huddled together in one corner. A priest was in the other, burning incense and intoning prayers. Nobody was bridled. After all, the damage had already been done.

Before Glory crossed the threshold, her way was blocked by Vargas himself. His eyes were bloodshot, his breath sour with fear.

'You are the girl, the witch-girl?' he asked in heavily accented English. 'The friend of Rosa, from England?'

'That's me.'

'You won't hurt him?' His eyes burned into hers. 'You will do only good?'

'No,' she said. 'I won't hurt him. I will – I will try to help.'

'Swear it. I have to trust you, I have no choice. *Swear.*'

'I swear.'

Rose gripped Glory's arm. 'I know you can do it. I believe in you.'

'I can only do me best,' she said, and felt a shiver of apprehension. The pressure of Rose's fingernails reminded her of last night's warning to stay away. As she walked into the centre of the room, the people around her fell silent, and shrank back.

She tried not to let it distract her. She needed to keep her attention on the child. Esteban was sitting bolt upright in the centre of the bed, which had been pulled into the middle of the room. As soon as she saw him, she could sense the fae rolling off him, like a toxic fog. His eyes were wide and unblinking. His body was shaken by shudders and pouring with sweat. She could hear the dull chatter of his teeth.

Rose had said that Esteban thought he saw a snake. That made it a figment – the type of bane associated with hallucinations. It had put the boy into a literal trance of terror. All banes were very difficult to undo; if the witch who hexed it was as strong as Glory, it might be impossible. Yet the bells over the doorway were silent and still. However had it been done? It was a question that must be contributing to the tension in the room. People must be wondering about the interrogations to follow.

Glory turned to the uniformed woman standing by the doctor and asked, in halting Spanish, if she was the fae-healer.

The woman nodded, and nervously held out her hand. A little mud-man was there, wrapped in what looked like a bit of pillowcase from Esteban's bed. It had been made in an attempt to draw the fae out of the boy and into a poppet. Glory would try the same thing, with a few amendments.

She beckoned Rose over. 'I'll need to make a poppet of me own. With blood from Esteban, if that's OK. Will you explain to his dad?'

The necessary arrangements were made, and the doctor passed her a sterilised scalpel. Someone else was sent to gather earth from Esteban's favourite play area in the garden, while Glory collected a marble from his toybox and dust from under the bed-frame. The earth was sandy, and the feel of it between her palms took her back to Dr Caron's therapy sessions, and the long hours fiddling with the sand-tray. She used it to build a mud-man around the marble, mixed with dust and a smear of blood she took from the boy's arm.

He didn't seem to notice her take it, any more than when she cut off a hank of his messy black curls. This she twisted into a strand of her own, moistened with spit, to make a bracelet. The audience watched intently, and in silence.

Glory's mouth was very dry as she climbed on to the bed to sit opposite Esteban. With the scalpel, she made a small nick in the centre of her forehead and then his. He didn't flinch. In her right hand, she held the poppet. With her left, she took one of his, and slipped the hair bracelet over their interlaced fingers. His skin was icy, despite the sweat pouring from his body. She leaned in to press forehead against forehead, blood against blood, eye meeting eye. His pupils were dilated and oddly clouded.

As her fae began to rise and tingle, warming the spot beneath her collarbone, she reached deep into her own dark secret heart. From here, the fae flowed out to the child; through the blood they shared, the ring of hair that bound them and the poppet she held. As she did so, she could feel the other witch's fae resisting her. It was a creeping coldness and sickness; a fuzz in the brain.

She stared deep into Esteban's eyes, trying to get past the haze that clouded them. The cut on her forehead burned. And, just for a moment, she heard it: a rasping slither and hiss, a squirm of darkness in her head . . .

She gasped, and flinched away. At the same moment, a scribble mark appeared on Esteban's lower left arm. It was a serpentine scratch, where beads of blood formed. Vargas cried out in anguish, and the other onlookers rustled and hummed. Rose was twisting her hands together and murmuring, as if in prayer.

Glory blocked them out. She took a deep breath and resumed her position. She didn't know whether the appearance of the snake-mark was a good or bad sign, but she clutched the child's hand more tightly, and the poppet more firmly. She started to whisper his name, over and over. There was a bitter taste in her mouth. As she began to sweat and shake, and a fearful coldness crept over her skin, she began to realise this wasn't something she could win. The bane was too strong for her. If she wasn't careful, whatever had infected Esteban would start to infect her too.

'I can't –' she choked out. 'I can't –'

All of a sudden, the pressure vanished. It felt like a warm breeze blowing through her body. With a crack, the marble fell to the floor, for the mud-man built around it had crumbled into a vile-smelling greenish dust.

Esteban gave a sharp cry. Then he blinked, and shook his head blearily, like someone coming out of a deep sleep. The bloody scribble on his arm had vanished. '*Papá!*' he explained. '*Vi una serpiente!*' Then he looked at the floor, clearly wondering where the snake had gone.

His father rushed at him, weeping and babbling, crushing him in his arms. Other people crowded around the bed. Glory was happy to step back, feeling shaky and confused. Several people came and pumped her hand, asking questions she was too dazed to respond to. But others, including the fae-healer, kept their distance. They seemed almost more nervous of her now than when she'd first entered the room.

Rose came and hugged her. Panic over, she was bright-eyed and pink-cheeked, almost giddy with relief. 'Oh, Glory! Thank you so, so, so much. You were wonderful! Miraculous.'

'I don't . . . I don't understand what happened.' Glory frowned. 'I thought I couldn't do it. I was *losing*. And then, out of nowhere –'

'Like I said, you're a miracle-worker! I shouldn't be surprised if you get a government honour out of this. Or a statue in the Plaza de la República. It's the least you deserve. As I'm sure the Senator will tell you . . .' She looked towards her boss, still cradling his son and barely visible through a knot of well-wishers.

'If it's OK with you, I won't stick around. I mustn't be late for work.' Glory smiled shakily. 'Could do with some fresh air too, if I'm honest.'

Rose glanced at her watch. 'Actually, I should be heading to the office too. I'll walk you out.'

'Bit past office hours, I'd have thought.'

'The Red Knights are on duty twenty-four-seven.'

'Wait – you're in the *militia*? I thought you was working for Vargas's campaign!'

'Oh, I am. But I also do some of the admin for the Senator's security detail. It's how I met my boyfriend, as it happens. He's a Red Knight lieutenant. I'll have to introduce you next time around.' Rose smiled. 'Maybe he should bring along a friend for you. No girl can resist a man in uniform!'

Raffi's family was very welcoming to Lucas. A noisy tribe of sisters crowded round to greet him, while Senora Almagro didn't stop beaming. The Comandante had the same small merry eyes and spiky hair as his son.

Bribery and corruption had certainly treated the police chief well. The penthouse duplex was stuffed with Louis XVI antique furniture and American pop art. Lucas and Raffi stretched out beside the swimming pool on a blue-tiled roof terrace, sipping coconut lemonade and eating savoury pastries brought out by the maids. The city sprawled below, rooftops shimmering in a smoky haze.

Lucas, however, was unable to relax. He didn't want to get Raffi too involved, yet needed his local knowledge and support. In the end, he kept Cambion out of the story, while explaining who Gideon was and why he was dangerous, particularly for a witch like Glory.

Raffi's response was not reassuring. He told Lucas that the militias were made up of ex-inquisitors and soldiers, mostly foreign, and all with shady pasts. The Red Knights were funded and administered by a consortium of Cordoba's wealthiest families. He suspected that Senator Vargas aimed to take them under state control if he was elected and use them as a basis to re-establish the Cordoban Inquisition.

It was no surprise Raffi distrusted Vargas's ambition to restore order to Cordoba's streets and integrity to its public life. His father owed his position to the current president, Ignacio De Aviles, a doddery old rogue who was embroiled in several lawsuits. This led Lucas to reconsider Raffi's departure from Wildings.

'You told me you were going home because the political situation had changed,' he reminded him. 'And that it would be safe for you here. But Vargas is ahead in the polls. He's still the favourite to win, right?'

Raffi smiled, and tapped his nose. 'Ah, but my *papá*, he hears things. Whispers that bad things are to happen to Vargas's campaign. Soon, he is to withdraw.'

'Is the source of these whispers reliable?'

'Some of them maybe yes, some maybe no. But one whisper is the most reliable of all.' Raffi lowered his voice conspiratorially. 'They call her La Bruja Blanca.'

La Bruja Blanca . . . the White Witch.

'I think I've heard of her,' Lucas said. 'Somebody tried to sell me a charm she made.'

'She is a fighter-hero from the revolution, many years ago. An ancient lady, though it is said she can appear young and beautiful, because she is so strong in her fae. She is hiding in the mountains. The peasant people, they think her very good and very powerful, and they tell her things. She has spies in the city too. Sometimes, they cause trouble for my *papá*. La Bruja Blanca does not like him. But she hates the Inquisition worse, and also the militias.'

Lucas dipped a hand into the gleaming water of the swimming pool. 'Sounds like a useful person to know.'

'La Blanca is no help to us here, though. If Glory gets in trouble with the militia, then that is very bad. Even my *papá* cannot control them. They make many witches disappear. You must warn her about this Gideon.'

'It's getting her to listen that's the trouble. She's . . . well, she's very angry with me.'

'Aha, but Glory is not angry with *me*. Tonight we will go party in the Carabosse, and I will talk to her. My family, we know the owner. So there will be no worries.' Raffi settled back on his sunlounger. 'Seriously, *amigo*, now is time to chill. I can make all things right.'

But when he and Lucas turned up to the Carabosse that night, they found the street closed off and the building evacuated. An excitable crowd had gathered behind the cordon, where a policeman was arguing with a soldier in a red uniform. The club had been raided by the Red Knight militia, said the man nearest to Raffi. A member of staff was accused of bane-hexing and assault. Some said she had escaped over the rooftops; according to other reports, she was already captive.

# CHAPTER 25

The vileness of Esteban's bane clung to Glory for a good while after leaving Rose. But after food and a shower, she felt more like herself. She didn't have to explain anything to her housemates, since it was Candy's night off and she and Todd were out. By the time Glory left for the Carabosse, her thoughts had turned to possible rewards. Maybe she could use Vargas's gratitude as leverage to get a better job. Or help with looking for her mum. Or a nice fat wad of cash. She wouldn't say no to a statue in the Plaza de la República either.

Not bad, for a girl from Cooper Street . . . !

Her revival was short-lived. Work was even more busy than usual and dominated by her least favourite type of punter: an English stag party. Fighting the bane had drained her more than she realised. After less than an hour the crush got too much and she slipped back into the staffroom for a moment's peace, on the pretext she needed supplies for a fascination.

'They are looking for you in the club,' somebody said from the passage outside.

It was the cat-woman, Sheba, dressed for her act in the silver leotard, the animal draped round her shoulders like a fur wrap. It was the first time Glory had heard her voice: a low and scratchy purr.

'Yeah, well, I'll be there in a sec,' she said irritably.

The woman's eyes shone yellowish in the dim light. 'It is the militia.'

Her cat opened its mouth and yowled. Glory stared at its white pointed teeth and ribbed red throat. And yet, somehow, she wasn't as shocked as she should have been. For hadn't she been tensed for this her whole life? Boots on the stairs, fists on the door. Rough hands, dragging her through the night.

Her thoughts flashed confusedly – Esteban's bane – Rose – the Red Knights –

It never occurred to her that there might be a reasonable explanation, or that she should try to face it out. Flee or fight: those were your only options in a witch-hunt. Hardly aware of what she was doing, she kicked off her spindly high heels and thrust her feet into the trainers she'd used for the commute. Fight or flee . . . But she had no weapon, and the basement was windowless. Helplessly, she moved towards the back door, knowing it was already too late. Of course they would have posted a guard there.

'Not that way,' said Sheba, blinking her golden eyes. 'This.'

She beckoned Glory into her dressing room. It was cramped and frowsty, smelling of cat. 'Emergency exit,' she said impassively, and pointed to a built-in wardrobe. Sounds of barked orders and indignant protests were coming from the main club.

Trembling, Glory opened the wardrobe and drew back a tangle of costumes to see that stairs lay behind. Sheba pressed something into her hand – a white feather, a knucklebone – before moving away to sit at her mirror. The last Glory saw of her, she was licking her hands to smooth her hair. The cat sat beside her, grooming its own sleek fur.

The stairs only went up one level. It wouldn't take long for the soldiers to work out where she had gone. But the rest of the building was used as an archive store and would be empty at night. Glory's hand closed more tightly around Sheba's parting gift. Though she didn't understand the feather, the bit of bone was important. If she could get on to the roof, she could use it as a lodestone. Witches, like cats, were good with heights . . .

She could feel the music from the club vibrating through the floor. She ran through a succession of storage rooms, the grandeur of their stone carvings and polished wood obscured by ranks of shelving towers.

Already, she could hear sounds of pursuit. She burst out into the entrance hall, lined by broken busts of inquisitors past, and headed up a sweeping marble staircase. The main door thumped and rattled. More soldiers.

The house to the north side of this one had a roof terrace. If she could get to a top-storey window, she could sky-leap across to it. The terrace would provide a flat landing, while the alley that ran between the buildings would put some distance between her and the militia.

A thunderous crash announced that the front door was

open. Looking down the shaft of the stairs, she saw a hand grabbing the banister only two flights below, then slide up towards her, fast.

On the next landing, she swung right into a dark corridor and then into a long gallery cluttered with more filing cabinets and shelving. Pounding feet were not far behind. In her desperation, she tugged at one of the towering stacks to try to block their way. The shelves crashed down behind her, with a flurry of yellowing papers and a satisfyingly solid crack. She pushed the next row down, and the next.

Finally, she reached the window at the north end. The shutters' heavy iron panels and rusty hinges were a struggle to open, and sickening to touch. But at least there were no bars. Glory picked up a chair and smashed it through the glass. She summoned the knucklebone to her sweaty palm and swung herself up on to the ledge, bent almost double to fit within the opening. Shards of glass were still sticking up round the frame. Her flimsy silver dress offered no protection and soon it and the glass were speckled with blood.

Behind her, men were clambering over the tumbled racks. There was a warning shout, a stutter of gunfire. Too late: Glory had hurled the lodestone with as much force as she could manage over the alley and on to the terrace below. In seconds, she swung after it.

She landed painfully, the impact jarring upwards through her feet, knees, spine. Nonetheless, she dragged herself to her feet and plunged unsteadily on. The next leap took her to a new building, and a slope of uneven clay tiles. It was as well she didn't delay. A thud and crack behind her alerted her to the fact she'd been followed. There was another sky-leaper, wearing the militia's red uniform. A big man, he was also swift and sure-footed, and equipped with a headlamp to illuminate his path.

The night-time city gave off a murky glow, but Glory had no idea where she was heading or how far she'd come. Her only option was to keep going, ducking and diving among the chimney pots in an effort to lose whoever was on her tail. Her breath came in harsh gasps; her heart banged painfully against her ribs. It occurred to her that the other sky-leaper probably had a gun. She hoped the need to manage his lodestone meant he would have little chance to fire it.

San Jerico's dilapidated rooftops were crammed with balconies and sun-terraces, and an attendant obstacle course of deckchairs, barbecues and washing frames. Glory stumbled on in a kind of daze, barely aware of twisted ankles and scraped shins. It was nothing like sky-leaping at Wildings. She'd been frightened then, but Lucas had been there, and even those last panicked leaps had been fuelled with a kind of elation.

Yet despite the clumsy desperation of the chase, with every sky-leap, hunter and hunted were briefly transformed – liberated – by a moment of unearthly grace. Suspended in the air, their straining, sweating bodies became a thing of miracle. To people watching from below, she knew they must seem like angels, dancing through the night.

There was little doubt, though, that the man was gaining on her. Glory was starting to falter, all too aware that with just one misguided throw of the lodestone, one lapse of concentration, and she could fall. She had no idea whether the militia was tracking their progress, but she needed to return to street level. Maybe then she could find some nook or cranny to hide in, or get lost in a crowd.

The air had begun to whir, distantly. She was too distracted to process the sound but it nonetheless filled her with a new kind of dread. Across yet another chasm, yet another wall reared up before her, its parapet dauntingly high. Two storeys down was a wide balcony, its French windows open to the night.

Glory only hesitated for a moment. She flung the lode-stone, pushing it with her exhausted mind through the open window and into the room. Swooping after it, she had to bunch her knees to her chest in order to skim over the ledge of the balcony, and then twist sideways to avoid getting trapped in the narrow window frame. She landed in a heap on the floor, her right hand once more locked in contact with the lodestone. Looking up, she saw a huddle of shocked people, wine glasses in hands.

Before they could react, she got to her feet and ran on. A thump, accompanied by the sound of breaking glass, told her that her pursuer had not landed as neatly as she had. A woman began to scream. Glory flung herself into a hall, where a little girl in her pyjamas stood staring at her. 'Outta my hexing way,' she shouted hoarsely. Skidding down the stairs, she found a corridor ending in a fire escape, but there was a police car in the street below and so she had to go up again, up once more into the night –

The whirring, roaring night –

At first she didn't understand. Then she felt the wind

on her face, whipped up by the helicopter's blades. A beam of white light swung through the dark, and when it found her, all she could do was twist and flutter, helplessly, like a moth caught in a flame.

# CHAPTER 26

Raffi had got on the phone to his father minutes after he and Lucas arrived at the club, but the police were as much in ignorance about the circumstance of the raid as everyone else. Nobody seemed to know the outcome of the Red Knights' witch-hunt. All the Carabosse staff had been taken away for questioning. There were many conflicting reports, and increasingly wild rumours. The most persistent ones were that the girl was a foreign witch, an Anglo, and the attack had been on an important dignitary.

In the end, they returned to the penthouse. Without knowing the facts, there was nothing else they could do. Raffi persuaded Lucas to try to get some sleep, after father promised to wake him if he learned anything new. Lucas grudgingly obeyed. He knew he needed to be as strong and alert as possible if he was to be of any use the next day.

He dozed fitfully, his scraps of dreams full of Glory's escape or capture. Sometimes he was the person chasing her, and she was always twisting just out of reach. In others, he watched, helpless, as she leaped over a dark stream to where Gideon was waiting. He argued with her too, in increasingly tangled crescendos of accusation and appeal.

The morning's news sustained Lucas's sense of living in a bad dream. Raffi's father, Comandante Almagro, was able to confirm that the suspect witch was Gloriana Starling, and that she was now in the hands of the Red Knights. Furthermore, Senator Vargas was about to hold a press conference to announce his withdrawal from the presidential race, following a bane attack on his son.

At eight o'clock, the Almagro family gathered round the television for the announcement. Vargas's face was ashen and his voice quavered as he began his speech. Raffi translated for Lucas. The Senator had reason to believe the attack on his son was a warning shot, and although the perpetrator was in custody, there would be worse to come if he continued his campaign. His loved ones did not deserve to suffer the danger attached to his position. Therefore, to his great sadness and regret, he would no longer seek election as president.

The audience around the TV whistled and clapped. Several jeered. But the Comandante looked troubled. He drew his son aside for a private word. When Raffi returned to Lucas, his face was grave.

'My *papá*, he is glad this man, Vargas, is not to be head of our country. He is glad the whispers he heard are true. But he is unhappy it happened in such a way. To put the bane on a little boy is very bad thing. It makes my *papá* full of worries. Especially if it is found out that I, his son, knew the witch.'

'Glory's as innocent of this as you or I am,' Lucas said, with a snap of angry impatience. 'There's no way in hell she'd hex a child.'

It was just possible that Glory had got mixed up with whatever shadowy forces had gathered to bring Vargas down. Someone might have taken advantage of her anti-authoritarian, anti-Inquisition beliefs. Someone like . . . Rose Merle? But Lucas couldn't begin to understand how or why.

'Either it's a terrible mistake,' he continued, 'or she's been framed.'

Raffi chewed his lip anxiously. 'Innocent or no, she will be made an example. The president must be supporting Vargas in this and so will my *papá*. Many of the people will be very angry at what has happened. It will be a big trial, most famous.'

'That's if Glory even gets as far as a courtroom,' said Lucas. 'I've told you what Gideon's like. He's a maniac. I can't leave her with him and his gang.' He looked at Raffi hopefully. 'Unless . . . perhaps your dad . . .?'

'No,' said Raffi, reluctantly but firmly. 'My *papá* cannot use his police against the militia, not for this. It would make civil war – *revolución*.'

Lucas had feared as much. 'OK. But what about your dad's informants? Is there any way of finding out where Glory is being held?'

Here Raffi was able to help. The Red Knights had a shiny new office in the centre of San Jerico, which they liked to show off to their clients, but Glory had been taken to a hacienda out in the countryside, just over an hour's drive to the north of the city.

'But Lucas,' Raffi finished, 'you cannot go *Smash! Bang!* into there. You are a kid, OK? Civilian. Not a special super army guy.'

Lucas took a deep breath. It was time to name-drop WICA.

At first, Raffi simply burst out laughing. Then he was stupefied into silence. Finally, he started asking questions. It took all Lucas's patience to answer them. But he knew he had to convince Raffi of his credentials. In fact, he managed to give the impression that he broke into military fortresses on a regular basis. After all, he still needed Raffi's help. He couldn't get out to the hacienda on his own.

He needn't have worried.

'You are one crazy *bastardo!*' Raffi proclaimed admiringly, slapping him on the back, and immediately offering to be the getaway driver. Lucas had to work hard to convince him not to accompany him into the Red Knights' lair.

'It'll be easier for one person to sneak in than two. And it's what I've been trained for.'

'OK, so what about your secret spy *amigos*? Can they not help?'

Lucas had already decided against telling WICA what had happened. If there were other British operatives stationed in San Jerico, he was worried they would hinder rather than help him, or at the least cause a dangerous delay. The post-Wildings debrief had made it clear how low a priority Glory was for the authorities back home. As for the Wednesday Coven's contacts . . . well, even Troy didn't trust them.

'All you need to do is drive me there,' he told Raffi, with much more confidence than he felt. 'Give me an hour to get Glory out, and if there's no sign of us after that, then you can start making emergency calls.'

# CHAPTER 27

Glory was unconscious for the duration of the flight in the helicopter. The last thing she remembered was an acrid-smelling cloth being held to her face, and the world collapsing into darkness. When she woke up, she was lying on a bed in a strange room, and Rose Merle was watching her.

She had no idea where she'd been taken, what time or even what day it was. The window was tightly shuttered and the room was lit by a single bulb. It was small and bare but didn't feel like a prison. There were blue patterned tiles on the floor, and an old-fashioned china washbasin in the corner. No noise could be heard from outside.

Her arms were oddly heavy, and she realised she'd been bridled. The iron cuffs came almost up to her elbows. Groggily, she sat up and turned to where Rose was primly perched on a chair.

'Oh, Glory,' she said, and her mouth quivered. 'How *could* you?'

Glory scrubbed her eyes with her hands, tried to collect her scattered thoughts. Her body ached all over.

'I saved Esteban.' Her tongue stumbled over the words. 'Saved him. If – if it weren't for me –'

Rose shook her head sorrowfully. 'That's how we knew it was you who hexed him in the first place. It was a black bane, Glory. Only the witch who cast it could undo it. After you left the mansion, the fae-healer confirmed it. And then the Senator was sent this.'

She passed her a photocopied piece of paper. Spanish text, with the English translation written below: *This time was a warning. Next time, we will not be so merciful. We are everywhere, and we are watching. Withdraw your campaign.*

'You've got what you wanted,' Rose said. 'An hour ago, Senator Vargas told the nation he was pulling out from the presidential race. Whoever you're working for must be celebrating.'

Glory didn't respond. Instead, she heaved herself out of bed and went to the basin. She splashed cold water on her face. The iron chafed her arms. Her bruises throbbed and cuts stung. She was glad of it. The pain focused her.

She was thinking hard about the lifting of Esteban's bane; how sure she was that she'd failed, and how relieved she'd been when she had felt the malign fae leave his mind and body. But it wasn't her that saved him. In that respect, Rose was right: it had been a black bane. The witch who'd hexed him was the witch who had cured him.

'I feel such a fool for trusting you,' Rose went on, twisting her hands. 'It's my fault you wormed your way into Vargas's home. I can't forgive myself.'

Glory gave a cracked little laugh. 'You've got front, I'll say that for you. You must've done the set-up for Esteban's bane while we was both in the Senator's house.' She eased herself back on the bed. 'Which conveniently placed me – an unbridled witch – at the scene of the crime. Of course, you'd know how to get round the basic security systems, thanks to your day job in the militia . . . but that still leaves the question of how you hexed a bane through a bridle, without setting off no bells. How d'you manage it, I wonder?'

Even as she spoke, she thought of Cambion. Cambion – and Endor. They were most likely one and the same. First they recruited witches to the cause, then they removed their allergy to iron. She couldn't imagine how they did it but the result was clear. Rose was an unidentifiable, untraceable weapon.

Rose had listened to her speech with a sad gentle smile. 'I really wish you'd cooperate.' She gestured to their surroundings. 'This isn't so bad, you know. Other people wanted to put you somewhere *much* less comfortable. That's why it's important that you tell me the details of how you committed the crime, as well as who you're working for. It will make everything easier. I promise.'

Glory snorted. 'Very easy, I'm sure. Starting with a phone call to me lawyer and a visit from the UK ambassador; finishing with cake and balloons and a first-class ticket back to Blighty.'

'People who reject human laws don't deserve human rights.'

'Nice slogan. You think up Vargas's catchphrases, as well as torture his kid?'

Rose sucked in her breath. 'This is what the fae does to people. People like you – it corrupts them. Blackens the soul.

I can feel it now, in this room . . . The shadow and stench of it . . .' She shivered. 'And I won't be part of it. I *won't*.'

She got to her feet and rapped on the door. It was opened by a solider with a gun.

When she looked back at Glory, there were tears in her eyes. 'I'm sorry. I liked you, Glory. I really did. I don't want you to suffer. But I can see you're past saving.'

Glory wasn't fooled by the tears. Only Rose had had the means and opportunity to set her up. There had always been something odd about her, something wrong, right from the start. But Glory had been too soft and stupid to see the danger.

She paced around the little room but got no closer to working out where she was, let alone for how long she'd been unconscious. The shock of the bridling, in combination with the drug used to abduct her, had probably knocked her out for a good while.

Her body had now adjusted to the iron, so she decided to test it by drawing on her fae. The only result was a wave of icy nausea, and she nearly blacked out again. It would have been even worse with a head-bridle. How in hell had Rose managed it?

Fight or flee, flee or fight . . . There was nothing to make a weapon from. The chamber pot under the bed was plastic. So was the plate of refried beans and cassava bread that had been left for her on the floor. Even the bedding had some kind of plastic coating. She realised that this, and the absence of her trainers, was to prevent her using shoelaces or sheets to hang herself. A cramp of panic gripped her chest.

As a diversion, she started to inspect her bruises and

scrapes, trying to be practical about it. Her dress was torn and bloodstained, and the remains of her make-up was smeared down her face. To use the washing things left out on the basin seemed a kind of defeat – as if Rose was right, and she had something to be grateful for. But she did feel slightly better after cleaning herself and eating some food. She even put on the long grey shirt that was hanging on the door. Much as she hated looking the part of a helpless prisoner, she didn't want the soldiers eyeing her through the tatters of her dress.

These activities didn't take long. Afterwards, she sat on the bed and tried to calm the thin continuous trembling that had set up under her skin. The light was controlled from outside and she wished she could turn it off. She would have welcomed darkness, and the illusion of hiding. She closed her eyes instead and gripped the grimy white fuzz that was all that was left of the feather Sheba had given her. It had somehow got caught in her hair.

*There is a real world outside this,* she told herself, *with real people.* They will find out what's happened, and help will arrive. It has to. It *must.*

But she could be anywhere. She could have been taken out of the country. And who would be looking for her, anyway? The cat-woman? Candice? Lucas . . . who she'd told to stay away from her for ever?

The idea of him was unbearable, and so was the hope. She knew it might already be too late. At any moment, she could be made to permanently 'disappear'. And though they'd always wonder – Lucas, her dad, Troy, Uncle Charlie and the rest – they wouldn't ever know what had really happened.

Yet in spite of everything, she didn't believe this was her end. It was impossible, sitting here in her warm strong body, her beating mind, to imagine the absolute finality of death. Not this way. Not now.

The soldiers came for her about an hour after Rose left. A black hood was put over her face and her hands were tied behind her back. She was hustled up and down several stairs and round several corners at such speed she soon lost all sense of direction. The floor underfoot was polished stone and tiles. It added to her impression that she was being held in a house, rather than an institution.

When the hood came off, she found herself in a big bare room. The dark oak furniture was scuffed, but handsome, and the stucco walls were hung with moth-eaten tapestries. There was a fair-haired young man in a red military uniform at a desk. Rose was seated a little way behind him.

'So it's the Starling girl,' the young man drawled. 'I'm Lieutenant Hale. I've heard a lot about you.'

Before now, the most Glory had seen of Gideon Hale was a blurry photograph in a newspaper. She wasn't as surprised to see him as she should have been. He and Lucas were connected in the same way that she and Rose were. It made a strange kind of sense that they should all come together, here at the ends of the earth.

'Yeah, and I've heard about you and all.' She spat ostentatiously on the floor.

Gideon's lip curled. 'Since I am the only British officer in the Red Knights, our Commander-in-Chief has delegated your interrogation to me. He and Senator Vargas agreed it would be appropriate, especially in light of our prior connection.' His pale eyes flicked over her disdainfully. 'By which I mean, the criminal plot formed by the Wednesday Coven and rogue elements of WICA to bring down the British Inquisition.'

'Nice spin.' Glory looked at Rose. She was in her smart office suit, poised to take notes. 'Might be harder to white-wash your latest cock-up, though – the one about you recruiting an Endor witch into the militia. Or didn't you know your girlfriend's a hag?'

Gideon yawned. 'Usually, prisoners save the wild accusations until a later stage in the interrogation.'

'It's not so much of a shocker,' Glory continued, 'when you take a look at the family tree. Bad blood runs deep. Yeah,' she said to Rose, 'turns out your old man's Vince Morgan. That makes the two of us cousins of sorts. Small world, ain't it?'

'As far as I'm concerned,' said Rose, all sorrow and solemnity, 'my father was Lord Godfrey Merle. A great man, who died a tragic death. Mummy was already disturbed, but the fae sent her mad. Evil. And if it ever, God forbid, came to me, I'd cut it out.' Her voice rose, throbbing. 'I'd rather bleed to death than suffer that pollution.'

Glory wondered how she'd ever fallen for this woe-is-me act. It seemed ridiculous now. But Gideon, she was pleased to see, looked a little uncomfortable.

'I'd watch me back, if I was you,' she told him.

'And if I were you, I'd hold my tongue. Else I'll get a bridle to muzzle it.'

shook her head. 'I want to see the Senator. He's
who ordered my arrest. There's some things he
o hear –'

'Well, he doesn't want to see you,' Gideon said crisply.
 disgust him. The next time you face him will be in
urt, after you've confessed. And you *will* confess. I'll make
sure of it.'

He paused for effect. He evidently had the same theatrical instincts as Rose.

'The trial will be conducted behind closed doors,
since we don't want to give you a platform to promote your
vile beliefs. Young blonde girls make such photogenic
martyrs.' He leaned forward, fixing Glory with those curiously pale eyes. 'Because your time in public will come, of
course. We'll burn you in the Plaza de la República for all
Cordoba to see.'

Even though she'd known this threat was coming,
Glory's vision was briefly dappled with unsteadiness and
dark. For the meantime, at least, it gave her the courage of
someone with nothing to lose.

She stared straight back at Gideon, and didn't flinch.

'The president will light the balefire himself,' he went
on. 'He knows the people are out of patience. You are the
symptom of a wider disease – a foreign terrorist, taking
advantage of their country's tolerance. As your flesh melts
from the bone, there'll be dancing in the streets.' He smiled.
'Perhaps Lucas will come and watch. Lay a wreath on behalf
of the British nation. Shed some discreet tears.'

Glory kept her face wooden. She knew her lack of reaction was annoying him. But she could feel the trembling

starting up under her skin, and didn't know for
she could suppress it.

'I'm curious about the two of you,' Gideon contir
know Lucas spent some time undercover in your cess,
a coven. So why is he in San Jerico? Government busine
Or something personal? Could he be driven by missiona.
zeal to bring you to the ways of righteousness?' He put his
head to one side, considering. 'Either way, I think he's going
to be *very* disappointed when he finds out what you've been
up to.'

Again, no reaction. Gideon got up and came round to
where Glory was standing, her hands cuffed behind her back.

'We had to study the famous Starling Twins, back in
the Inquisition's training centre. They were a pair of deviant
sluts, and you're the same. Bringing you to the balefire will
be the latest victory in a long crusade.'

She managed to laugh. 'A crusader? Don't flatter yourself. I've known rent-a-thugs like you me whole life. Paterson
used you before, and Vargas is using you now. And so's she.'
She jerked her head at Rose. ''Cept you're too dumb to see it.'

Gideon hit her across the face, so hard her eyes watered.

'No –' Rose put her hands over her ears, her eyes
screwed up tight. 'I mustn't – I can't –'

Gideon ignored her. He took hold of Glory's face by
the chin and squeezed, hard.

'Don't cry, little witch-girl,' he said softly. 'Save it for the
balefire.'

The strange thing was, if Glory hadn't known better, she
would have seen Gideon and Lucas as two sides of the same

coin. They had the same kind of voice, the same kind of manner. There was even something familiar about the way Gideon wore his clothes and sat in his chair. But even if Lucas hadn't got the fae, and had become the High Inquisitor he believed he was destined to be, he and Gideon would still have been poles apart. Different species. Glory knew that with certainty now.

Gideon only hit her once. Afterwards, she was taken back to her room and left to 'consider her options'. A bit of mental softening-up before the main event. Rose had said nothing more, just blinked and quivered in the background.

She was put in a head-bridle. The effect of the iron was much stronger than when it was just the cuffs. A sleepy coldness flooded her veins. It took ice and water to drag out the stain of fae, fire to purge it. Fire and ice . . . It wasn't as if she hadn't been warned. Those dreams of the Burning Court had been a foreshadowing, after all.

Her mother had been in many of those dreams, yet during the long lonely wait that followed, Glory barely thought of Edie Starling. She wanted to think of flesh and blood people, not shadows or ghosts. The people who knew her and loved her, and had made a real difference to her life. The people who would remember her. She remembered them, and tried to be strong.

# CHAPTER 28

Witchwork was all very well, thought Lucas, but what he really wanted was one of those cunning and sinister gadgets the agents in MI5 and 6 used. Something with poisoned needles and electroshock shooters, hidden lasers and blades.

They're not going to kill her, he kept telling himself. They'll want to keep her for a show-trial. I can still fix this. I will find her and save her and make things right.

In the absence of hi-tech weaponry, he had to rely on another kind of asset: inside information. They knew Glory was being held in the grounds of an abandoned sugar cane plantation. The estate had changed owners many times in the past decades but had recently been bought by one of the Red Knights' clients. He planned to turn the place into a luxury hotel, but in the meantime allowed the militia to use it as an unofficial base. The police knew about it thanks to a tip-off from the caretaker.

Raffi had told his family that he and Lucas were spending the day trying to get help for Glory at the British Embassy. But after an off-the-record chat with one of his dad's lieutenants, he took Lucas to the caretaker's dilapidated bungalow on the edge of the city. At first, the man was reluctant to talk, but the wad of cash – Troy Morgan's cash that Lucas had brought – proved very persuasive.

He told them that the estate's owner employed him to keep an eye on the place when it was unoccupied and to tidy up after the soldiers had been there. Yes, he knew 'bad things' happened at the house, and he didn't like it, but he needed the money, and what was a poor widower to do? Yesterday evening, he saw they were getting the place ready for one of their 'special visitors', and was told not to come into work until further notice. After another helping of cash, he drew them a map of the place, including the room where the 'visitor' was going to be held. He was vague on the security details, but did warn them that bundles of barbed wire had been thrown on the roof to deter sky-leapers.

A plan was already forming in Lucas's head. It was not a particularly sophisticated one, and the risks were substantial, but it was probably his – and Glory's – best chance. It involved purchasing camouflage trousers and a jacket of the kind the Red Knights wore while on hacienda duty, as well as night-vision binoculars, a rope, a small sledgehammer, a chisel and a crowbar. And a knife.

Map secured and shopping done, he phoned Troy to break the news. It was a relief when the call went to voicemail. Then he paid a visit to Casa de la Armonia. Once the militia discovered Candice's connection with Glory, she might be in trouble, and he felt it only right to warn her. He also wanted to get access to Glory's things, preferably without having to root around in the rubbish.

He found Candice and Todd loading bags into a taxi.

'Hi, you don't know me but I'm a friend of Glor—'

'We don't know anything about her,' Candice gabbled. At the same time, Todd said, 'It was obvious she was trouble, right from the start.'

There was an embarrassed pause. 'What's Glory to you?' Todd asked suspiciously.

'We met at the club last week and had started to, well, hang out. Then I heard she'd been arrested. I just wondered if you'd —'

'There's rumours of a witch-hunt,' said Candice, taking a swig from a hip flask. 'We've gotta get out while we still can.'

'You're leaving the country?'

'Absolutely.' Todd slung a guitar case into the boot. 'Place is a hole anyhow. Sooner we're outta here the better.'

Candice hunched her shoulders defensively. 'It's not like there's anything *we* can do. Not if Glory's been messing with witch-crime. She'll drag the rest of us down with her.' Something about Lucas's expression gave her pause. 'Here,' she said, fumbling around her neck. 'Take it. I won't be needing it any more.'

It was a charm, of the kind the hotel receptionist had tried to sell him.

'I got Glory to craft it for me,' Candice said distractedly. 'Kept telling her she should make a business outta them. It's the real deal – not like the rubbish they sell on the streets.'

'Uh . . . thanks.'

She readjusted her oversized shades. Her hand shook a little. 'We'll be more help to her back in England. My family have connections, you know? Maybe we can send out a lawyer or whatever.'

'C'mon, babe,' called Todd, who was already sitting in the car. 'Check-in closes in an hour.'

As their taxi sped off, Lucas looked at the little glass bottle in his hand. It was on a chain and looked pretty flashy: a dab of blood congealed at the base, a piece of mirrored glass, some dried fern. Glory would have only made it to please her cousin, for there was little evidence such trinkets worked. But the raw ingredients of another witch's work could be useful – more useful than anything he might find in Casa de la Armonia's rubbish bin. Candice's parting gift was more precious than she knew.

Five minutes later, Raffi's car drew up. 'Hey, *amigo!*' he hollered from the window, music blaring from the stereo. 'Time to go kick some Red Knight ass!'

Glory lost track of time in that bright, empty room. She had no idea how long she'd been waiting before Rose came through the door and abruptly removed the bridle.

'So it's good cop, bad cop,' she said. The bridle had a tongue-prong to prevent speech, and her mouth was sore. 'Why bother? You know I ain't got nothing to say. I've been stitched up good and proper.'

Rose was muttering to herself; shaking her head, pacing the floor.

Glory watched her disgustedly. 'You was right to say your mum was a nutter. But you're a different kind of crazy. Endor got to you in Wildings, didn't they? Made you into a proper little fanatic –'

'SHUT UP,' Rose shouted, and put her hands round her ears. 'I can't even *think*. For God's *sake* –' Then she slumped down on the chair. 'I'm just . . . so . . . tired,' she said emptily.

Glory eyed the door. There would be soldiers outside it, but if she jumped Rose now, and if the girl was carrying a weapon, then maybe –

'I'm going to help you,' Rose announced. 'I have to . . . I can't stand this any more.' She got to her feet again, resumed her quivery pacing. 'I'll try . . . try to show you the way. The odds, though . . . it's bad . . . Dangerous.' Her head twitched. 'Should you – *could* you – risk it?'

Glory felt that if she made any sudden movement, or said the wrong thing, then the chance would be gone. She nodded, very slowly, forcing herself to be calm.

'I ain't got nothing to lose.'

Raffi and Lucas aimed to get to the hacienda by early evening, as the light was fading. Every minute of delay was another minute where Glory was at the mercy of Gideon, but Lucas had to be practical. Staging a break-in in broad daylight was not an option.

They drove out of the city, past the shanty towns with children selling fruit on the side of the road, and into a grassy open landscape. As the miles slipped by, the scrubby bushes and small twisted trees began to grow denser and taller.

Finally, they came to a sprawl of evergreen forest not far from the hacienda. Raffi parked deep within the trees. If the car was found and he was questioned, he'd say he'd got lost and was waiting for a friend to come and collect him.

Lucas hoped Raffi's identity would be protection enough. Even the militia couldn't afford to have the Chief of Police on the warpath.

For his own safety, he was wearing a personal alarm. If he got into trouble, he could send a signal to Raffi's monitoring device. Raffi would then call for back-up. He would be scrying on Lucas too; although they knew that much of the house would be iron-proofed.

*I can still fix this. I will find her and save her and make things right.*

He knew very well that the odds were against him. All he had was the white-hot certainty that he would do whatever it took.

The hacienda's grounds were enclosed by a high wall, whose top was lined with decorative yet vicious iron barbs. In the gathering darkness, Lucas prowled the perimeter, looking for an access point. He found one to the east of the property, where a tree's lower bough, thick and solid, overhung the top of the wall. He sky-leaped on to it, and then down into the greenish-black gloom. The ground was swampy, the undergrowth matted with brambles.

Trying to be as quiet as possible, he struggled through the thicket until the main property was in view. A weed-green drive wound round to the house, whose vaulted arcades and mottled mustard-coloured walls might have been romantic in other circumstances. All the windows were shuttered, and the doors hung with rust-spotted iron bells. The paved terrace was patrolled by militiamen.

*A good place for someone to disappear*, thought Lucas, lowering his binoculars.

At least it didn't have the defences of a purpose-built prison. The caretaker had said that only the ground and first floor were in use. Lucas also knew which entrance to target: a service yard at the back of the house, where an outside set of stairs led to the former servants' quarters. Shrinking back into the cover of the thicket, he began to work his way round. A guard was stationed in the doorway to the enclosure, but he had expected that. It helped that the man looked distracted and fidgety, his thoughts elsewhere.

Crouched behind a mass of rubbery ferns, Lucas took out one of the two coins he had been holding in his mouth and flicked it towards the soft mud by the guard's feet. The coin had been cleaned and polished to a bright silver. The shine drew the guard's eye and then, irresistibly, he was drawn to pick it up. *Gotcha*, thought Lucas. He took the other coin out of his mouth, slick with spit, and began to flip it from finger to finger. The tingle of fae sparked from his fingertips, turning both coins' gleam to a dazzle, a fleck of light that danced in the guard's eyes. The man stared at the silver in his hands, entranced.

When Lucas judged the guard's face to have sufficiently slackened, and his eyes sufficiently dulled, he got up from his hiding place and quickly and smoothly moved past the man and through the entryway. The longer he played with the coin, the longer the guard's trance would last, but he only needed a few minutes. It helped, of course, that he was wearing an elusion. If someone did get a glimpse of him in the dark, chances were that it would be too smeared and uncertain to make an impression.

Lucas ignored the door into the main house. There

would be a guard the other side, and in any case, he wanted access to the deserted upper storey. The door at the top of the stairs was locked, but he'd been practising his lock-picking since Wildings. Just over a minute after leaving his hiding place among the ferns, Lucas was in the building. The guard, meanwhile, was blinking and shaking his head. He put the coin in his pocket, conscious of a moment's inattention; that was all.

This part of the house was cramped and plain with a floor of rough wooden boards, as befitted servants' quarters. Lucas peeked out of the sagging shutters, judging the distance from the window to an outhouse rearing up from a tangle of brambles and rhododendrons. It would be a long leap, but not an impossible one.

He trod very quietly, knowing there could well be militiamen in the rooms below. When he put his ear to the floor, he thought he could hear rough male laughter, and was relieved. It meant he would be able to tell if Glory had company.

He was wearing a belt containing the tools for the non-witchwork aspect of his activities. They had learned Tap code as well as Morse code back in WICA, and once he knew Glory was below him, and alone, he would tap out a signal on the bare boards to alert her to his presence. Then he would take up the floorboards and knock through the plaster to make a hole in the ceiling of her cell. As long as they found some way of concealing or getting rid of the fallen plaster, they could hide the hole with a fascination. She would be bridled, of course, but his picks should deal with that – the locks on those cuffs were never very complicated. The plan was to pull her up through the floor and then sky-leap out of the window.

First, though, he had to find out exactly where she was. The caretaker had seemed sure of where she would be held, but Lucas couldn't leave anything to chance. When he reached the spot marked on the map, he lay down and once more listened with his ear to the floor. Silence. From inside his jacket he brought out a forked twig, sourced from a rubber tree near where Raffi had parked the car. A witch hazel was the traditional choice for blood-dowsing, but any tree would do, as long as the wood was still green with sap.

Lucas produced the charm that Candice had given him and which contained Glory's blood. He scraped the two ends of the forked twig against the reddish-black smear, then made a small cut in the centre of his palms. He held the two ends of the forked side in each hand, with the stem pointing straight ahead. Walking slowly, holding a picture of Glory in his mind, he waited for a dip or twitch as the dowsing-rod sensed the flow of her blood. Nothing.

He retraced his steps, moving from abandoned room to room. Still nothing. Either the caretaker was wrong and Glory was being held in an entirely different part of the building or, more likely, Glory wasn't in her cell because she had been taken away for questioning. The idea of her being frightened or in pain was choking, so that he suddenly couldn't think, almost couldn't breathe, and the flow of fae faltered. The effort it took to bring it back, and with it a picture of Glory – whole and unhurt – made his surroundings grow even darker and hazier, as if he was dowsing in a fog.

'Hold it right there,' a voice barked. 'Hands up.'

Slowly, very slowly, Lucas turned around. A Red Knight was pointing a gun at him. Gideon was standing behind. He looked amused. 'Really, Lucas,' he said, 'we must stop meeting like this.'

Lucas pressed the button on his silent alarm. Outside the hacienda, in a grove of rubber trees, the distress signal flashed its warning from Raffi's dashboard. Raffi had been scrying too, so as to be sure to be ready for the getaway. But it was too late for him to respond or even react. A brawny arm was encircling his neck. With a gun pressed to his head, he was dragged from the car.

While Lucas was cuffed and bridled and his clothing searched, Gideon prowled restively around the room. 'Your breaking and entering technique has got more ambitious,' he observed. 'Shame you didn't spot the security camera in the yard. This place might be a little rough around the edges, but it's not completely medieval.'

Lucas squared his shoulders. It was pointless, but he might as well go through the motions.

'I'm here in Cordoba on a counter-witch-terrorism assignment. I have a mandate from the British Inquisition as well as WICA, and am working alongside the Cordoban police –'

'Spare me the résumé,' said Gideon. 'I'm really not interested.' But although his voice was as languid as ever, Lucas sensed he was on edge. He kept touching things: the shutters, the wall, a pile of dust sheets. His face was flushed, his eyes bright. Excited, but jittery.

'And as a matter of fact, your timing's good. As a representative of Her Majesty's government, it's only appropriate that you should witness the judicial execution of one of its citizens.'

Lucas's mind raced. How long before back-up arrived? Could Raffi's father scramble a helicopter? There must still be things he could do, help that would come. The alternative was unthinkable. So he swept past it. 'You're to be judge, jury and executioner now? That's not multitasking – it's megalomania.'

Gideon shook his head regretfully. 'I'm afraid in this case justice will have to be applied retrospectively. The hag-bitch is already dead. You're too late in that respect – she died an hour ago, while attempting to escape. But we intend to burn the body all the same.' He laughed. 'You always wanted to be an inquisitor, didn't you, Stearne? Well, this way, you still get to watch a balefire.'

# CHAPTER 29

Lucas was tugged back to consciousness by a dull pain at the back of his skull. For a moment it wasn't so bad, because he couldn't work out where he was and why. Then reality crashed back. He had lunged at Gideon, a rush of hate surging through his body, and then something had knocked him into darkness.

When he was able to raise his groggy head, Lucas found he was tied to a chair set in front of a pair of French windows. Beyond the glass, he had an impression of high walls covered in vines, carved stone columns, a mossy fountain. The view, though, was dominated by the pyre set in the middle of the courtyard.

It was lit up like a film set. As the Cordoban national anthem played from a crackly stereo, two Red Knights secured a body to the stake. The limbs lolled awkwardly, like those of a broken doll. Under the grey prison shift the body looked both frail and lumpen. Lucas couldn't see a face, only a spill of bright blonde hair. Then the soldiers stood back.

At that, Lucas made a sound he didn't recognise: raw

and animal. And Gideon, who was standing by the window, laughed again.

Rose was beside him, his arm around her waist. There were chairs for them too. Unlike the lowly henchmen who were gathering under the colonnade, the pair of them would recline in comfort behind the glass. They wouldn't want the smoke stink getting into their clothes.

Gideon moved to check the camera he had set up on a tripod. The film would be something for his private viewing pleasure but also, presumably, for the good folk of Cordoba. Justice must be seen to be done – even though it wouldn't be half as exciting with a dead body. Clever Glory, to spoil his fun.

Lucas stared and stared, trying to imprint her face on to his brain for all time, even though his last glimpse of her was already disfigured. There was an ugly bruise on one cheek. And blood too around her eyes and nose.

'How – did – she – die?' he asked laboriously, one resisted word at a time.

Gideon shrugged. 'She must have tried to work her fae through the iron. It brought on some kind of haemorrhage.' He eyed Lucas with genuine curiosity. 'A girl like that . . . Did you really care for her? Or was she just a bit of coven rough on the side?'

Lucas barely heard him. There was white static in his head, a violent shaking building up in his body.

Rose had been staring fixedly through the glass. 'I'm sorry,' she mouthed to the body on the pyre. Her voice was a whisper, her face white. 'I never wanted –'

'What's the matter with you?' Gideon said irritably. 'You've been acting out ever since we got down here.'

She didn't respond, just shook her head, as tears welled in her violet eyes.

However, Gideon's exasperation didn't last long. The jittery excitement Lucas had sensed in him earlier was still there, still fizzing in the air around him. Lucas briefly wondered about Raffi, and what could have happened to him, but he didn't have the strength to think about it. It was too late, anyhow. Everything was too late.

Gideon said something into his two-way radio, and there was a flurry of action around the pyre. He made one final adjustment to the camera and took his seat, pulling it right up in front of the window. 'Burn time.'

As the balefire was lit, Rose gave a small muffled cry.

Lucas kept silent. Though he couldn't move away, he could close his eyes. He tried to block out the hiss of the flames, the crackle of the wood. Tried to ignore the tang of smoke he could already sense – or did he just imagine it? – clinging to his nostrils and hair.

Instead, he tried to remember Glory as she truly was. The pride and grace of her, swooping through the night skies above Wildings, dancing through the London chimney tops. How her eyes could look so black, yet be so bright. The waxing and waning of her Devil's Kiss, as she leaned towards him in candlelight. Loss spilled through him, unstoppably now.

He felt a clutching pressure on his arm. He thought it was Gideon, forcing him to watch. But it was Rose.

He looked: he couldn't help it. The flames had already caught the hem of Glory's clothes. Flames were licking greedily at her bare feet. But some of the wood must have been damp, for the smoke was so thick it was soon almost hiding the pyre.

Rose bent down and whispered to him. He twisted away, tried to block out whatever poison she wanted to pass on. Her guilt or regret was almost as repulsive to him as Gideon's gloating.

'Lucas,' said Glory's voice in his ear. 'It's me.'

'Should you – *could* you – risk it?' Rose had asked, back in the prison room.

And Glory had said yes, because anything was better than this, and what would come after. Even though she thought Rose was probably mad as well as bad, and was clutching her head with twitching hands.

But then, as so often before, Rose snapped into efficiency.

'Sorry,' she said. 'One of my headaches. Such a bore . . . Here – you know what to do, right?'

She produced colouring pencils and paper from her handbag, like someone getting ready to entertain a child. Or a witch, preparing a glamour.

'I'll say you overpowered me with your Dark Arts,' she said, as she set about undoing Glory's cuffs, 'and stole my identity. These people are too stupid and arrogant to understand witchwork. I won't be able to give you long, though: half an hour at most.'

Glory eyed her dubiously. The risk wasn't just hers; Rose was endangering her own position. Rose saw and understood her look.

'I *have* to do this. I really must. And,' she took a deep

breath, 'It's difficult to be sure but I think this is what I really want. For *real*. Do you understand?'

She didn't wait for Glory's answer, just pressed her knuckles against her eyes, took another steadying breath. 'All right. Once you're disguised as me, your best route out is through here.' She was using chalk to sketch a map on the floor. 'I often walk in this part of the grounds if I've got a headache and Pedro, the guard stationed there, isn't too bright. There are cameras about the place, but it's very hit and miss. You should be OK if you head to the walled garden on your right. From there you can hide in the forest, or get to the main road, hitch a lift. I don't really care. That's your problem.'

Glory nodded through this and other instructions, though she was struggling to keep up. The iron had left her limp and drained, and she was worried about the glamour. Witchwork wasn't much better at altering body-shape than it was at disguising age. A glamour could clothe her body with an impression of Rose's taller, slimmer frame, but the measurements wouldn't stand up to inspection. Would they get away with it?

Rose, however, was already sketching her face, examining her features with impersonal concentration. Glory picked up her pencils and began to draw. Her own portrait first, followed by the other girl's. Red hair, purple eyes, white cheeks. Then the details: the puckered burn marks on Rose's right hand, the faded lilac blot on her neck, the shiny rounded tips of her fingernails. The effort it took to use her fae was dragging. Her Seventh Sense, numbed by the iron, was sluggish and thin.

Rose was the first to finish. She sat back on her heels, drawings in her hands.

'Are we really some kind of cousins?' she asked. 'Is Vince Morgan really my father?'

'Uh-huh. Your Granny Lily was my great-aunt. So you're a Starling girl, same as me.'

Rose frowned. 'I know that should mean something. That it's something I should *feel*. But I can't. At least, not very often.' She smoothed down the paper restlessly. 'Sometimes I don't think I really exist.'

Glory worried Rose was about to flip out again. Yet despite Rose's bizarre pronouncements, this was the first honest conversation they had had. She couldn't let the chance go.

'Can you tell me what happened, when you went to Cambion's clinic and had the surgery? Do you really not remember?'

'I honestly don't. It was to do with Alice, I think. Then there was something about – about a gingerbread man.'

'Alice? Is that who gives you your orders?'

'It's what I called my fae. Back at the school, with Dr Caron.'

'So who've you been working for all this time?'

The girl's eyes widened. 'Oh, it's just me. And Alice, in my head.'

'Alice . . . talks to you?' This wasn't anything like Glory's experience of the fae.

'Not exactly. I feel her words, like an echo. A dark echo. It's because of the gingerbread man.' She sighed. 'I know that doesn't make sense. But Alice wanted me to hex

Esteban, and then she made me put the blame on you, after I asked you to help cure him.'

'But I couldn't take off the bane,' said Glory. 'You must've done it yourself.'

'Yes.' Rose rubbed her head distractedly. 'Sometimes I can boss Alice, instead of her bossing me. But it never lasts. That's why we have to hurry, you see . . . before things change again.' She gave herself a shake. 'Ready?'

Rose pulled out a single red hair, tore off a piece of fingernail, and smeared Glory's picture of her with moisture from her eye and sweat from her palm. Glory reciprocated. They struck a match, burned their self-portraits, and mixed the ash with the other material. Then they pressed the amulets between their palms, and whispered each other's names as they stared into the other's eyes. In different circumstances, the set-up might have been almost comical. Yet Glory had never performed witchwork with such seriousness.

Seconds later, she was gazing at her own face. Rose had done a good job. The eyebrows weren't quite dark enough, perhaps, and the nose was slightly too hooked. But she'd got the bruise where Gideon had hit her, and the scratches and cuts on her arms.

Rose examined her handiwork in a compact mirror, before passing it to Glory. Glory looked into the glass and saw that she was beautiful. Her very own fae-tale transformation: from witch to princess.

Quickly and silently they exchanged clothes. Glory's prison shift was shapeless enough to hide the change in build, and Rose must have dressed with this in mind. She wore loose-fitting trousers and blouse. The shoes pinched Glory's feet, and the trousers were too long, but she wasn't making any complaints.

Rose pinned the glamour's amulet into the roots of her now blonde hair. Glory tucked hers into the belt of the trousers. She put Rose in the cuffs, as gently as she was able, and picked up the bridle.

'It wasn't Mummy's fault, you know,' Rose said abruptly. 'She thought she was helping me. She didn't want me to suffer like she did. She was a different person before she became a witch. So was I,' she said, as Glory prepared to lock her in to the head-cage. 'Before Alice took over. Please . . . will you take my hand?'

Glory hesitated. She didn't like to look at her; this mirror-sister, this crooked twin. But though she kept her eyes lowered, she did as Rose asked. The hand had her own chipped red nail polish on the bitten-down nails, but it was Rose's warmth she felt under the illusion.

'I'm glad this is nearly over,' Rose said softly. 'And when it is, I want you to forget me. This isn't who I am. The person I was disappeared long ago.'

The guard outside had been tranced, or something similar. He was leaning against the wall with his eyes glazed and body motionless. Rose had made her preparations well. But at the end of the corridor, Glory lost her nerve. It was somehow more frightening being outside the cell than inside it. She had a sudden fear that the whole business was another of Rose's traps. She thought of all the questions she should have asked her while she had the chance, and in the midst of her confusion turned right when she should have turned left. It took several long sweaty minutes to put herself back on the right path.

The house was vast and rambling, badly lit, and with a derelict air. She tried to walk like someone who knew exactly what she was doing and where she was going. Rose had said that Gideon was on a conference call with his superiors, but Glory knew if she ran into him it would all be over. She might be able to manage an approximation of Rose's cut-glass accent that would fool a foreign soldier. With Gideon, she'd have no chance.

Finally, more by luck than good management, she approached the outside door Rose had directed her to, the one with carved stone vines around the frame and a pug-faced soldier, Pedro, on guard. She started the performance; clutching her head and grimacing, Rose-style. The guard stood to attention and opened the door. Giving him a distracted smile, she moved past into the warm damp night, her heart speeding so fast she thought she was going to be sick.

One step into freedom. Then another, and another one after that –

And then, the shouts. The pounding feet, the cries to stop. 'Miss! Witch-attack!' the guard was shouting at her, over a crackle of static from his radio. 'Miss, you must return. Big danger! *Atención, peligro!*'

Almost before she knew it, she was hustled back into the house, along a corridor and up some stairs. A door was slammed behind her, and another soldier took up position outside. This time it was for her own protection.

What had Rose tried to do? Or had there been some attempt at rescue? From the guard's excitable Spanglish, it sounded as if the captive harpy had tried to work some evil, but been struck down in a faint, and they were trying to revive her now . . . There had been something final and foreboding in the way Rose said goodbye, and it chilled Glory to think of it.

Rose's room wasn't much more luxurious than the one Glory had been imprisoned in. The window was open and overlooked the front drive, but was too small to squeeze out of. While she tried to work out her next move, she turned the lamp down low and held a damp flannel to her brow, as if she really did have a headache. Pretending to be too ill to speak or move wasn't much of a cover but it was all she had.

Her usual decisiveness had deserted her. The bridling had left her weak and cold. For possibly the longest half an hour of her life, she lay on the bed trying to think of what she should do, while every nerve and muscle was tensed for the door to burst open, for the shouts and threats and fists to start.

Incredibly, they didn't come. Rose must still be alive and her amulet still hidden. At one point Gideon looked round the door, face tight.

'You've heard the news. Stay here till we know more, OK? I've got to phone the wretched Senator –'

Glory lay in the shadows. She rubbed her forehead, let out a faint moan.

Gideon made a sound of annoyance. 'Really, you need to sort these migraines out. You're no use to me if you're ill.'

She risked a faint whisper. 'Sorry.'

'Here.' He put a small pistol on the bedside table. 'If we're under attack, you should be armed.'

And then he was gone again, and with him the guard at the door, and after another five jittery minutes, she decided to make a move, only for Pedro to come rushing back with the news that an intruder had been captured, and the hag-bitch was dead.

In the viewing room, Glory stood rigidly by the window, forcing herself not to look at Lucas strapped in the chair. Having him there, so perilously close, was almost as wrenching as watching Rose on the balefire.

For her vision had come true after all. Here was the Burning Court and balefire, here was the audience behind the glass. There she was at the stake; and also here in the viewing chamber, staring into her own face as the first flames spat upwards. And although some things didn't belong – the marble columns, the lush vines, Gideon's arm curled loathsomely around her waist – they only made the experience more surreal, more nightmarish, than any dream.

She couldn't forget the feel of Rose's hand in hers or the emptiness in her voice as she said goodbye. She had been fortunate that Gideon was too preoccupied to pay much attention to her, but listening to him relate events over the phone, she gathered that when a solider had gone to check on the prisoner, she had uttered a piercing cry and then collapsed. Blood had run from her eyes and nose, but there had been an uncanny smile on her lips. She had remained unconscious, possibly in a coma, for nearly an hour before her heart had stopped.

Depending on the temperature of a fire, it could take anything from one to three hours for a body to burn. A glamour could survive the destruction of its amulet, and even the death of its witch, as long as the witchwork was strong and had been worn close to the body for a substantial amount of time. Rose had collapsed about ten minutes after Glory left her. She had remained alive, but unconscious, for another forty-five. Glory calculated the illusion would outlast her by about forty minutes. By the time the pyre had been built, Lucas captured, and the fire lit, there were perhaps only fifteen minutes to go before the glamour expired.

Or maybe her own glamour would be the first to fail. The bridling had sucked the life out of her fae, and although the effect was temporary, she knew the witchwork on her amulet was dangerously weak. She could be imagining it, but the burn marks on her hand already seemed a little faded.

'I'm sorry,' Glory whispered to the ghost of Rose Merle. 'I never wanted –'

Smoke from the damp wood had begun to billow, black and thick. The Red Knights stationed at the hacienda's main entrance points were still on duty, but the others were all watching the balefire. Soon they, and most of the garishly-lit courtyard, were hidden by a rancid fog.

It was time for Glory to make her move. When she took Lucas by the arm, she was shaken to see him recoil from her with such hatred. But as soon as she said his name, Lucas squeezed his eyes briefly shut, and the juddering tautness she could feel in his body dissolved away.

Their hands touched when she loosened the rope binding him to the chair. Then Glory went to Gideon, leaned her head against his. As he turned round, she felt the curve of his cheek. That was when she stuck the barrel of the gun in his ribs.

'You're burning the wrong witch,' she whispered into his ear, a loving smile on her face, in case somebody caught sight of them through the smoke. She pulled him up and round so that his back was to the window. 'Now you're going to escort us outta here. Keep quiet and play nice, and you might make it out yourself.'

Lucas got to his feet. He was dazed but calm, though he avoided her eyes. She understood. She didn't want to look at him either – not so long as she was hiding behind a dead girl's face. And yet the impulse to go to him was immediate; she could feel the movement of springing forward gather in her body. She forced it down.

Gideon, meanwhile, seemed emptied of everything but stunned horror. She had expected threats, snarls, bravado. Instead, he was limp and unresisting.

At Glory's direction, he fumblingly picked up the chain attached to Lucas's cuffs and opened the door. She walked beside him, holding the point of the pistol to his side. The soldier outside stood to attention and Glory smiled Rose's dazzling smile. 'The prisoner's getting agitated. We're taking him back to his cell,' she said in her best posh voice, hustling the trio past. Gideon kept his silence, although she thought she could hear his teeth chattering. Coward, she thought with contempt.

Somehow she got the three of them down the hallway and round the corner. Lucas came to a stop.

'I came with Raffi. Is he a prisoner here too?'

'Raffi?' She shook her head. 'No. No, I ain't heard nothing about that.'

Lucas bit his lip, but they kept moving through the shadowy depths of the house. Glory was worried that the glamour on Rose was already wearing off; that lines of red hair had begun to streak the blonde. Or that her own brown-black eyes were showing through the illusion of their violet covering. And as soon as anyone else saw Gideon they would realise something was wrong. His skin was a sickly green and he was panting as if he'd run a marathon. His legs buckled, and he swayed drunkenly in her grip.

Glory gave him an angry shake. 'Get a grip of yourself. We ain't done with you.'

He barely seemed to notice. 'Can you hear it?' He clutched at her with clammy fingers. 'The hissing . . .'

'What's he talking about?' Lucas asked.

'I dunno,' she said, but she felt a creeping in the pit of her stomach.

'Playing ill now, are you? Think you can trick us?' Lucas was whispering – they all were – but with a stab of violence in his voice.

'It can't be a trick – I can *see* them.' Sweat was pouring down Gideon's face. '*We have to keep them away –*'

'Keep who away?' Lucas asked.

His eyes darted fearfully. They were clouded, with a

greenish tint. 'The *snakes*. In – in the shadows there. There! I can hear them . . . the slithering – they're getting closer . . .'

Glory swallowed hard. 'He's been hexed.'

'What?'

'It's the same bane . . . the bane what Rose cast on the Senator's kid.'

'And Rose is dead,' said Lucas. They looked at each other in fearful understanding. It meant the bane was irreversible.

Somehow, Rose had known her time was up. Even before coming to see Glory in her cell she must have made her preparations. Vengeance had been done and Glory, raised in the tradition of coven blood feuds, should rejoice. Instead, she remembered reaching into Esteban's mind, and how the bane had nearly overcome her. The rasping darkness, the taste of bile . . . She felt a wave of exhaustion and disgust. For it seemed she had been here before: fleeing through a strange house with a captive inquisitor, while another witch was engulfed by flames. 'Lucas – I don't – I – what shall we do?'

'Where's the nearest exit?'

'Through here.' She had been heading for the door she'd gone through earlier, with the vague idea of forcing Gideon to requisition a car, and tell his henchmen they were taking Lucas to another detention facility. No chance of that now. 'There's a guard, though, and –'

'So let's get him to help.'

Glory released Lucas from the cuffs he'd kept on for appearance's sake and the two of them dragged Gideon into a small anteroom. He didn't attempt to resist them, instead he clutched at them with desperate hands. The bane was progressing much faster than Esteban's; bloody scribble marks had started to wriggle up from under his skin. The horror of it was catching: they were both sweating and shaking too by the time they managed to disentangle themselves.

Lucas took up position behind the door. Glory ran to summon the guard.

'Oh! Help me, please help – Lieutenant Hale's been attacked. More witchwork – *hurry* –'

The Red Knight pounded after her and into the room where Gideon was rocking and moaning on the floor; snake marks, like living tattoos, writhing over his face. The man didn't even have time to cry out before Lucas struck him over the head with a chair.

He staggered and fell, and between the two of them, they managed to disable him. Lucas tied him up with the cuffs and rope that had been previously used on him, tearing a strip off the man's shirt for a gag.

Glory was watching Gideon. He needed no restraints: his eyes were nearly completely clouded over, and soon he would be locked in the bane's trance.

'Help me,' he rasped. 'You . . . can . . . *help me* –'

'I can't,' she said with a tremor of pity, in spite of herself. 'The only person who could is dead on your balefire.'

'Leave him,' said Lucas harshly. 'We have to go.'

They took the Red Knight's set of keys, and his communications radio. One of the keys opened the door with the carved vines around the frame. Together, they slipped through it.

One step into freedom. Then another, and another one after that.

# CHAPTER 30

There were no shouts, no gunfire, no alarms. The identity of the girl on the balefire hadn't yet been discovered, Gideon and the guard hadn't yet been missed. Everyone was still enjoying the show.

Glory seemed to know where she was going and Lucas followed her blindly. Thunder growled in the darkness, the air was hot and close. They ran into the ruins of a walled garden, and then an overgrown orchard. The top of its walls were barbed, but half-fallen in, and they sky-leaped into the tangle of trees beyond.

Lucas thought they were to the north of where Raffi had parked the car. He felt another twist of anxiety, but there was nothing for it but to keep going: a headlong scramble through the undergrowth, tripping over roots, ferns, brambles. Rain began to patter overhead, then drum against the leaves. It seemed as if they had been running for miles, for hours, for ever.

'Stop,' he called out at last, in a muddy clearing. 'Where are we going?'

Glory turned. Rose turned. Two girls in one. He was

chasing a ghost. 'I don't know. I just – we have to get away.'
Her breath came fast. 'We have to keep running –' She made
a stumbling step towards him. 'Lucas . . .' Tears glittered in
her eyes. Rose's eyes.

'No. Wait –'

She flinched.

'I still can't believe . . . I have to see you. The real you,
I mean.'

Lightning flared as, haltingly, he reached out to touch
her hair. It seemed as if the rain was washing the red away,
but it was the witchwork that was fading. As he stroked the
damp strand curling by her cheek, it lightened under his
fingertips, gleamed blonde.

Glory gave a small gasp. She closed her eyes; when she
opened them, another streak of light revealed the lilac dark-
ening to blue, then brown. He traced the line of her brows,
and watched them darken too, grow straight and strong
beneath his touch. As he cupped her face in his hands,
brought it close to his, its features shifted and blurred . . .
the last of Rose Merle vanishing into the night.

There were tears on Glory's face, but no blood. He
brushed his lips against the bruise, livid on her cheek. He
bent his head to kiss the bloom of fae on her collarbone. The
rain crashed through the trees. He said her name. Her arms
tightened fiercely around him, even as her mouth trembled
under his. Then she was kissing him back.

The roar of water was deafening, the trees seemed to be
cracking under its force. Red mud and black leaves sloshed
around their ankles. They were streaming with water,
dissolving with it; into the night, into each other.

A beam of brightness swooped through the downpour and caught them in its light.

'Good to see the two of you are on top of the situation,' said a voice. American, amused.

And behind it, 'Lucas, you dirty dog! This is hot stuff, *amigo!*'

Raffi, and Jenna White.

The voicemail that Lucas left for Troy Morgan had produced results. As soon he'd picked it up, Troy got hold of Zoey Connor at WICA and Jonah Branning at the Inquisition, demanding action. 'Your cousin,' Jenna remarked drily to Glory, 'appears to have quite a forceful personality.' WICA knew that Section Seven had an agent in Cordoba on the trail of Cambion. After some inter-agency haggling, Jenna White was contacted and tasked with finding Lucas and Glory's whereabouts. She had arrived at the hacienda just in time to intervene in Raffi's capture by a Red Knight. 'This spy-girl is super kick-ass! She takes the *bastardo* down!'

Raffi and Jenna were debating whether to stage an intervention themselves or wait until Comandante Almagro and the police arrived, when the scrying-bowl showed Rose – or so it appeared – turn on Gideon. The police were now on their way to the hacienda, but Lucas, Glory and Raffi were travelling south in Agent White's armoured jeep. Section Seven had a lead on the location of Cambion's clinic, and Jenna had been heading there before the diversion to the hacienda.

Now and again Raffi would turn round in his seat to

look at Glory and Lucas in the back, and grin at them broadly, or give the thumbs-up. They were sitting a respectable distance apart, though their hands rested casually against each other in the space in between. Whenever they caught the other's eye they smiled, then looked away, collusive and a little shy. They were very tired. Lucas thought how good it would be to fall asleep, knowing Glory was beside him.

Her voice dragged with exhaustion as she recounted what had happened between her and Rose. 'She were being controlled in some way. Voices in her head. And that thing with the gingerbread man – it didn't make no sense at first, but now I'm thinking she might've meant a poppet.'

Jenna shook her head. 'You can tell if a poppet's at work. It's that dead-eyed look people get, and the way their bodies jerk about, like they're on strings. Rose may have been a bit schizo, but it's clear she passed for normal most of the time.'

'And if a witch was directing her through a poppet, they would have had to keep close by,' Lucas pointed out. 'You need to be within viewing distance.'

Glory bit her lip. 'Whatever it was, she must've got free of it in the end. Though I think she guessed, somehow, that she weren't going to recover.'

'Well, I've had enough of guesswork,' Jenna said shortly. 'It's time for solid facts. Let's hope Cambion HQ can provide them.' She still had her high ponytail, and a trace of pink lipgloss, but the cheerleader peppiness was long gone.

So far, there were no signs of pursuit. By now the police would have reached the hacienda, where the Red Knights must be struggling to contain the fallout from their lieutenant's condition and the exposure of the balefire witch. Jenna said that Gideon had overstepped the mark in any case. Neither his superiors in the Red Knights nor Senator Vargas would have been happy with the extent to which he had taken matters into his own hands. 'The guy probably had a few screws loose even before the hexing.'

Lucas was mostly conscious of the ache at the back of his head where he'd been knocked out, and the steady warmth of Glory's hand. He did not want to think of Gideon or his fate. A bane of that nature was too powerful for the mind and body to withstand. Gideon would not live long under such pressure. Lucas searched himself for pity and found none. It would come later, perhaps. He supposed that would be a good thing.

At last, he allowed himself to float into sleep. In the front of the car, Raffi was renewing his charm offensive on Jenna. 'But how old are you *really*?'

'Too old for you,' she said, with a flick of the ponytail. 'And too smart besides.'

It was mid-morning before they reached their destination. The rain poured all night, turning the roads to churning red mud, the potholes to oily ponds. As the sun came up, a smudge of mountains loomed ahead, their peaks dusted with rose.

They stopped only once, at a run-down petrol station attached to an even more dilapidated motel, to use the bathroom facilities and get food. Jenna had a medical kit in the car to deal with Glory's scrapes and bruises, but when Raffi heard of the blow Lucas had taken to his head, he asked, with uncharacteristic diffidence, if he could lay his hands on the spot. As he did so, Lucas could feel the fae flowing through, warm and faintly tingling, and the last of his headache vanished. 'Maybe I will become super-kick-ass-spy-doctor,' Raffi said. 'Fighting evil and mending bones!'

At long last, the jeep jolted along a steep stony track into an Amerindian village on the outskirts of the forest. Earth paths wound round small houses of bark, mud and thatch. Most of the inhabitants were out tending to their crops, leaving behind a few elderly women chewing plantain in the sun, and toddlers scuffling among scrawny chickens. Nobody seemed particularly interested in their arrival.

Perhaps the locals were used to strange visitors. There was a tiny airstrip just outside the village, and near to that, a very different kind of construction. It was a low white house, built on sleek modern lines, and approached by a rhododendron-lined drive. The sign above the porch said *Rising Sun Health Spa & Holistic Retreat*.

The door was wide open. Jenna and Glory went in first, as they were the only ones who were armed. They found themselves in a reception as plush as any Harley Street clinic's: high-end lifestyle magazines on the table, ornate – though wilting – flowers in a vase. There was nobody on guard, nobody on duty behind the gleaming glass desk. A chair overturned on the floor struck an oddly discordant note.

As the foursome moved through the building, they saw more signs of a hasty but efficient exit. The office had been cleared of all paperwork, and there were no computers or telephones, just a few wrenched-out cables. They found a few curls of shredded paper on the floor in the corridor, which Jenna carefully scooped up and put in an evidence bag. There was a small guest house attached to the back. Its rooms didn't look as if they'd ever been inhabited. The surgery and consulting room drew another blank.

While the others continued to search the place, Raffi went to talk to the locals. He came back shaking his head. 'The receptionist and the doctor – *americano*, the lady said – left last night in a little plane.'

They had regrouped in the surgery. There was an operating table, an empty trolley full of empty trays, and some impressive-looking machinery.

'They must have left in a hurry if they had to leave all this behind,' Lucas said. 'It looks top of the range stuff.'

'Yes,' said Raffi. 'To put implants into brains. I saw a very good film about this. They use microchips to make an army of robot-people to take over world.'

'You don't need science for that,' said Jenna slowly. 'Witchwork could do it just as well. Only with golems, not robots.'

Lucas frowned. 'Golems? They're just a fae-tale version of a person who's being controlled by a poppet. I thought we ruled that out.'

'No, golems are different. I've been thinking about it. OK, the fae can get into a person's mind through a poppet, but it doesn't have as much control over the victim's thoughts as it does over their actions. On one level, the person is aware of what's happening to them.

'With a golem, now, there's no crafting dolls to stick

pins in or tie into knots. It's about possessing the heart and mind. Creating a body without a soul.'

'So how d'you build one of these bad boys?' Glory asked in her most sceptical tone. She was usually only too eager to believe in the wonders of witchwork. Jenna, however, was bringing out her prickly side.

'In the stories, a golem is created from dust and fae,' Jenna said. 'The witch gives it life by inscribing sacred words on its body, or sealing them inside its mouth.'

Glory scowled. 'Rose was a real person. As real as you and me.'

'Well, this isn't a fae-tale. But maybe Rose did have something sealed inside her. Maybe Cambion used modern surgical techniques to plant something in her head, something crafted with fae. Something that would suppress her own powers and bind her to those of another witch.'

'Aha!' Raffi exclaimed. 'Is that why Rose's banes set off no bells and why she could wear the bridles?'

'You got it,' said Jenna, with a brief return of her cheerleader twinkle. 'Iron doesn't react to the act of witchwork, but to the source of its fae, right? So whoever was hexing the banes was doing it at a distance, too far off for the iron to sense them. Endor is creating witches who can't be detected.'

'And who don't even know they're still witches,' Lucas said. 'Let alone that they're being used as some kind of . . . weapon.'

'Rose knew she were being manipulated,' Glory insisted. 'That's why she used to get so weird and twitchy. And she managed to get free of it to help me. She must've used her own fae then.'

Jenna shrugged. 'Rose told you she got some kinda virus after the surgery. Then there's the way she died, which sounds like a brain haemorrhage. So maybe something went wrong during the operation that wasn't ever put right.' She gestured to the machines around them. 'I bet half this junk is just for show, anyways.'

'You know others that have had this procedure?' Raffi asked.

'Section Seven has some ideas.' She looked at Lucas guardedly, and he guessed she didn't want him mentioning her initial lead: Chase Randolph Parker III, the Supreme Court judge's son. 'Wildings was the main recruiting ground. At the moment, we believe Dr Caron was working alone there, and that the school governors hired her in good faith. The next stage is to get a warrant to shake the place down.'

'Why use kids?' said Raffi. 'Why not the grown-ups?'

'Because kids are much less likely to arouse suspicion,' Lucas answered.

'Yeah,' said Glory. 'And we're s'posed to be easier to push around and all. The perfect recruits. Endor, WICA and the Inquisition – great minds think alike.'

Lucas heard the edge of bitterness in her voice. 'The thing about Wildings,' he said quickly, 'is that everyone's so well connected. Take Rose. Stepdaughter to Godfrey Merle, one of the world's most powerful media tycoons. Look at Mei-fen, and her family connections to China's ruling party. Or you, Raffi – son of a Police Chief. In the normal course of things, most of us would have ended up in powerful positions ourselves, or at least moved in those circles.'

*Like me*, he thought. Son of a High Inquisitor. For Endor, I'd be the perfect catch.

'D'you know if the procedure can be reversed?' Glory asked Jenna grudgingly.

'Could be, if it's just a matter of digging out the mystery implant. But it's not like we're going to get any answers here. Those bastards obviously knew we were on to them. They've even wiped the place clean of prints.'

'Hang on.' Lucas's eye had been caught by a pearly glint under the operating table. It was a small button, possibly from a shirt cuff. 'Maybe we could try scrying on this.'

Jenna wrinkled her nose. 'It coulda been lost days ago. And a button isn't exactly a personal item. Do you even know who you'd be scrying for?'

'Dr Claude, at a guess. He's the *americano* the locals told Raffi about, and who checked Rose out of the clinic back home. I know he's probably miles away by now, but it's worth a try, isn't it?'

Lucas said he would go back to the jeep to fetch the glass bowl Raffi had used to keep an eye on him in the hacienda. It gave him an excuse to get some air, for being in the surgery was making him increasingly claustrophobic. He kept returning to the idea that, in different circumstances, it could have been him. A Stearne in the service of Endor.

Jenna had parked downhill from the building. Lucas was getting ready to open the boot, when his ears picked up a faint mechanical hum. An unmarked stealth helicopter suddenly whirred into view, hovering in the air like a vast shiny black beetle. Another division of the Red Knights? Or – worse – Endor? There was no time to give a warning.

Before his appalled eyes, a squad of black-clad men was already dropping from the craft; spreading out to surround the clinic.

The next thing he knew, a hand was clamped on his mouth, his arms were pinned behind his back, and he was dragged into the shadow of the forest.

'Sssh,' said his captor, as he thrashed about. 'You are safe.' This man wasn't in black. He was wearing a camouflage suit, with a white feather pinned to his chest. 'La Bruja Blanca wants to see you.'

As Lucas was taken deeper into the rainforest, two more men in camouflage emerged from the trees, silent as smoke.

'Take me back,' he said, still struggling furiously. 'My friends – they need *help* –'

'Your friends will not be harmed,' said his original captor, pulling a hood over Lucas's head. 'That helicopter is of the UCI, military division. They seek the same people you do.'

The United Council of Inquisitors . . . Lucas did not find this news hugely reassuring. They were the governing body of the world's inquisitions, and had their own witch-hunting task force. Who had called them into Cordoba? He was in no hurry to meet the mysterious 'White Witch' either. From what Raffi had said, she was an elderly female version of the witch-outlaw Robin Hood.

At least he hadn't been hit on the head again. He was on a forced march of incredible speed, a man holding him up on either side, so that in many places he skimmed the ground. His ears buzzed with the sound of the rainforest:

300

the roars and keening of the howler monkeys mingling with a cacophony of bird calls, cricket whines and the screeching of numerous mammals. The air smelled green and mossy; its humidity meant his clothes clung damply to his skin.

Finally, they came to a halt and the hood was removed. The forest had begun to thin, for they had reached the foothills of the mountain range. Sunlight filtered in sequins through the trees and into a small clearing. There was a group of efficient-looking tents, but the encampment had a temporary air. Wherever the guerrillas had their base, this wasn't it.

Lucas's hands were untied. More people emerged from the tents. Then the flap to the largest tent was untied from the inside, and an elderly woman emerged. 'La Bruja Blanca,' she announced.

# CHAPTER 31

'You look just like your father,' said the woman who stood before him. Her voice was British and she had a pale, fine-featured face. 'But I suppose everyone says that to you.'

Lucas didn't speak. He couldn't. He was face to face with Edie Starling, in the middle of a South American jungle.

And when he finally found his voice, he blurted out, 'I thought you were old.'

The guerrillas laughed softly.

'A young beauty one day, an ancient crone the next – that's the story, isn't it? Neither true, I'm afraid. The first La Blanca was old when I met her, and had been in the mountains with her revolutionaries for many years. But with one blonde witch-woman succeeded by another ... well, people are easily confused. And then there's Ana here.' She indicated the elderly woman who had introduced her. 'Ana stands in for me on occasions. No witchwork; just sleight of hand.'

Although Edie's platinum hair was threaded with silver and the skin around her eyes was lined, her figure was girlish and slight. Lucas couldn't see Glory in her face. Her daughter's sallow colouring, her strong jaw and dark brows, came from elsewhere. But there was a jaunty red scarf tied around Edie's neck, at odds with her utilitarian clothes, and he thought, well, Glory would like that.

'Why have you brought me here?'

'We've been watching you since you first arrived in San Jerico. And my daughter, of course.'

Lucas shifted uneasily. He wondered how much she knew about his and Glory's history. Perhaps this meeting was about to turn into an ambush, as part of some complex revenge plot against his father. Edie Starling's manner seemed almost too casual to be true.

'You see, I have a number of informants,' she told him. 'One of them works at the Carabosse Club, another for Senator Vargas. They, and many others, are troubled by the idea of the Inquisition returning to Cordoba. But a society where witchwork runs riot can be a kind of tyranny too.'

He cleared his throat. 'Which is what Endor's after.'

'Yes. Endor wants this country to slip even further into anarchy. It's the ideal base for the crime that funds them, and the terror they export. They're hoping to establish a stronger presence here, which is why they were determined to sabotage Vargas's campaign. My friend in the Senator's household had his suspicions about Rose Merle from the start. The hexing of Vargas's child proved him right.

'I have something to show you. Come.'

She beckoned Lucas out of the clearing, and he felt another prickle of nerves. Before she left, she stopped and spoke softly in Spanish to the old woman, Ana, and then to one of the men of her own age. He was grizzled but handsome, and as she moved on, caught her hand and smiled.

*Ah*, thought Lucas. *Poor Patrick*. His thoughts flashed back to London, to his and Glory's old lives, and the subsequent lurch of incredulity made him stumble. He suddenly couldn't think what he was doing here or how it had happened. Yet he had no choice but to keep going.

Edie Starling led him through the trees to a small but steep ravine. There was a woman's body lying in the creek at the bottom of it. Her head had been cracked open on the rocks. It was the fallen glasses Lucas recognised first; large and unfashionable. Then the missing finger-joint.

'You knew this woman?'

'Um. She was a . . . therapist. At this school I went to. With Glory. We think she was working for Endor.'

Edie's face was impassive. 'I used to know her too. Many years ago, by a different name. We had reason to believe she was Rose Merle's handler. So when I heard of Glory's arrest, it was time to bring your so-called therapist in.' Lucas barely had time to register how Edie skimmed lightly over her daughter's name. 'My men intercepted her the day before yesterday. She died last night, in the course of trying to escape. By then, fortunately, she had already given us most of what we needed.'

She sat down on a stone outcrop and invited him to sit too, producing a small plastic bag from her pocket. It contained two small curved pieces of metal, and a sprinkling of dirt.

'This was her ring. It turned out to be hollow inside, and filled with sand.'

Lucas remembered it. Large and plain, like everything Dr Caron wore. 'She used sand in her therapy sessions. For us to, er, play with.'

Edie smiled thinly. 'Sand-play is a recognised therapeutic technique. Dr Caron's use of it was not.'

Dr Caron might not have been a real therapist, but the feelings she had drawn out of him in their sessions had been real enough. Lucas thought back to those long hours in the tower room, fingers trailing in the sand, forming it into shapes, crushing it into nothingness . . . burying his conflicted feelings in its depths.

'When my men found her,' Edie continued, 'she was on her way to the southern border, to meet with another Endor operative. As you know, Endor has no command centre. Once an integrated network, it has fragmented over the years into a loose association of regional groups. Dr Caron and her associates feared their base here was no longer secure. Perhaps they were aware that my people had begun to watch the place. Either way, they were already preparing to evacuate. The aim was to establish a new clinic elsewhere, with a new source of patients. And so Dr Caron was in talks with another Endor cell. She needed their support for the enterprise.'

'You know about Cambion, then? And Wildings?'

'I do now. Dr Caron was not going to her meeting empty-handed. She intended to demonstrate the success of the Cambion project.'

Edie drew out a slim laptop from within her shoulder bag. 'Encrypted, of course. Luckily, this jungle is home to an

expert hacker or two.' She gave another thin smile. 'Some of the data was lost or corrupted during the decryption process, and it's not the full story by any means. Still, there are a number of things of interest.'

She switched on the machine and clicked on a picture file. It was an X-ray of a human skull, face on. There was a little white splinter above the right eye.

'There – one of the so-called "implants", though it hasn't been planted particularly deeply. Only the outer layer of the membranes around the brain has been breached.'

'What . . . what is it?'

'A fragment of bone,' Edie answered coolly. 'Any kind would do, but it's a finger bone in this instance. Not exactly high-tech.'

Lucas felt queasy. 'I thought Dr Caron damaged her hand in a car crash.'

'No. The removal of the fingertip was self-inflicted. But the crash was real enough. It's what induced Rose's own collapse.'

'So last year, when Rose came home after the surgery, and it seemed she'd literally lost her mind – when she was without memory and sensations and emotions –'

He was thinking of Jenna's description of a golem: a body without a soul.

'Dr Caron was in a comatose state; Rose was feeling the effects. The witchwork she had undergone was not as straightforward as its pioneers believed. When they bound the heart and mind of one witch to the bone of another, they failed to anticipate there would be a strong physical connection as well as the mental one.

'Dr Caron recovered and so – to a certain extent – did Rose. However, the connection between them must have been weakened. Rose began trying to mentally resist, to fight back, using her own fae. Her struggle intensified last night. As a result, Dr Caron grew confused and distracted, and therefore much easier for us to manage.'

'But then the doctor made her own bid for freedom.'

Edie frowned. 'I admit we let our guard down. She might have been confused, but she was still Endor-trained. Unfortunately for her, it was dark and raining and she didn't see the drop.'

From where he was sitting, Lucas couldn't see it either, or the broken body in the creek. He was glad of it. 'Rose heard a voice in her head. She told Glory it was her fae. She'd even given it a name, Alice. But it was Dr Caron, right? Using some kind of telepathy?'

'Yes. There are recordings of the process stored on this computer, and I will show them to you. I've already downloaded all the uncorrupted data on to a USB stick. By now, it should have been delivered to the inquisitorial squad at the clinic. Once I am sure of their intentions, I will give them this laptop and the ring. Their forensic team will want to take a look.'

Lucas blinked. 'You're putting this in the hands of the United Council of Inquisitors?'

'This is an international issue, and only they have the necessary resources.'

So Edie Starling the outlaw wasn't so revolutionary after all. Lucas should be glad she wasn't some mad-eyed jungle queen. It was clear she had influence and authority,

as well as mystique. What would Glory make of her, though? How could she be prepared? His heart tightened. For a new possibility had occurred to him – that this life was something Glory might want too. Edie might want it for her. She could be La Bruja Blanca the Third: righting wrongs, fighting tyranny, folk-heroine and celebrity.

Edie cut into his thoughts. 'I don't intend to deal with the UCI directly and I'm sorry they arrived before we could reach the rest of your companions. I would have preferred to have met you all first.' She turned to face him. 'Nonetheless, I'm glad of the opportunity to speak to you on your own.'

Lucas tried to prepare himself. Though he didn't think this was an ambush any longer, it was still a reckoning. 'My fath—' he began.

'Can you tell me –' Edie said at the same time and he felt silent, not least because of the unfamiliar hesitation in her voice. 'Can you tell me . . . Glory . . . what is she like?'

He could feel the intensity of her gaze, like heat. It took a moment to collect himself. 'She's strong and she's brave.' He paused. 'An extraordinary witch, though you probably know that already. Stubborn as hell, but not quite as tough as she thinks she is. Exasperating. Generous. Loyal. She's – well. She's the best person I know.'

'Thank you.' Edie suddenly looked, and sounded, very tired. 'Ashton and I . . . we talked about the two of you. It was a long time ago.'

'I'm sorry about what my dad did.' The words came easily now. 'I found out how they blackmailed you – he and the others at the Inquisition. I know he regrets it. It was a shameful thing.'

Edie nodded slowly. 'When I met your father,' she said, 'he was in the grip of a terrible grief. Sometimes it seemed like anger. Behind it all, I thought he was a decent man.'

Lucas felt a great unclenching inside, like a cluster of knots untying itself. But he had one more confession to make.

'Endor wanted to do it to me – what they did to Rose. But there's nothing genuine about the Cambion treatment, is there? The fae can't be blocked.'

Edie shook her head.

'But if it could be . . . if the procedure was known to be safe . . . if things had been different . . . I would have said yes.'

'And now?'

'No.' The last knot had loosened. He smiled. 'I'd say no.'

Edie Starling smiled too, then sighed. 'I think it's time I met my daughter.'

# CHAPTER 32

'Surrender yourselves!' boomed the man with the loud-speaker. 'This witch-hunt has been authorised by the United Council of Inquisitors! Cease and desist all witchwork! Lay down your arms!'

Glory put down her gun in the doorway of the clinic and followed Jenna and Raffi outside, hands behind her head. One instant they were surrounded by hulking black-clad men bristling with weaponry; the next, they were pushed to the ground, arms wrenched behind their backs and cuffed in iron. *Here we go again*, she thought.

It took a lot of arguing, explaining and telephone calls before it was accepted that Glory, Jenna and Raffi were not Endor terrorists. On the way out of the building, Glory had ordered the others not to breathe a word about Lucas if he wasn't already in custody. She was boiling with frustration and anxiety about him. Would she be able to sense if something bad had happened to him? And could Jenna be trusted to keep her mouth shut?

The leader of the squad was a stocky German. Glory recognised him from the fundraising party for Senator

Vargas. He curtly introduced himself as Major Carsten von Dernbach, Witch-Hunter First Class.

'Senator Vargas requested our intervention – the police here are impossible and he's lost confidence in the private security firm he was using. Then we had a tip-off from the WSA regarding this facility.'

The WSA was otherwise known as the US Inquisition. Jenna did not look happy. 'This is a Section Seven-led operation. The WSA has been appraised of our progress but –'

'I think you'll find most of the leading was done by WICA,' Glory put in. 'It were us who made the breakthrough at Wildings, and then with Rose Merle.'

Jenna's ponytail swished. 'Oh, so you're WICA again, are you? As opposed to AWOL?'

'And hey,' said Raffi, jabbing an indignant finger at the Major, 'don't you speak badly of the police. You have no authority in this country. We Cordobans threw you out once, we'll do it again.'

Busy with recriminations and resentments, nobody paid much attention to the villagers quietly gathering at the end of the drive, or the elderly lady at their head.

'La Bruja Blanca,' she announced in a high cracked voice, 'has something she wishes you to see.' She held up a straw basket. 'It is for the girl called Gloriana Starling.'

'That's me!' One of the inquisitors put out a restraining hand but Glory shook him off.

When Major von Dernbach strode over to take the basket, the woman moved back. 'I do not question La Bruja Blanca's bidding. Neither should you.'

She looked Glory over, then beckoned her near. After

handing her the basket, she kissed her on both cheeks. 'Your friend is safe,' the old woman whispered in her ear. 'Come to the edge of the forest in one hour and I will bring you to him.'

Then, so that everyone could hear: 'If La Blanca's gift pleases you, there will be more to come. She has chosen the girl Gloriana to be her courier.'

'Senora!' the Major interjected, as the old woman shuffled off. 'Who gave this to you? We need to talk –'

The woman paid no attention, hobbling towards the village with surprising speed. Her assembled neighbours murmured softly. When the Major sent one of his men after her, he had to push through an uncooperative crowd. He came back a few minutes later, shaking his head. The crone had vanished into thin air.

'Get these people rounded up,' the Major told him irritably. 'We'll need to take their statements. Some of them must have had an idea about what's been going on round here.'

Glory looked inside the basket. There was a USB flash drive in a padded envelope, and a white feather, like the one the cat-woman had given her.

'You are a special one,' Raffi told her solemnly. 'La Blanca's favour is very rare thing.'

'Special's one word for it,' Jenna muttered.

Glory suppressed a smile. She knew she owed Jenna for their escape from the hacienda and for bringing them here. That didn't mean she had to like her. Glory suspected that the S7 agent would have preferred to keep the trip to Cambion a solo gig. Just as the Major would have preferred to snatch the USB stick and fly off in his shiny black helicopter. But to both their irritation, Glory was turning out to be a valuable resource. They needed to keep her on their side.

A computer was fetched from the helicopter and brought inside the building. There were two folders stored in the memory stick, and a statement from La Bruja Blanca in a separate Word document. It said that the contents of Folder A pertained to the final hours of the Endor agent known as Flavia Caron, now deceased. Folder B contained material taken from her laptop. The laptop and other 'items of interest' would be passed over in due course, via Gloriana Starling, and only on the condition that Gloriana could personally testify to her colleagues' good faith in 'pursuing the matter with diligence and integrity'.

Both the Major and Jenna White made harrumphing noises when they got to this part.

Glory started with Folder A. There was a photograph of Dr Caron's body, splayed among rocks, with a bloody gash on her head. Another photograph of two halves of a ring, and a sprinkle of sand. Finally, a short film that appeared to have been taken on a mobile phone.

The image was fuzzy, but Dr Caron was easily identifiable, sitting cross-legged in a tent. She looked sweaty and dishevelled, and was shaking a little as she took the thick metal ring she wore on her left hand and moved it to the index finger of her right. It was the finger with the missing joint, and she made a beckoning motion with it. The poor sound quality meant the audience around the computer strained to hear her words. 'Rose,' she said, 'this is Alice.' She waited, and closed her eyes. Then she began to rhythmically twist the band around her finger. 'Hear me. Feel me. Set me free . . .'

Folder B, with contents taken from the Endor laptop, provided more pieces of the puzzle. Even so, it would have been difficult to make sense of them if it wasn't for the information that had already been gathered. There was an article from a Cordoban tabloid, with a photograph of Senator Vargas making a speech, and Rose and Gideon standing among his supporters. An X-ray of a skull, with a splinter of bone. A second film-clip.

This clip was of much better quality. It had been taken inside the clinic's consulting room. The people in it had their faces digitally disguised, but Glory recognised some of the voices. She knew Rose, who was sitting at the table, from the burn mark on her hand. There was a tray of sand next to her, just like the ones in Dr Caron's study, and a tiny shard of bone.

'So how do you feel, about to perform your last act of witchwork?' Dr Caron asked off-screen.

'Hopeful,' answered Rose.

Her mother was sitting beside her. Although Lady Merle's face was pixelated, Glory would have recognised her voice anywhere. 'I'm so happy for you,' she said. 'So happy and proud.'

'We'll repeat this test,' said Dr Caron, 'after you've had the procedure, to ascertain its success. That's why, even though I know it makes you uncomfortable, you must use your powers to their full extent. You know what to do?'

'I do.'

Rose Merle summoned the piece of bone to her hand, and expelled it with a little cry. It was a lodestone now: the receptacle of her Seventh Sense, part of her body and soul and fae. It also formed the backbone of the human figure she began to mould from the sand, damp with spit and blood from her finger.

A poppet, with a lodestone at its heart. Rose summoned the lodestone again, and it carried the sandman with it. The figure moved sluggishly, but unstoppably, towards her hand.

'Look, Mummy,' said Rose. 'It's like in that fae-tale. A gingerbread man!'

Soon the sand would be sealed in Dr Caron's ring, and the bone sealed in Rose's head, uniting them for ever. Bonded by bone and earth, blood and fae.

'Oh, my darling,' said Lady Merle. 'Imagine – you're going to be free.'

# CHAPTER 33

The inquisitors did not want Glory disappearing into the jungle. Neither did Jenna. But they didn't have a choice – not if there was a chance of gaining further information from the White Witch. Their priority had to be finding the other Cambion victims, and the Endor agents controlling them. So approximately one hour after receiving the memory stick, Glory walked alone into the forest, taking the path marked by white feathers pinned to trees.

Lucas was waiting for her a little way along. His face was dappled by sun and shadow; what she saw most of all was the blue of his eyes. She knew her face lightened foolishly, that she pulled him towards her too eagerly. She didn't care. If only they could always meet like this: alone in the wilderness, free from regulations and obligations and everything else that divided them . . .

Very gently, he pushed her back, holding her face between his palms. For the first time she became aware of the other people emerging from the trees. Lucas's expression frightened her. It was more searching, and serious, than she had ever seen before. 'I have something to tell you,' he said.

The deeper they moved into the rainforest, the more dream-like the journey became. A flock of rainbow-coloured macaws swooped above, followed by a scatter of neon-bright butterflies. In the treetops, what looked like thin black branches turned out to be the limbs of spider monkeys. Glory walked through more shades of green than she knew existed.

The old woman, Ana, led the way. Lucas kept a few steps back, giving Glory her space. She was glad of it. She was in a state of almost hallucinatory anticipation. Nothing felt real, nothing mattered, except what waited for her at the end of this journey.

Finally, her escort dropped behind. So did Lucas. Ana pointed ahead, to where the trees thinned and the ground grew stony. Glory's dreamy haze evaporated. She smoothed her tangled hair and Rose's ill-fitting, sweat-stained clothes. She wished she had something to do with her hands.

A muddy path led to the lip of a ravine. There was a small, slim woman standing on the edge, looking across to the horizon. It seemed an eternity before she turned around.

'Hello.'

'Hello.'

They looked at each other. Each took a step nearer, then another. But not too near, not too close. To cross that final short distance was impossible. It was not just space, it was years and memories and irredeemable loss.

Edie's eyes were moving carefully over her. Edie's face

was very calm, very pale. She was not the wary young woman in the photographs, with her distant smile and flyaway hair. Yet Glory would have known her anywhere.

She was afraid that if she touched her, she might vanish. This woman was the last in a sequence of potential mothers, different ghosts. Edie the feckless runaway. Edie the coven queen. Edie the martyr of the Burning Court. Edie the terrorist. Edie the revolutionary. Edie the Starling Girl . . . She didn't look like any of these. She could have been all of them.

'I've been looking for you,' Glory said at last, with a catch in her voice.

Edie closed her eyes briefly. 'Yes.'

'I didn't know what happened.'

'No.'

'I knew you was probably dead. But I couldn't believe it. Not truly, not inside. Then with me coming to this country . . . well, it's like fate, ain't it? The white feather, I didn't know what it meant, but it was you, protecting me –'

Edie was so very still. So very watchful. 'Of course,' she said formally, 'I would do everything within my power to help.'

''Cause you *are* powerful, ain't you?' said Glory, too eagerly. 'With all these people following you, thinking you're some kind of – of super fae-godmother. Then there's the stuff you got off Endor. Them UCI prickers couldn't believe it.'

'I'm glad it was useful. There is a document that was damaged during the decryption but might still be recoverable. I think it relates to the identities of the other victims.'

Glory nodded distractedly. Somehow, the meeting had already gone wrong. Somehow, she must have said the wrong thing, in the wrong way. For why else was her mother still talking of work? And with such deadening politeness?

'Dr Caron told me of two others, apart from Rose Merle. An American boy and an Iranian girl. Each has their own Endor handler, of course. It's possible the witchwork can be undone, if the implant is removed and the controlling ring or equivalent destroyed. It will take a good fae-healer as well as a surgeon.'

The words marched on, relentlessly. Glory barely heard them.

'Did you know Rose is – was – family?' she tried. 'Uncle Vince's kid. She was a Starling Girl too. I didn't know it at first, but I felt a connection. So did she, in spite of everything. Candice Morgan's been in Cordoba too.' She knew she was babbling, yet she couldn't stop. 'She's a bit of a wild child. Been running rings round Troy and the rest.'

'How are they all? The Morgans?' Edie's voice was strained. But there wasn't a trace of the East End in it.

'Um, well, the Wednesday Coven's still top of its game.' She wondered about explaining the story about Charlie and the Goodwin Trial, Silas Paterson and the rest, but maybe Edie already knew it. None of it seemed important anyway. 'Cooper Street is on its uppers, though. Auntie Angel's lost the plot. Me and Dad moved out.'

Surely the mention of Patrick would be a cue?

Nothing. Just another polite nod.

Glory looked over the ravine, and its treacherous

plunge. There was a dark stain on the rocks below. Back to business, then. 'Is this where the doc fell?'

'Yes. We've moved the body. It was a pity; we'd been making progress with her, and I'm sure there was more to come. She wasn't a strong woman – she could have been made to talk.'

'But Rose and the doc was linked in bodies as well as minds, right? If you'd been . . . forceful . . . with her, then Rose might've suffered too.'

'I've done worse,' Edie said. Not casually, exactly. Wearily. Matter-of-fact.

'That's not surprising, is it.' Indignation warmed Glory, pushed her on. 'I know how them pyros at the Inquisition stitched you up. Strong-arming you into Endor, so you'd do their dirty work.'

Edie sat down on the rocks. 'It was a long time ago.'

'But . . . Mum . . .' They both flinched at the word. 'They *stole* you from us. Stole you from me and Dad. It *broke* him.' She felt the old anger flood back. 'This is what Lucas don't understand. All this "end justifies the means" – it's crap.'

'He does,' said Edie.

'Does what?'

'He does understand.'

'Oh – he told you that? Made a formal apology on behalf of the British nation, did he?'

'It wasn't his fault. We can't be responsible for our parents' actions.'

Tears sparked in Glory's eyes. Nothing was making sense.

Edie made as if to put out her hand, then thought better of it. 'You're right,' she said slowly, carefully. 'The Inquisition treated me, and others like me, with ruthlessness and contempt. But even though I owed them no loyalty, I knew Endor was the bigger threat, just as it is today. I did my duty. And then I found I liked the responsibility, I relished the challenge. So when I had the chance to do bigger, better things – take bigger risks – I took it.'

'No. You couldn't have chosen. You was *forced.*'

'At first, perhaps. Later, I got free of the Inquisition, free of Endor. I swore to myself that I would never be at anyone's beck and call again. But there was no going back.'

'Why not? What – what about your old life? What about me and Dad?'

'My life before . . . I tried to make it work. I really did. I resented the covens' expectations – all the intrigue about my mother's legacy – and Patrick was the only person who understood. He was so kind and gentle; so easily contented. I thought he could make me like that too, but –'

'I get it. We weren't enough.' Glory didn't try to keep the bitterness from her voice. Auntie Angel had been right, after all. *The kind that always leaves, never looks back.*

'I wasn't enough. I didn't know how to be a wife, let alone a mother. Your gran had a talent for lots of things; parenthood wasn't one of them. I never knew my dad. His identity changed from one of Cora's stories to the next. And they were always great stories, full of craziness and colour, and unhappy endings. Like my mother herself.

'I told myself I'd come back for you, when you were older. It was the only way I could live with myself, at first.

But the childhood I had – assignations, midnight flits, border crossings . . . I didn't want that for you. I didn't want to pass on that kind of damage. I thought it would be easier for you, for everyone, if I disappeared. You could start over without me.'

'Quite some vanishing act. Not so much as a hexing Christmas card in twelve hexing years.' The words scorched her throat. 'Growing up in Cooper Street weren't exactly a picnic, you know. It broke Dad's heart when you went. Angeline . . . she's half-mad. She hates everyone, including me now. Drunks and loonies and mobsters – that's the family you left me to.'

'It was still better,' said Edie, 'than anything I could give.' She bowed her head.

Glory drew a shaky breath. 'I kept having this dream . . . of the Burning Court . . . sometimes it was me on the stake, sometimes it was you. For years, I thought the Inquisition might've got you. And then, yesterday – with Rose – watching her, watching me –' She swallowed painfully. 'Well. I guess you did save me, in the end.'

Edie made a small tentative movement. Then she placed her hand, very carefully, on Glory's. Her head was still bowed. 'I'm sorry I'm not what you were looking for. But you have grown into everything I could have hoped.'

Glory had to take a couple of moments to control herself. Blindly, she fixed her gaze on the blur of green on the other side of the ravine. Her eyes and throat throbbed and stung. She knotted her hand with her mother's, so tightly they both shook. One more step across an impossible distance.

Glory was the first to move her hand free. Her mother's face was wet with tears, which she wiped away neatly and resolutely, though they kept falling.

Finally, Glory asked, 'You like it here? You're happy?'

'I've made a life for myself,' Edie replied, after a pause. 'And now – well. Senator Vargas has asked for my help. An intermediary got in touch this morning.'

'Back in the presidential race already! That were quick.'

'Cordoba needs a strong leader, a man of integrity, if Endor is to be kept out.' Edie's cool efficiency had already started to return. This time, though, Glory could see the effort it took. 'The fact Vargas has reached out to me is a good sign. He knows he needs to unite the country.'

'So he wants La Bruja Blanca's endorsement.'

'He wants my advice. To restore order, he'll need to establish an Inquisition of some kind. And if he could be persuaded to appoint witches to senior roles within it, we could perhaps create a new kind of security agency.'

'An Inquisition led by *witches*?'

'It's just an idea.' She shrugged. 'I haven't agreed to anything yet. I'm not sure I can. After so long in the wilderness, of being an outsider, I don't really know how to come in. To stop . . . resisting.'

'I find it hard too.'

'You're very young,' Edie said quietly. 'Too young to turn your back on the everyday world, or cut yourself off from its people. My mistakes shouldn't be yours.'

At that, Glory lifted her chin. Her face was calm, her smile fearless. 'Don't worry. They won't.'

# EPILOGUE

The two runners on the roof were barely visible in the evening light. The sky was low and grey, except for a burst of gold at the horizon. In the street below, a child gaped and pointed. 'Look!' he said to his mother. 'Sky-witches!'

The woman frowned and pulled the child along hurriedly. Soon the sky-leapers were out of sight, the fluorescent Ws on the back of their uniforms ducking and weaving through the dusk. Autumn had brought a chill in the air and their breath plumed like smoke. So far from the ground, they were conscious only of their own sharp gasps, the thump of their feet on slate, brick and stone.

It had been an even race, but now the boy was drawing ahead. In one smooth bound, he flew across the gap between the dome of a library and a neighbouring bank. When the girl landed after him, he caught her in his arms.

They were both pink-cheeked, panting. Lucas pushed the hood back over Glory's head. Her hooped earrings were tangled in her hair. Her eyes flashed. He tugged the neck of her T-shirt, touched the dark kiss-mark under her collarbone.

'Witch,' he said, smiling.

Smiling, she slid her hands up his back, to the secret spot under his shoulder blade. 'Witch,' she said.

The rooftops were a different country. Hand in hand, they walked to the edge of a parapet and surveyed their kingdom.

Lucas sighed. 'I don't want to come down.'

'We mustn't be late,' said Glory. 'It's the first time Dad's had a birthday party since he were a kid. And I can't leave all the preparations to Peggy.'

Lucas knew she had received a letter from Edie yesterday. The letters weren't frequent, and they didn't say much, but they still came. Patrick had had his own letter, a long one, soon after they returned to London.

'How's he doing?'

'Good. Yeah. Makes me think I maybe underestimated him all this time. He don't need protecting, not the way I thought.'

'You make a good minder, all the same.' He squeezed her hand.

'Reckon we both do. "Starling & Stearne: No Witchcrime Too Large." Remember?'

'I'd say "Stearne & Starling" has a better ring to it.'

She laughed. 'You wish. Come on, then – I'll race you.'

They ran on. Over walls, down slopes, across chasms. Sometimes one was ahead, sometimes the other, leaping effortlessly through the dark.

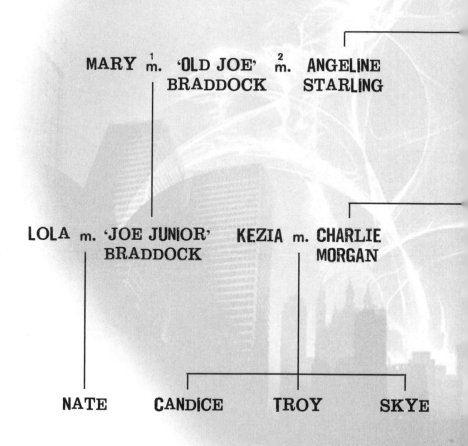

MARY m.¹ 'OLD JOE' m.² ANGELINE
BRADDOCK STARLING

LOLA m. 'JOE JUNIOR' KEZIA m. CHARLIE
BRADDOCK MORGAN

NATE CANDICE TROY SKYE

# THE STARLING FAMILY TREE

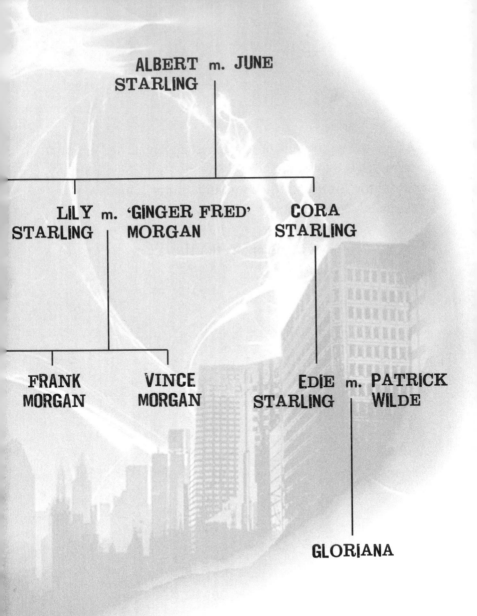

# Acknowledgements

A writer's equivalent of a witches' coven is her editorial team. And so I would like to thank my agent, Sarah Molloy, my editor, Emma Matthewson, and Emma Bradshaw, Isabel Ford and Diana Hickman at Bloomsbury.

**www.laurapowellauthor.com**